SAY
I BOO

An Abby Spector Ghost Mystery

MORGAN SPELLMAN

MEADOW CAT

Published by Meadow Cat Press
An imprint of Meadow Cat, LLC

ISBN: 979-8-9885795-0-2 (print)
ISBN: 979-8-9885795-1-9 (ebook)

For permissions, inquiries, or questions, please contact:
meadowcatpress@gmail.com

First Edition: September 2023

Cover design by Holly Dunn Design

1 2 3 4 5 6 7 8 9 10

www.MorganSpellman.com

*For those of us left behind
when the ghost of a loved one
moved on.*

AN ABBY SPECTOR GHOST MYSTERY

SAY
I BOO

MORGAN SPELLMAN

Chapter One

Abby Spector was a magician. Not a supernatural sorcerer or a slick con woman, but the real deal: a performer, an illusionist, a stage artist who sparked wonder and joy in a captivated audience with the smallest sleight of hand.

So what if she worked for children's parties and could barely afford her share of a small apartment's rent? She could evoke smiles with a flourish of flowers, conjure applause with a flick of cards. Her routines brightened children's days, brought families closer together, and drew even the most cynical audience into a world of endless possibilities, if only for a moment. That was enough for Abby.

At least, it usually was. Today was different. Today, she was working at 104 Blackthorn Lane.

There was nothing wrong with 104 Blackthorn Lane, except its uncomfortable proximity to 103 Blackthorn Lane, which haunted Abby every time she peered out an eastern window.

A vine-ridden oak blocked most of her view, but the chipper yellow facade was unmistakable. The front garden had been pulled up, replaced with a single row of boxy shrubs. In the kitchen, a girl sat reading. Sheer curtains blurred her face. For a moment, Abby's heart almost believed that after all these years, Chelsea had returned home. A black cat jumped onto the windowsill, her tail widening the gap between the curtains, and the image vanished. The girl at the table was too thin, too young, too *dull* to be Chelsea, and the walls were a crisp, solid white.

Abby turned away from the window and gripped the sink with trembling hands. The logical part of her knew that houses sold all the time and just because some new family had moved in and painted over Chelsea's gorgeous kitchen murals didn't mean that the world had moved on.

But it sure felt like it.

Of all the houses in her large suburban town, why did she have to work so close to *that* one?

Abby shook herself out of her thoughts and focused on her reflection in the decorative mirror. Tears glistened in her hazel eyes, threatening to smear her eyeliner. That wouldn't do. Not today, not when Abby had an audience to please.

Taking a deep breath, Abby shut her eyes and plucked happy thoughts as if Peter Pan were waiting on her to learn how to fly. She thought of her favorite cat at the local cat cafe, and the funniest lines in her favorite TV show. When she opened her eyes, she wasn't exactly soaring with happiness, but her hands were steady as she pulled big purple robes over her jeans and T-shirt, donned a droopy moon-and-star hat over her short brown hair, and headed to the stage in Mr. Wiltshire's living room.

The house pulsed with raw, uninhibited energy. Scents of buttery popcorn and pizza wafted down halls lined with bright banners, and tufts of cotton candy clung to the carpet.

All Abby had to do was keep her eyes off the eastern windows and perform.

Plastering a show-winning smile on her face, Abby strolled into the center of the living room where wide-eyed kids peered up at her through layers of clown makeup. They met her with a round of applause followed by hushed silence as she began her act. This was her twelfth performance—she had practiced long enough that she had memorized every flourish and perfected every pause, holding anticipation just long enough to heighten the joy at revealing a vanished object reappearing in the palm of her hand and the thrill of guessing which object was going to emerge from her hat next. And—most importantly—as it was *only* her twelfth performance, the boredom had not creeped in. Reaching in and out of the hat didn't carry the monotony that scooping ice cream had, and changing up her tricks provided more autonomy than repeating the same welcome greeting at the county fair ever had.

It helped that the kids were a good audience. They giggled and clapped as she pulled flowers and toys from her hat. They waved balloon-animals through her card tricks and gasped when she made a rope disappear. For the big finale, she produced a tray of cookies seemingly from midair. The kids went wild. Cheering, they jumped from their seats and rushed toward the brightly frosted cookies.

Abby stepped back as kids crowded the counter, and parents attempted to herd them into some semblance of order.

She smiled. This was what she loved most about performing—the joy that simmered in her audience and filled the room with the warmth of a freshly drawn bubble bath. The kids were bouncing up and down, radiating happiness.

Abby's phone vibrated in her pocket. She slipped it from her jeans and grinned at the number.

Lucas Clark, her childhood best friend, was finally calling *her* for once.

Her grin soon turned into a frown as the magnitude of Lucas Clark calling spontaneously washed over her. The man scheduled his trips to the grocery store. He would never call without texting first. Was something wrong? Was he back in Virginia? His graduate program was supposed to be finishing soon—Abby glanced at the date. It was December 7th. Had he said he was returning December 3rd or 13th? All Abby remembered was that the date had a three in it.

Abby slunk toward the door, hoping no one would notice— or care—if she disappeared for a minute.

By the time she stepped onto the front porch, the phone was dark and still.

She took a seat on the bench swing and called Lucas back, shivering as the breeze tousled her robes.

The phone rang twice before he answered with annoyance. "I just had a conversation with your voicemail."

Abby's eyebrows creased before she remembered she had recently changed her voicemail to a fake conversation that started with "Hey, what's up?" and ended with "Actually, why don't you just leave a message, so I can decide if this interests me enough to call you back?" She had recorded it months ago on a whim, but her mother had had such a strong reaction that Abby kept the concept, though she changed up the exact words to keep her mother on her toes.

Abby pictured Lucas talking to her voicemail and laughed.

"For once, I'm jealous of my voicemail. It's been forever! How have you been? Are you back home?"

"I'm back in the States, yes," Lucas said. "But not home. I'm in Pennsylvania."

"In Pennsylvania?" Abby wrinkled her face. That was a good distance from their large suburban town outside of DC. "What are you doing there?"

A weary sigh answered. "You remember my sister, Michelle?"

"Of course." Abby recalled the tall, skinny girl with corkscrew curls who made amazing chocolate chip cookies, wore the same pair of lavender sneakers every day, and ranted about the environment. Of course, that was years ago. She must be thirty by now. Abby wondered if she still wore the same pair of sneakers. "Why? Is something wrong?"

"Well, she's getting married—"

Abby jumped to her feet with a grin. "Seriously? Good for her! Are you going to be best man? Or man of honor or whatever? How come I'm just now hearing about it?"

"Uh, there's been so much going on. I'll fill you in later, but I wanted to ask—"

"You couldn't find a date, so you want me to be your plus one?" Abby squealed. "Count me in."

"No, I—I hate to ask this, but I need a place to stay for a few days." Lucas's tone sounded serious. Abby's compassion was dampened by her—admittedly selfish—joy at the opportunity to see him in person for the first time in two years.

"You can stay with me."

"Don't you have an aunt who lives in Philly?"

"I did, but she moved to Portland. Come stay with me. It'll be fun. Just like old times! We can stay up late watching movies—didn't they make a new *Pirates* one?"

"Years ago."

"Great. It should be online, then. We can have a marathon."

Lucas smacked his lips. "Are you sure? If it's too much trouble—"

"No trouble at all," Abby said quickly. She would text her roommate later and let her know he was coming. If she had a problem with him staying on the couch, he could sleep on the floor in Abby's room. She didn't have another birthday party for two weeks, and she could swap shifts at the coffee shop so she could spend more time with him.

"Thank you." Lucas's voice sagged with relief. "It's just until the wedding, next Saturday."

"Stay as long as you like. Where are you? I'll come pick you up."

"I'm four hours away. I'll take the bus."

"Don't be ridiculous. You know how much I love road trips. I'll be there by dinner time."

"I'm in the middle of nowhere—"

The front door cracked open. A blonde girl with a big crown that read 'Birthday Girl' in pink letters slipped outside.

"I can and I will," said Abby, nodding toward the birthday girl. "I've got to go. Don't you dare get on that bus. And don't even think about paying me for gas. Text me the address."

Abby hung up and turned her attention to the newcomer. What was her name again? Lizzy? Lacey?

Abby grinned. "Hey, birthday girl."

The girl rocked back and forth, squinting up at Abby with tear-stained eyes.

Abby frowned. Was something wrong? It wasn't her performance—Abby had put on a flawless magic show, one of her best yet. Even the parents had gasped and applauded at all the right places. The birthday girl had been just as entranced as the rest of the audience. But now that she thought about it, even when Abby had handed her the stuffed white rabbit, the girl's smile had trembled. Something had upset her, and Abby wasn't cruel enough to walk away from a seven-year-old on the verge of a breakdown, even if her best friend was waiting for her. "What can I help you with?"

The girl twisted the hem of her shirt. "Can you really find things?"

With a subtle smile, Abby reached behind the girl's ear and pulled a chocolate coin out of thin air. She held it out as an offering, a demonstration of her gift.

The girl took the chocolate with a weak smile. "Can you find something for me?"

"Depends," Abby said. Technically, she was paid to work until noon, which was about seven minutes ago. But she could spare a few minutes for the kid. "What are you looking for?"

"A necklace."

Abby forced a smile. The girl was after a missing necklace? While Abby had several sweets and trinkets hidden in her sleeves, she didn't have any necklaces, and she wasn't about to go tramping through her client's house to find a specific one. If the girl wanted a necklace, all she had to do was look down.

"You already have a lovely necklace." Abby pointed to the silver locket at the girl's neck. Then she pointed to the window. "And look at all those presents! I bet one of them might contain a necklace—or something better, don't you?"

The girl shook her head. "Not just any necklace." She glanced over her shoulder at the living room window, through which the party was still in full swing. "Ms. Cynthia, my stepmom, gave me a necklace on my birthday."

"This morning?" Abby asked.

She shook her head. "On my actual birthday. On Tuesday. And now I can't find it. My parents think Katie—my sister—took it. But Katie didn't take it. She *didn't*. But they won't listen. They won't let her out of her room, and she's missing my party." Her eyes filled with tears that she hastily brushed away. "Can you find it?"

Abby leaned down so she was on eye-level with the girl. The sight of her tears tugged at her heart. She hated when anyone cried, especially kids. She wished she could find the girl's necklace, but knew that was out of the question. There had to be another way to cheer her up.

The door creaked open. Ms. Cynthia, a tall blonde woman in a red wool dress, stepped on to the porch and shivered fiercely. "Lilly! There you are. What on earth are you doing out here? Come back inside."

Lilly—that was her name—flashed Abby an expression that clearly said 'help me' as Ms. Cynthia dragged her back through the door. "Why don't you leave the magician alone and get ready to open some presents, okay?"

Abby followed them inside as Lilly protested, "But Katie—"

"Katie's just fine upstairs." Ms. Cynthia ushered the girl toward the fireplace. "Now, go sit down."

"Mom!" Lilly rounded on a woman in the back, who bore a striking resemblance to her. They had the same light brown hair, freckled skin, and rounded facial features.

This must be the girl's birth mother. Abby studied her. She looked tired where she stood with her arms crossed, wrapped in an oversized sweater and fraying dress pants. Receiving a pleading look from her daughter and a fierce scowl from Ms. Cynthia, her steps faltered. She bowed her head, fidgeting with the inside of her sleeve.

"This is my house," Ms. Cynthia whispered harshly. "Your mother is a guest here. She has no say over the rules."

Abby chewed her tongue as the tension between family members grew uncomfortably stiff. As she packed up her magic supplies, she kept her attention on the family.

"She's a feisty one, isn't she?" the girl's dad commented as he chugged a glass of lemonade.

Abby's brows knitted together. She knew better than to get involved with another family's personal business, especially when those families happen to be paying her to keep things light and joyful. But something was amiss here, and Abby wasn't one to walk away from such an alluring puzzle.

"Your daughter, your wife, or your ex-wife?" Abby asked.

The dad snorted. "All of them." He shook his head, leaning back against the counter. "They're all upset about this necklace. If I'd known it was going to cause this much trouble, I'd never have let Cynthia buy it in the first place."

"Is it possible she just misplaced it?" Abby asked.

He shook his head. "It was on her nightstand when we put her to bed last night. She was in her pajamas all morning— didn't get dressed until just before the party started. She wasn't even going to wear the necklace—said it was too fancy for her outfit. Cynthia went to get it, and it was gone."

"It couldn't have fallen behind the nightstand?"

He shook his head again, faster this time. "Cynthia's convinced Katie took it. Once she's got her mind set on something, there's no changing it."

"What do you think?"

"I think Lilly's too young to have a thousand-dollar necklace."

Abby's jaw dropped. "The necklace was a *thousand* dollars?"

She knew this neighborhood was wealthy, but what in the world did a seven-year-old need a thousand-dollar necklace for?

He nodded. "Now you see what the fuss is all about."

Abby surveyed the room, from where kids ran their messy fingers over white carpet to where a couple preteens refilled the buffet bar. No one looked like they had stolen a thousand-dollar necklace. Still, Abby asked, "You're sure her sister took it? There's no one else who could have?"

He grunted. "No one even knew about it except the family, and maybe the cleaning lady. But Cynthia's got much more valuable jewelry lying around and none of it's missing. Hell, we've got dishes more valuable than that. What kind of thief would go sneaking into a kid's room for a single necklace when there's easier loot lying around?"

Abby scrunched up her eyebrows, trying to picture dishes worth more than a thousand dollars. Were they studded with diamonds?

Abby watched Ms. Cynthia set a big birthday present down in front of Lilly. Lilly picked at the velvet ribbon, buying time before she pulled it open. Ms. Cynthia sat beside her, smiling. Lilly's mother stood behind them, a patch of dim sunlight streaking her hair gray as she frowned. Was she also upset her eldest daughter was missing the party? Or was she upset that she was overshadowed by Ms. Cynthia at her own daughter's birthday party?

Abby had a feeling it was the latter.

"It was nice of you to invite Lilly's mother," she said. One thing Abby knew about men like Lilly's father was that they appreciated a good compliment.

"Hmm? Oh, well, Lilly begged for her to come. Who am I to say no?"

"She and Cynthia seem to get along pretty well." Another thing Abby knew about men like Lilly's father was that they loved to correct others. Prying questions might shut them out cold, but a statement with implications will get them talking.

He scoffed. "Give it an hour and let's see what you think. This is the longest I've heard 'em go without sniping at each other."

"That must be rough for the girls." Abby took her time moving the last of her trinkets into the briefcase that held her magic supplies.

"They can handle it." With a side-eyed glance at Abby, he straightened up and gestured to her briefcase in a clear declaration that the conversation was over. "Need a hand?"

"I'm almost finished. All I need is the check."

"Ah." He slid a leather wallet from his back pocket and paid Abby her full fee in cash, plus a tip that was stingy considering the size of the event, but which Abby appreciated nonetheless.

She pocketed the money with a quick "thank you," locked up her briefcase, and headed toward the door.

As she reached the far end of the living room, Abby adjusted her hat in a way that sent it tumbling to the floor, brushing Lilly's mother's shoes.

"Sorry."

"It's fine." Lilly's mother picked up the hat, holding it out to Abby as if it were a wet dishrag.

Abby took it with a polite smile. "You know, your daughter asked me for a favor," she said softly, lowering her voice to a little more than a whisper, "to find her missing necklace."

The mother's face paled. Outside, wind surged through the trees, sighing against the windows. She tucked herself deeper into her sweater.

"You see, her stepmother thinks Katie stole the necklace. She's being unfairly punished now, locked up in her room, missing all the fun."

"Why are you telling me this?" the mother asked sharply.

Abby shrugged. "Your daughter is very kind and considerate. Katie's lucky to have a sister like her."

The woman's features relaxed. She nodded. "They are both lovely girls."

"They are." Abby snapped her fingers. "And another thing—I bet they'd be relieved if someone were to *find* the necklace on the floor."

The woman's face paled. "What exactly are you implying?"

Abby seized the mother's arm and pulled her into the hallway. She tugged at the woman's sweater, rolling up the sleeves until a silver chain glittered in the dim light.

The woman gasped, pulling the edge of her sleeve down.

Abby let out a sigh of relief. She had been about fifty percent sure Lilly's mother had taken it, but if she had been wrong at least she could leave with her money before anyone made a scene.

The mother's lips quivered. "Does Greg know?"

"Who?"

"Lilly's father."

"Ah, I don't think so. But it's only a matter of time before he realizes it. You're one of the only ones who knew about the necklace, you had reason to be in Lilly's bedroom, and it's clear you and Cynthia don't see eye to eye."

"This—" the woman clenched her fist around her left sleeve and hissed "—is far too expensive to give to a seven-year-old. That woman will spoil her rotten. She treats her like she's a damn princess."

She had a point. But not a point good enough to merit stealing from her kids. "And you—what, prefer she play the role of an evil stepmom?"

"I want to be able to bond with my daughter." She squeezed the chain around her arm with pained disgust as if it were a vine of thorns digging into her skin. "I can't afford this kind of luxury."

"You still have that chance," Abby reassured her. "But you'll lose it if you steal from her."

"What are you going to do?"

Abby sighed. "Well, I was going to go home and watch some sitcoms, but my best friend needs a ride—"

"I meant about the necklace."

"Oh. Nothing."

"Nothing? You won't tell Greg?"

Abby shrugged. "It's not my business. I just came to offer some friendly advice. Right now, Lilly trusts you. If you don't want to lose that, you better try harder."

With a final nod, Abby stepped through the big front door of the Wiltshires' house.

She walked down the narrow sidewalk between frost-laden lawns to her small blue car and turned on the heat. As she waited for the car to warm up, she noticed the reflection in her rearview mirror.

103 Blackthorn Road.

Chelsea's house.

Abby shut her eyes. When she opened them, she locked her gaze on the pale stone facade of the Wiltshires' home, refusing to let it drift to the house in its shadow. Lilly stood near the window, the diamond necklace sparkling at her neck. Grinning, she embraced a girl who could only be her sister.

So the mother returned the necklace after all. Abby smiled in silent appreciation.

She leaned back in her seat. The roaring heat and the familiarity of the neighborhood stirred more than frost on her window—it woke long-dormant memories of snowball fights and campfire tales, late-night adventures with starlit bike rides and whispered secrets, and a longing for something. Or some*one*.

Abby shook herself from her thoughts. She shouldn't have worked a party so close to *that* house. She shouldn't let old memories get the best of her like this.

Rubbing the half-formed tears from her eyes, Abby turned her attention to her phone. There was a single text from Lucas with the address to a place called Kensington Manor. Abby plugged it into her GPS and grinned.

Sad time was over. Now, it was best friend time.

After putting the car in drive, she floored it out of the neighborhood, watching 103 Blackthorn Lane fade in the rearview mirror.

If only she could leave her sorrow behind as well.

Chapter Two

Abby had forgotten how much she hated solo drives. Road trips were one thing, with endless conversation, a plethora of music playlists, and frequent snack breaks. But the dull stretches of highways followed by narrow winding roads made her antsy to get out and stretch her legs.

Several times she considered turning around and letting Lucas catch the next bus, but then she remembered this was *Lucas*—her best friend, who she would do anything for, including a four-hour drive.

An hour in, she stopped at a gas station for hot chocolate. Two hours in, she called her cousin to catch up and ended up singing nursery rhymes to her three-year-old niece. Three hours in she did something that proved just how desperate she was for conversation: she called her mother.

"Hello, this is Rebecca Spector," her mother answered in her professional tone.

"Hi, Mom."

"Abby, darling—" Roaring wind crackled through the speaker. Abby pictured her uptight mother driving through town in her black BMW with the windows cracked just enough to let in the wind but not enough to mess up her hair. "What's wrong?"

Abby straightened in the driver's seat. "Nothing's wrong. Can't I just call to say hi?"

"If it's money you're after, ask your father. I don't have my—"

"I don't want money."

"Everyone wants money."

Abby sighed. "I'm not calling about money. I just wanted to catch up. You know, see how you're doing."

"I'm doing fine, although my back is killing me. My usual Pilates instructor was out yesterday and this new woman didn't have a clue what to do. She ruined my back."

"I'm sure your back is fine."

"It's not fine, it hasn't been fine since I was thirty."

"I'm sure she didn't ruin it."

"If it's not better by Monday, I'm going to have to make an appointment with the chiropractor." Her turn signal clicked.

Abby tapped her thumb against the wheel. A quick glance at the clock showed only a minute had passed. It felt much longer. Wasn't talking to someone supposed to make time feel like it's going faster? She had forgotten her mother was an exception to that rule.

"What's wrong?"

"Nothing's wrong," Abby insisted.

Her mother sighed. "I know you didn't call to hear me complain about my Pilates. If nothing was wrong, you would have made a joke or changed the subject by now, but you're just letting me prattle on—"

"I'm being polite."

A heavy pause followed. Abby could picture her mother pursing her lips.

"Is this about Chelsea?"

Her mother said her name in the same dismissive way she had said it all those years ago, when Chelsea was still alive and 'a bad influence' on Abby. Abby's heart clenched. Even after all this time, it hurt to talk about her. Hurt to remember what she had lost. Abby tightened her grip on the wheel. "I saw her house today."

Her mother took a sharp breath. "What in the world were you doing there?"

"I worked a party next door."

"I told you this job was no good."

"It's not the job's fault."

"Of course it is. If it weren't for that silly magician thing, you never would have driven past her house. And on Shabbat! You're supposed to be resting."

Abby let out a heated sigh. "You grade papers on Saturdays."

"Only when I'm in a pinch, and I feel guilty about it. *And* I get paid well. They pay you what—twenty bucks an hour? For three hours a week? That's not a living wage, Abby."

Abby worked more hours and got paid more than that, but there was no point in arguing with her mom. It wasn't enough. It was never enough. "That's why I work at the coffee shop."

"If you could just get a normal, stable, nine-to-five job—"

"Mom—"

"—you wouldn't have to worry about going by that house. What if your next party is in a movie theater?"

"No one wants a stage magician to perform in a movie theater."

"Are you going to have another breakdown?"

"I haven't had one in years."

"You haven't stepped foot in a movie theater in years."

Abby took a deep breath and held it until her chest burned.

The background noise coming through the phone stopped. Her mother must have stopped driving. When she spoke next, she sounded crisper and clearer. "Are you alright?"

Abby shook her head. On the verge of tears and frustration, she tried to force the pain in her heart into words: that even after all this time, she missed Chelsea. That she wished she could go back in time to before the tragedy, before the heartache. But what good would saying these things out loud do? Her mother couldn't change the past, couldn't bring back the dead. "I'm fine."

"Good. Did I tell you my friend Amy's husband is looking for an office manager—"

"I *have* a job, Mom. Two of them. I'm not looking for a new one."

"Well, if you change your mind—"

"You know what, I've got to go."

"Wait," her mother said sternly. "Your father and I are going out of town next weekend. Could you stop by Sunday morning to water the plants, take down the trash, bring in the mail—the usual. Around noon, maybe?"

Abby frowned. Why noon? She envisioned showing up to her parents' house at the same time as a recruiter, or worse—some unsuspecting blind date her mother was trying to set her up with. She shook her head. "I'll think about it."

Abby huffed as she ended the call and blasted her favorite music, trying to think of anything except her mother, Chelsea, and the house Chelsea used to live in.

At long last—after half an hour of driving down an old country road with no other cars in sight—the GPS finally chimed that her destination was on her left.

Abby slowed as she turned into a stone driveway marked by an iron sign swaying ominously in the wind. It read: *Kensington Manor.*

Pine needles and feather-light snow sprinkled Abby's windshield as she followed the crescent driveway to the front of a large Victorian house that loomed over a hill, its Gothic trim poking a dark sky. Twinkling lights hugged the hedge and winked around the branches of a bare oak.

Abby double-checked the address. *This* was where Lucas was staying? The house was the biggest Abby had ever seen. The garage alone was the size of her childhood home. What was Lucas Clark doing in a place like this?

Abby parked her blue Volkswagen at the bend in the driveway and turned up the heater as she attempted to text Lucas that she had arrived. Her phone had such low signal, the message didn't go through. After several minutes of watching snowflakes melt against her windshield, she scrambled out of her car and ran to the front door.

Snow whipped around her, stinging her eyes. She pulled her magician's robes over her head, but it did little to stop the cold.

Hurrying to the front porch through billowing wind stirred memories of trick-or-treating—of racing Lucas to the houses that gave the best candy, and playing rock paper scissors on the scariest decorated driveways to see who would knock first. Her heart ached to go back to that time, when her worst nightmares were of rubber spiders coming to life and she would wake to find the world as it should be, with everyone she loved alive and well.

She shook snow from her shoulders as she reached for the doorbell, which was guarded by an elaborate wreath tied with a red ribbon.

She rang once.

Twice.

Three times.

Stepping back, she shivered and watched the glow of electric candles fill the upstairs windows. At least someone was home.

The front door opened.

Abby blinked. While she had been hoping to see Lucas, she wouldn't have been surprised to see a butler, well-dressed CEO, or sophisticated elderly person greet her on the doorstep of the extravagant manor. Instead, the woman who greeted her looked like a bouncer at a club.

In her dark leather jacket and combat boots, Abby almost thought she was a security guard, but brightly painted butterflies on her shoes ruined the effect. She stood a few inches taller than Abby, in dark jeans, a loose graphic tank top, and a deep purple leather jacket, looking incredibly out of place against the ornate porch trim. Pale light glistened off her warm brown skin, illuminating highlights in her dark wavy hair and sparkling against her nose ring. An amused smirk lifted the corners of her lips. "What the hell are you supposed to be?"

Abby's tongue slid across the roof of her mouth as she tried to think of a witty retort or a tasteful flirtatious remark. When nothing came to mind, she shrugged and said, "I'm Abby, Lucas's friend. I came to give him a ride."

"Not in this weather, you aren't," Not-Security-Guard said. She pulled the door open wider and grimaced at the blackening skies. "Come in before you freeze."

Abby ran her fingers through her hair in an effort to flatten the frizz. She wiped her sneakers over a monogrammed entry rug that looked nice enough to belong in an art gallery—at least, it had until Abby smeared mud across it.

Not-Security ushered Abby inside. "I'll get Lucas. Wait here."

She gestured to an opulent open living room across the hall, with a marble fireplace, high ceilings, gold-tinted furniture, and a crystal chandelier.

"Do you live here?" Abby asked, gawking at the elegance. She had not stepped foot in someplace this formal since her eighth-grade field trip to the White House. In the nearest corner, a Gothic Victorian cocktail bar gleamed in the firelight. Alcohol lined the lower shelves, while fancy dishes were flaunted in the center. Glass bowls rested on the counter, brimming with candy, nuts, and dried berries ripe for the taking. A large Christmas tree filled the opposite corner, its reflection twinkling in the dark windows.

The only sign the place was lived in was a fluffy white cat sprawled across the couch nearest to the fireplace. She glanced lazily in Abby's direction and lowered her head, as if Abby wasn't worth the time or effort to get to know.

Not-Security snorted. "I wish."

"Is this a hotel?" Abby ventured, extending a hand toward the cat.

The cat tentatively sniffed her and stretched, rubbing against her outstretched hand. Abby wondered if she could smell the candy she had hidden in her pockets, or the potato chip crumbs she had spilled on herself in the car. Either way, the cat gave a satisfied purr at Abby's touch.

The woman shook her head. "Private estate. Try not to drip

on the furniture or Michelle will have another fit."

"Michelle? Michelle *Clark*?" Abby tried to envision Lucas's sister, a mild-mannered perfectionist, 'throwing a fit.' She would have had an easier time imagining Mickey Mouse as a serial killer.

"The one and only."

"Is she prone to having fits?"

"She's prone to kissing up to Mrs. Kensington." Not-Security smirked as she rapped her knuckles against the archway. "Don't make a mess. She'll kill you if you do."

She retreated down the hall, her painted boots thumping against the polished floors.

Abby frowned. Each answer to her questions had raised even more questions. What were Lucas and Michelle doing here? Is this where Michelle was getting married? How could she afford to rent a place like this? Her fiancé must be loaded.

Abby shook the thought, giving the cat a final stroke before moving toward the candy bar.

She took a handful of what she thought were chocolate chips, which turned out to be chocolate-covered blueberries. They were good, despite the unexpected tartness.

Firelight danced across the rug, gleaming off picture frames over the mantle. Abby stepped closer to study them. Some were modern, with two white guys in business jackets and warm smiles standing between a stern-looking old woman and a distant old man. Then there were older pictures. Some looked like they were taken in the 80s and 90s, while others went *way* back. Several featured an old-fashioned horse and carriage. Each picture showed a family in front of the house, posing under the same oak tree.

"Some in-laws, huh?" a voice said behind her.

Abby turned as Lucas stepped into the living room, grinning. He looked...*sophisticated.*

His soft gray suit complemented his dark complexion. Despite the baggy shoulders and the slightly frayed edges, it suited him. His curly black hair was longer than the buzz cut he had worn when Abby had last seen him and his chin sported stubble a touch stronger than a five o'clock shadow. But he was still Lucas, with his too-big grin and familiar warm eyes.

"Did you just come from a James Bond audition?" Abby teased.

"Interview." Lucas clasped his hands behind his back. "For a teaching position."

"Spy would have been a lot more interesting."

"I know, right?"

Just like that, it was like they were ten again. Like he hadn't been living out of the country the last two years. Like they weren't in some super fancy mansion in the middle of rural Pennsylvania. They were just two best friends, spending time together.

Abby leaped across the couch to throw her arms around him. "What's this about in-laws? You didn't secretly get married while you were away?"

Lucas laughed. "Nothing like that. I mean Michelle's future mother-in-law. She owns this place."

Abby's jaw dropped. "*What?*"

Lucas pointed to a framed photo of two teenage boys in sophisticated polo shirts and chinos with a fluffy white dog. "The one on the left is Michelle's fiancé, David. He grew up here."

Abby stared at the picture of the boy who looked like he was on the set of a Banana Republic commercial. She supposed people would find him attractive, if they were into polished, sophisticated men—or men in general. "Michelle did good. Who's that next to him?"

"His brother, Robert."

"I meant the dog."

"Oh." Lucas scratched his head. "I don't know. I haven't seen any dogs around. Just Marie Antoinette."

"Who?"

Lucas gestured at the cat, who had returned to sleeping in the center of the couch, but was now stretched out luxuriously, spilling pale fur across the upholstery.

Abby rubbed her chin. "And that's it? That's the family? There's no sister or anything?"

"Nope, just the two brothers and their mother."

"Is the brother single?"

"Since when are you into guys?"

"Since they're millionaires, apparently." Abby reached for another bowl of chocolate.

"He's married," Lucas said with a disapproving tone, as if he couldn't tell Abby had been joking. Or—*mostly* joking.

"Well, then you've got to find me some cute cousin or someone, get me in the family— Hey! I was eating that."

Lucas set down the bowl of chocolate he had taken from Abby and glanced over his shoulder. He tugged on Abby's arm. "Let's go."

"Why? You can't seriously be in a hurry to leave this place."

"I am." Lucas glanced right and left, before answering with a voice like he was confessing a great crime. "I was in town for an interview."

Abby frowned. "I thought you came for the wedding?"

"I tried to schedule them at the same time, but the latest I could get was yesterday. I figured I could crash here until the wedding, help Michelle out—but she wasn't onboard with that plan."

Abby wrinkled her nose at his cologne—or, more likely, the previous owner of the suit's cologne. It smelled like mothballs. "Seriously? She hasn't seen you in two years, and she isn't happy you came early?"

Lucas shifted his weight. "It hasn't been two years."

"She visited you in England?"

Lucas scratched at his collar. "I, uh, came home a few weeks ago."

Abby stared at him, her stomach going cold. "You came home and you didn't tell me?"

"I was busy," Lucas insisted, but it didn't soften the blow. Abby had been fantasizing about his return for months, and he hadn't bothered to call her and let her know he was back. That hurt.

"Dad's driving me up the wall. All this 'you should have gotten a business degree', 'come sell insurance with me, son' nonsense. I'm twenty-six years old, I'm not working in insurance! And I'm definitely not working with my dad. *Again!*"

Abby tried not to show how dejected she felt. "I work for my dad sometimes."

Lucas sighed. "I didn't get my master's in English literature so I could go back to working for *my dad*."

"I get it, I get it. You need a big-boy job."

"I *need* to live on my own again." Lucas moved away from her and began to pace, his voice rising with each word. "And a nice private library wouldn't hurt. But I'd take anything, even teaching grade school at this point. I'm tired of wasting away in my parents' guestroom. Mom's started making my lunches again."

"She makes the best chicken salad sandwiches."

"Yes, but the point is—I'm not in first grade anymore. I can make my own lunch." He collapsed into an armchair, rolling up the sleeves of his suit. "Anyway—as I was saying—I thought I could come and stay with Michelle for a bit, but she's not as happy to see me as I'd planned."

Abby raised an eyebrow. "Why not?"

He held up his index finger. "I didn't tell her I was coming." He raised his middle finger next to his index finger. "I invited Mina Amir." He raised his ring finger as well. "I didn't tell her Mina was coming. That's three strikes."

"Who's Mina Amir?"

"Michelle's friend. They did everything together in high school. She's the one who let you in."

Abby recalled the bouncer-like woman as Lucas stood and poured himself a drink of sparkling water from a fancy bottle.

"Her maid of honor backed out last minute, and I told her I'd handle it. I thought it'd be nice to surprise her with Mina, but apparently they had a falling out or something and—" He shook his head. "Here we are."

"Why did Mina come if they aren't friends anymore?"

Lucas shrugged. "Beats me. Let's get out of here. I'm starving."

"I brought snacks." With a magician's flourish, Abby reached into a hidden pocket in her robes and pulled out a box of his favorite snack: packaged chocolate sponge cake.

Lucas's only response was a minimal brow crease.

Abby frowned at his lack of enthusiasm. She tossed him the package. "There's more in the car."

"Thanks," Lucas said, setting the cake aside, "but I'm in the mood for real food. Maybe we can stop for dinner somewhere.

Know anywhere I can get a good salad?"

Abby's frown deepened. Never in her life had she seen Lucas Clark pass up an opportunity to gorge on sweets, especially cakes.

Michelle stepped into the room, crossing her arms. Abby almost didn't recognize her. Granted, the last time she had seen her, Michelle had been covered in mud and sweat from a stream cleanup gone wrong. That had been six years ago, but still—in a delicate lilac dress that hugged her curves, she looked like she was headed to the Oscars. Her corkscrew curls had been relaxed into straight shoulder-length strands that framed a face heavy with makeup. Fancy bracelets circled her wrists and a huge diamond ring covered half her ring finger.

"I'm afraid you'll have to wait." Michelle's eyes narrowed as she flicked her manicured nails against a thin watch amidst her bracelets. "The blizzard is getting bad. Mrs. Kensington called and said she's getting a hotel. A tree fell over the main road. You're lucky you made it before then."

Abby had been stuck in worse places. Her date with her TV would have to wait—one of the large screens in this mansion would do just fine. And she would trade a night alone for some time to catch up with Lucas any day.

Michelle glared at Lucas like the storm was his fault. "Guess you got what you wanted, one big *happy* reunion." She spat the last few words.

Abby inched forward, attempting to defuse the tension. "I'm just happy to see you both. Congratulations on the engagement!"

Michelle's shoulders softened. "Thank you, Abby. You're welcome to join us for dinner if you'd like. I have some clothes you can borrow."

"I'm good." Abby pulled the oversized robe over her head and hung it over the back of an armchair. Thankfully, her jeans and T-shirt were still mostly dry.

Grimacing, Michelle pulled the robe off the armchair. "I'll just hang these in the closet. Lucas, show Abby to the dining room."

"This isn't the dining room?"

Lucas shook his head, strolled across the wooden floors, and shoved open a pair of double doors. "This is."

Abby was prepared for some fancy dining room she would expect to find in a five-star hotel, but unlike the living room, the dining room was elegant in its simplicity. A long candlelit table rested in the center of the polished floor. A crystal chandelier loomed over it, smaller than the one in the living room, but by far the most impressive thing in the room was the view. The curtains were drawn back, revealing large snow-splattered windows overlooking a veranda and garden that bled into fading twilight. The third wall held a cozy fireplace that kept the room feeling toasty.

Across the room, a small door opened and a middle-aged woman entered, carrying a tray of bread and a large pitcher of water. Despite her graying blonde hair, she had a youthful demeanor, with rosy cheeks and a simple apron over an artsy dress that reminded Abby of a watercolor painting.

Lucas rubbed his hands together. "That's what I'm talking about. Thank you, ma'am! These rolls look delicious."

The woman smiled at Lucas as she set the tray down in the center of the table and filled their glasses with water.

Lucas pulled out a chair with his back to the fireplace. He placed a napkin in his lap and prepared a roll by cutting it precisely in half and spreading a tiny smear of butter across one side.

Abby sat next to him.

Michelle took the seat across from her brother with her back to the window, flashing him an annoyed glance. She turned to the woman filling their water. "Sorry about the extra guests, Sandra. Don't worry about anything fancy for them. They'll be fine with whatever you have."

Lucas's brow wrinkled in confusion, as if he was trying to decide if this was a compliment or insult.

"That might have been a problem if the boys were here," said Sandra, "but with this storm, I have three dinners that would have gone to waste."

"Three?" Abby asked.

"Mrs. Kensington's stuck in town," Lucas explained. "Michelle's fiancé, David, and his brother, Robert, were supposed to fly in tonight, but that's not happening. So do you want to split the third meal or—?"

"Lucas." Michelle pointed a fork at her brother. "Manners."

"I'm asking if she wants to share—how is that not polite? Does anyone want to share the extra dinner?"

Michelle buried her face in her hands as two others joined them in the dining room. Mina slipped to the head of the table, where she had the perfect view of all windows. Marie Antoinette jumped into the empty chair at the foot of the table and sat tall, wrapping her tail around her. Her blue eyes and crystal collar sparkled in the overhead light.

"Is she having dinner with us?" Abby joked.

Michelle sighed, pinching her forehead.

"That is Miss Antoinette's chair. Mrs. Kensington likes the company when she dines, and as it's usually just the three of us…" Sandra gestured between herself and the cat, before returning to the kitchen.

"Sounds like an interesting family," Abby said, patting Marie Antoinette.

The cat slid out of her touch and raised a paw, locking eyes with Abby as if daring her to touch her again. Abby returned her hands to her lap. Bossy cat.

Sandra moved in and out of the kitchen, returning with several bowls of steaming butternut squash soup, and finally—canned fish for Marie Antoinette. *That* had the cat purring.

Once everyone had food in front of them, Sandra removed her apron and slipped into the remaining empty chair.

"You live here?" Abby asked, attempting to make conversation. She had assumed Sandra was a hired cook, but now that she took a seat at the table, Abby reconsidered this assumption. "Are you related to Mrs. Kensington?"

Sandra poured a glass of wine, licking her lips as if she had to think about it. After several seconds, she shrugged and explained, "We're roommates. She needed help taking care of this place and I needed a place to stay."

"Sandra's an honorary member of the family," Michelle said fondly. "I don't know what I'd have done these past few months without you."

Sandra's hands went to her heart, her smile growing. "Aren't you a dear? Eat before the soup gets cold."

"Don't have to tell us twice, do they?" Abby asked, reaching out to stroke Marie Antoinette.

The cat hissed, slapping her hand away, as if she expected Abby to steal her tuna.

Even if Abby had been hungry enough to consider the thought—which she hadn't—there would have been no need, for as soon as the bowls were drained, Sandra returned to the kitchen and brought everyone—including the cat—platters of

fish, with the head, scales, and eyes still intact. Abby expected
Lucas to gag, but he surprised her by tucking his napkin into his
shirt and digging in with sophistication. This was the same guy
who had run out of a sushi bar twice with an upset stomach
from just *seeing* raw meat. Something had changed.

Abby didn't like it.

Attempting to ignore Lucas's odd behavior, Abby tasted the
fish cautiously. Mina, Sandra, and Marie Antoinette devoured
their dishes. Michelle merely batted hers around the plate,
cutting it into smaller and smaller pieces without actually
taking a bite.

Lastly, came the dessert—decadent chocolate tiramisu that
everyone (except the cat) gushed over. Abby asked Sandra for
the recipe, but promptly handed it to Lucas when she saw how
complicated it was. When it came to baking, Abby preferred
her endeavors to be of the break-and-bake variety.

The candles burned low, stomachs grew full, and the
windows darkened with night. Sandra retreated upstairs and
the remaining guests moved to the living room, savoring their
drinks. Abby indulged in a luxurious peppermint hot chocolate decked out with whipped cream and chocolate shavings
that melted on her tongue. It was to die for.

Mina tossed a toy to Marie Antoinette, who batted it lazily
across the polished floor. Michelle snuggled into a thick white
cardigan and took out her laptop, while Abby and Lucas took
seats on the couch, across from the flatscreen TV. Before they
had settled on a channel, a loud *pop* startled them all. The TV
flickered off, along with the lights.

Lucas shrieked and leaped from his seat as if expecting an
intruder.

Marie Antoinette growled menacingly in the dark.

When several strokes of the grandfather clock ticked through the dim firelight, Mina voiced what everyone must have been thinking, "The storm must have knocked out the power."

"No, no, no." Michelle groaned, clutching her laptop to her chest. "I'm almost out of battery!"

"I'm sure David's fine," Lucas said reassuringly.

"I'm not worried about him," Michelle cried. "I've got a report to finish."

Lucas gave her a quizzical look. "Didn't you take time off?"

"Yes, but we're launching a new product Monday and I promised to review the press release."

"I'm sure your team can handle a press release without you," said Lucas.

Michelle looked like she was about to disagree, but sighed and sank deeper into her chair. She twisted her large sparkly engagement ring and shut her eyes with another heated sigh.

"This is a nice place to get hitched," Mina commented, sipping her beer like it was fine champagne.

Abby licked whipped cream from her upper lip. "How come I didn't get an invitation to this wedding?"

Michelle frowned. "Sorry, Abby, it's nothing personal. We had a strict limit on—"

"I was talking to him." Abby elbowed Lucas. "Am I not your plus one?"

He sputtered into his tea.

Abby mimed getting shot in the heart. "You didn't get a new best friend, did you?"

Firelight flickered across his brow, revealing a prickle of sweat.

"Dude?" Abby glanced at Michelle and Mina for assistance. "He doesn't have a new best friend, does he?"

Michelle shifted in her chair. "He's bringing someone he met online."

"What?" Abby turned back to him, holding back a laugh of disbelief. "Is she for real?"

He shut his eyes, nodding like it pained him.

Abby elbowed him harder. "Who is this? Like a date? Online where? A dating app?"

He took a very long, slurpy sip of tea, side-eyeing Michelle.

Snow spilled down the windows. It was too dark to see more than a vague outline of the bushes outside, but the fire's crackle couldn't drown the wind's eerie moaning or the rattling of bare branches against the house.

Abby gently nudged Lucas's arm. His stalling time was up. "Spill."

He muttered something quieter than a cat's footsteps.

"Speak up."

"We roleplay together."

Michelle's jaw dropped. For a moment it looked like she was about to scream in horror, but then she clapped her hands together and cackled so hard she clutched her side like it pained her.

Abby raised an eyebrow. She didn't find his response to be funny. Lucas loved his online roleplay games. She had dabbled in them herself, but never had the attention span to carry on novel-length plots like he did. Sure, she was hurt that Lucas hadn't mentioned his online roleplay partner before, but she was Lucas's friend through and through—she would defend every last choice of his, even if she didn't necessarily agree. "Well, I'm sure this person is very responsible if they've kept up with one of your games."

Michelle wiped tears of laughter from her eyes. "Of course

you're bringing a stranger to my wedding. Why am I even surprised anymore?"

Lucas tugged at his collar as if it was suddenly too tight. "We're not strangers. We talk at least once a week."

"Friend or date?" Abby asked him. "How long have you been playing together?"

"Six months. Date-ish." He fidgeted nervously. "At least, I hope so. I like her, but I haven't exactly asked her out yet."

Mina's eyebrows shot up. "But you asked her to a wedding?"

"Yeah."

"And you somehow didn't make it clear this was a date?" Abby prompted.

"I told her it was my big sister's wedding and I didn't want to go alone. It just so happens there's a comic con up the road this weekend, so we're going there after."

"What?" Michelle straightened. "You better not show up to my wedding in costume."

He held his hands up in a sign of surrender. "We just got tickets for Sunday." He mouthed to Abby, *"Fifty percent off."*

Abby gave him a thumbs up. As much as she agreed a wedding was not the best idea for a first date, his logic made sense. And who was she to comment on dating lives when hers had been dead for nearly a decade?

"Is she hot?" Mina sat on the armrest of the couch, bathed in candlelight.

Lucas loosened his collar. "I don't know. I, uh, haven't seen her before."

Michelle nearly choked on her drink. "Seriously? I swear, Lucas, if you ruin this for me—"

Though the threat remained unspoken, Lucas gulped. Abby didn't blame him. The flickering firelight heightened Michelle's glare, making her look all the more menacing.

Finally looking away from her brother, Michelle carefully rested her drink on a crystal coaster and stood. Folding her arms across her dress as if she was wrapping herself in an imaginary shawl, she crept toward the window and peered into the dark.

She was silent for so long, Abby feared she was thinking of tossing Lucas out into the storm, but when she spoke at last, she said, "I hope this doesn't destroy the rosebushes."

Abby stifled a laugh. She exchanged a glance with Lucas that was part affirmation that worrying about the roses was ridiculous—they were flowers after all, they could survive a little snow—and mostly relief that Michelle had diverted her attention away from Lucas.

"It's a vicious storm, isn't it?" Mina said with admiration. She passed through quivering shadows to stand beside Michelle, where she rested a palm against the glass pane and flipped the lock. Under Mina's steady fingers, the window creaked open.

Michelle stiffened. "What are you doing?"

Mina leaned forward, sticking her head out into the storm. "What's it look like?"

The storm crept in, splattering snow across the windowsill. The Christmas tree protested as the wind surged, its ornaments rattling. Mina threw her hands up in appreciation. In the firelight's golden-glow, with her flannel shirt drooping low on her arms and fanning out behind her like wings, she looked majestic—like a phoenix about to take flight.

Marie Antoinette hissed, fleeing the room.

Michelle snatched Mina back and slammed the window shut. "Like you're about to flood the living room."

"Lighten up." Mina turned back to the room with a hollow

expression that made Abby's heart twinge. A snowflake melted down her cheek as her grin faded under tired eyes and sagging shoulders. Abby recognized the look of someone longing to escape some unwanted emotion. Mina was carrying something that made feeling anything—even the sharp sting of freezing rain—an improvement. "I was just appreciating the storm."

"Look at this!" Michelle stomped on glitter-sized droplets of snow melting across the hardwood floor. "Do you know what kind of damage you could do?"

Mina shrugged. "It's just water."

Michelle lifted a hand to her forehead and pressed her fingers against her temple. "Yes, but do you know what water does to hardwood? To *rugs*? I think it's time we go to bed."

"It's barely past nine," said Lucas, who had this uncanny ability to know precisely what time it was without looking at the clock.

"Yeah, and I have to get up at 7 a.m. to pick up my wedding dress."

"The dress stores aren't open in the evening?"

"They are, but I also have to pick up the bridesmaid presents and place cards, and six dozen candles—stop by the florist to make sure they got my order correct—"

"We get it." Mina clapped Michelle on the back, leaving a wet handprint on her white cashmere cardigan. "Take it easy. Get some sleep. I won't open any more windows."

Michelle chewed the inside of her cheek. "You promise?"

"Pinkie promise." Mina wriggled her pinkie finger in Michelle's face.

Michelle took Mina's finger with a sigh. Her dark eyes swept across Abby and Lucas as she left the room. Pausing in the doorway, she glanced back over her shoulder. "This place better be in tip-top condition tomorrow morning."

"Of course," said Mina.

"Don't worry!" Lucas called back.

"We'll behave!" Abby replied.

With a shake of her head, Michelle slipped into the shadowy hallway.

The others sat in silence as the stairs creaked, then the ceiling, and then finally a door upstairs clicked shut.

Lucas let out a sigh. "Someone's uptight."

"She's getting married," Abby pointed out. Although she agreed the bride-to-be was overreacting, she could imagine the pressure she must be under with a future mother-in-law who lived like this. "That's gotta be stressful."

"Sounds pretty sweet to me." Mina carried a candle to the bar, taking her time to peruse the labels. "Weekend-long celebration of you and your loved one? What's to stress about?"

"You know Michelle." Lucas made a gesture like he was pushing up his glasses even though he was wearing contacts. The familiarity of that gesture made Abby smile fondly. It had been too long since she and Lucas had hung out in person. For over a decade, they saw each other daily, and now they were lucky if they saw each other once a year. The thought made her heart ache. This was her opportunity to change that.

"Hell yeah I do. She needs to lighten up." Mina picked a black bottled drink with a poisoned-looking apple on the front. She took a swig and stuck her tongue out with a sound of disgust. "Either of you want this? It's nasty."

"No thanks." Lucas stroked his mug of tea like it was a cozy kitten. "I'm good."

Mina shrugged, picked up the candle, and went back to browsing the labels of beer, cider, and wine bottles.

Abby turned to Lucas. "Want to play a board game? I think I saw Clue in the library."

"No thanks." Lucas yawned. "I'm not a fan of board games."

Abby's jaw nearly dropped. "Since when? You used to beg me to play Clue with—"

"Careful, Mina," Lucas said sharply. "Don't burn yourself."

"With this?" Mina laughed, waving the candle around like a baseball bat. She brought it to a halt in front of her and trailed her fingers mesmerizingly over the open flame. "I've breathed fire with bigger flames."

Lucas shifted away from her.

Abby felt her eyes widen in amazement. "You can breathe fire?"

Mina grinned. She tossed the candle from one hand to the other, evoking a startled shriek from Lucas. "I'll show you if you have any corn starch."

"No." Lucas got to his feet, wringing his hands and keeping his eyes on the ceiling where Michelle's footsteps had last been heard. "Absolutely not."

Mina set the candle down, holding her hands up in a sign of surrender. As Lucas returned the candle to its original position, Mina snatched a small bottle of whiskey and took a swig. At first, Abby thought she was being dramatic, but Mina's cheeks puffed out, and she spat the dark liquid over a neighboring candle.

The flame shot up in an explosion, bursting over the coffee table like a miniature firework. An orange glow lit Mina's smug expression as crackling and hissing filled the room. Lucas spun around in alarm, but by the time he faced Mina, the fire had receded to an ordinary candle flame again.

Abby stared at her. She could use someone like Mina in her

magic act. Of course, parents probably wouldn't want their kids so close to fire, but if Abby ever landed a gig for grown-ups, she knew who to call. She clapped in appreciation.

Lucas's face pinched. "Really?"

"It's better with corn starch." Mina flicked a spec of ash off the bar. She recapped the whiskey and sipped out of the poisoned apple bottle. "You know, this drink is growing on me."

"Where did you learn that?" Abby asked.

"To drink?"

"To—" Abby mimicked spitting over the candle.

Mina smirked. "A guy at a party taught me."

"A guy…like a boyfriend?" Abby's stomach knotted as she wished for a sign that Mina was single and at least a little gay.

Mina shook her head. "More like a one-night stand."

"Oh," said Abby, the knot in her stomach tightening.

"Or maybe two nights." Mina scratched her head and shrugged. "I don't remember. I can't remember half the people I've slept with."

People, not guys. That was promising. The fact that she didn't remember the names of said people was less promising.

Lucas rubbed his thumb under his chin. "What happened to you?"

"What do you mean?"

"I mean this—" He held his palm toward her, waving his hand in a gesture that looked like he was offering to wipe down her car. "The punk clothes, the rebel attitude, spitting fire across the carpet."

Abby thought it was a bit judgmental of Lucas to be calling out other people's clothing choices when he dressed like he was cosplaying a professor from the 1950s, but he had a point about her attitude. Abby admired the way Mina dove into every moment, inspired and wholehearted, but her brash attitude appeared to stem from desperation rather than confidence. Desperation about what, Abby wasn't sure—perhaps she was desperate to stand out in a world that pressured her to conform. Or perhaps, like Abby, she was desperate to escape the discomfort of grief.

"You don't like my clothes?" Mina feigned insult, bringing her hand to her heart. "Guess I should return the matching shirt I bought you."

Lucas clicked his tongue.

Abby laughed. "Don't mind him. He's just grumpy that Michelle isn't happy he invited you here."

Mina stiffened. The bottle in her hand slowly slipped to the counter, landing with a clank. It echoed through the room, which suddenly felt stale and stiff like it had been sealed off from the rest of the house.

"Michelle isn't happy I'm here?"

Abby winced at the note of pain in Mina's voice, even as Mina's jaw tightened into a stoic expression. She instantly wished she could take those words back.

Lucas kicked her under the table—a warning too late—adding pain to her regret. She glared at him, massaging her knee.

"I'm sure she's happy you're here." Abby tried to recover the situation quickly. "She's just not happy with Lucas."

"For inviting me." Mina's eyes narrowed. She turned to Lucas. "She did ask you to invite me, right?"

Lucas shook his head quickly, the way he did when he was trying to hold back a secret. She had seen it many times, usually right before he spilled a confession to his parents about something Abby had roped him into. How hard was it for the guy to lie? He should have at least learned how to *evade* questions by now. But instead he stood there, sweating uncomfortably while Mina's face grew colder.

"Uh, well, you see, the thing is…" Rocking nervously, Lucas fidgeted with his pockets. "Maybe you should ask Michelle that question."

"I'm asking *you*." Mina started toward Lucas with a menacing glare. Shoving her nose inches from his, she demanded, "Does Michelle want me here or not?"

"I, uh—" Lucas backed away until his knees met the couch, and he sank back into the seat. "I don't know! I thought so…"

"But?"

Lucas bit his lip and shook his head three times before he finally said, "You used to color coordinate your exam note-cards."

Mina scoffed. "Are you saying my outfits are not coordinated enough for her?"

"No!" Lucas sighed. "Forget about Michelle. When did you become so—so—"

Mina's locked jaw and clenched fist dared him to finish his sentence. She growled, "So what?"

"—different."

Mina's shoulders relaxed. She turned her back to the others while she retrieved her bottle and took a final swig before slamming the empty bottle into the recycling. When she returned, the firelight picked up a shimmer of tears in her eyes.

"What are you avoiding?" Abby asked softly.

Mina's eyes narrowed as she turned to her. "What?"

"Did you lose someone?" Abby studied Mina's dark eyes. They were harsh and stoic, holding back a storm of emotions that Abby might have missed if she had not been swept away by the same storm years ago. "Someone close to you?"

Her gaze softened. She shut her eyes, choking back a word or emotion. When she opened them again, her eyes gleamed like daggers. "Don't talk to me like we're friends. You don't know *anything* about my life."

She snatched a water bottle and stormed upstairs.

Lucas sighed. "You've got to stop doing that."

"Doing what?"

"Pushing people to share intimate details about their life."

Abby shrugged. "What was I supposed to say? It's obvious she's grieving. I was just trying to help."

"Some people aren't ready to be helped." Lucas leaned back and took a sip of tea. He grimaced. It must have gone cold.

Abby chewed her lip. She didn't like seeing people in pain, and Mina's grief pulsed through her brighter than a New York billboard. But that seemed too private to share with Lucas. He wouldn't understand—he had never lost anyone. She asked instead, "Why did you invite Mina without asking Michelle?"

Lucas rubbed his chin, frowning. "Can we drop it? I told you; I invited Mina because I thought Michelle would want her here. Turns out, she didn't. And I'm starting to see why." He gestured to the counter where the candle burned. The polished wood around it glistened with drops of alcohol.

Abby's curiosity was dampened only by Lucas's solemn mood. His shoulders were stiff with tension. He cupped his mug without drinking it, even though it was still at least a third full.

Forcing a grin, Abby moved closer to him on the couch and slid her arm over his shoulder. "Want to see a magic trick?"

Lucas pinched the bridge of his nose. "Not tonight. Sorry, but I'm exhausted. Let's get some sleep and hopefully we can get out of this place tomorrow. There will be plenty of time for games back at your apartment."

"But it's nice here," Abby said, looking fondly at the bowls of candy.

"You won't think that way when the Kensingtons return." He stood, put down his tea, and picked up a nearby candle. Holding it away from himself like it was a dangerous object capable of exploding at any moment, he retreated into the darkened hallway.

Abby grabbed another candle and followed. "You're sure you don't want to stay down here by the fire? This is like the perfect place to tell ghost stories. Is that a hot tub?"

"Probably." The stairs creaked as Lucas started up them. "They have everything here."

"A swimming pool?" Abby asked. "A roller coaster?"

"Wouldn't surprise me," Lucas grumbled as they reached the second floor. He turned off the stairs and led Abby down the hall to a wooden door with a suitcase out front. Sighing, he pushed open the door, set his candle on a nightstand, and picked up the suitcase.

Abby followed him into the room. It was cold, cramped with a large desk, wardrobe, and leather loveseat. Burgundy wallpaper filled the space between them. Abby wrinkled her nose at the musty smell.

"I'll take the bed, you take the loveseat," Abby suggested.

Lucas glanced up from where he was carefully removing his folded clothes from his suitcase. "There are a ton of rooms here. Take any one of them. Just make sure it's unoccupied first."

A twinge of sadness stung Abby's heart at the thought that her reunion with Lucas had been hijacked by his sister and the snowstorm. Instead of laughing, catching up, and singing along to show tunes in the car, they were going to bed early like old ladies. The fact they were going to bed in a *mansion* softened the blow, but only a little.

"Okay." Abby stretched, surprising herself with a yawn. Maybe the drive had taken more out of her than she'd thought. Maybe sleep was a good idea. There would be time to catch up tomorrow, she supposed. For now, she would see what fancy rooms awaited her.

"And here—" Lucas handed her a pair of sweatpants and a T-shirt. "For you to sleep in."

Abby considered protesting, but her jeans were a little stiff and it was far too cold for her to sleep in her underwear. And the shirt was so *soft*.

"Thanks," she said, tucking the clothes under her arm. "Sleep tight. Don't let the bedbugs bite."

"I doubt they have bedbugs here." He shut the door gently behind her.

A hollow silence enveloped Abby. Her candlelight flickered off the stained wooden door and the intricate brass knob as Lucas's footsteps retreated behind it.

She tucked the borrowed clothes under her armpit. This wasn't at all the reunion she had hoped for. Four years ago, Lucas would never have shut the door in her face. Abby felt a tug at her heart, like she was losing her best friend.

Shaking her head, Abby started down the hall. He was just tired, like he had said. It wasn't *personal*—just like it wasn't personal that he hadn't called since he arrived home. He had simply been busy. Tomorrow, things between them will be better. Tomorrow, they will catch up like old times.

Abby tried the door beside Lucas's. It opened to a room slightly larger than Lucas's and just as elegant. Mina stood at the far end, near the window, a large pair of headphones over her ears, workout clothes covering her curves as she punched invisible opponents. Abby shut the door quietly and was careful to knock gently before opening the remaining doors. Once she assessed every unoccupied room on the floor, she picked a nice big room with a four-poster bed and its very own wood-burning fireplace.

She searched around for some matches before remembering the pack in her pocket that she kept for birthday cake candle emergencies. They were damp, and the first two struck out, but the third sparked and burned. It took her a few more tries to get the wood to catch, but soon enough she had a decent fire.

Abby's candle dripped wax onto the small wooden night-stand as she parted a lace canopy and climbed into a creaky bed. Cold night air and the scent of old-lady perfume tickled her nose, but the sheets were soft and inviting. She quickly snuggled under a warm down comforter.

Across the room, two large windows peeked out behind half-drawn curtains. It was too dark to see anything more than occasional bursts of snow outside, and a pair of blue eyes gleaming at the foot of the bed.

Abby started, before noticing the white fur surrounding them.

"Marie Antoinette." She gasped, pulling her hand over her heart. "You startled me."

Marie Antoinette gave a commanding meow and swiped at Abby's feet.

Abby frowned. "Do you want something?"

With a hiss that sounded awfully dissatisfied, Marie Antoinette hopped off the bed and trotted to the door, where she meowed incessantly.

Sighing, Abby let the cat out.

She returned to bed, blew out her candle and pulled the comforter up to her shivering nose.

ABBY HAD BEEN deep in the midst of a pleasant dream about her childhood cat supplying her with tickets to Disney World when she woke with a sharp pain in her throat.

She tried to breathe, but her lungs wouldn't let her. Coarse lace scraped her lips and tongue. It flooded her vision, crinkling against her eyes as pain seared down her neck.

Snatching the lace, she attempted to pry it off. Something— or someone—held it down.

Cold hands clasped her neck, digging into her skin like a chain. Someone was strangling her. She reached for their hands but she gripped only air.

Blinking back pain, Abby stared into the darkness, attempting to pull the lace from her neck. It wouldn't budge, only tightened until dark spots shot across what little vision she had.

Abby had been here before, in the throes of death, with nothing but herself and the inevitable fate that beckoned the end of all souls closing in on her, dragging her deeper and deeper into darkness.

Only this time, she wasn't about to wake up from a nightmare: this was *real*.

Was she having a heart attack? A stroke? Abby's medical knowledge might have been made up primarily from medical dramas, but she was pretty sure that life-threatening illnesses didn't come with the feeling of cold, dead hands pressed against her skin. At least, not the common kind.

Illness or not, Abby refused to give up without a fight. Writhing under the velvet blanket, she struggled against her invisible attacker. She tugged and snatched at the lace, but it held tight. She clawed, shoved, and kicked until her lungs burned and her vision swam.

Desperate, she kicked the bedpost as hard and as loud as she could. It shook, the sound lost against the storm. Flailing her arms, Abby knocked at everything she could reach. Her hands closed around a cord and pulled.

A lamp crashed against the nightstand. Objects clattered together, crashing to the floor in a series of loud sounds that ended with shattering glass.

The pressure lifted from Abby's neck. Cool air filled her lungs. With trembling hands, Abby pried the lace from her face and took a deep shuddering breath.

The door creaked open. A pale, thin woman in an old-fashioned nightdress stood in the doorway. She held a candle that illuminated a blood red necklace and messy blonde hair.

Abby screamed.

The woman screamed louder, in a series of short, startled gasps that sounded like blaring hiccups. The candle flickered in her trembling hands.

A flashlight beam soared in from the hall, bathing the green-sponged wallpaper in golden light.

Abby winced at the brightness.

"Abby?" Michelle's voice came from the doorway. "What are you doing here?"

"You mean what's *she* doing here?" Abby pointed at the woman in the corner, whose scream-hiccups dissolved in the flashlight's glow.

Michelle stepped forward, tentatively, arms folded across her silk robe, flashlight clutched in her hand. She frowned at the stranger. "Annabelle?"

"You know her?" Abby asked.

"Of course. She's a bridesmaid." Michelle shot the flashlight around the room as if expecting something sinister to dart out. When nothing did, she turned the light back to Abby and hissed, "Abby, what are you doing in Mrs. Kensington's room?"

Abby's heart steadied. She sat up, leaning against the headboard and taking slow, deep breaths. She pointed her thumb at Annabelle. "I thought she was a ghost."

Annabelle bit her lip. "I thought you were a burglar."

Abby shrugged, giving a heavy sigh. "That wouldn't be the first time."

Footsteps sounded in the hall. Mina rushed in, barefoot in sweatpants and a baggy T-shirt, with her phone sending out a light brighter than Michelle's flashlight. She waved the light around, bouncing it off the walls like they were in some kind of rave. "What's wrong?"

"Is everyone okay?" Lucas shouted from down the hall.

Michelle raised a hand to her forehead. Massaging her temples, she muttered, "That's what I'm trying to find out."

Annabelle stepped forward, her hand over her heart. "I thought I heard a burglar. I heard something break."

Something crunched under Michelle's slipper. Her flashlight darted to her feet, where shards of a porcelain vase sprinkled the mustard carpet. Her sharp intake of breath was as effective as if she'd screamed her disapproval.

Three pairs of eyes landed on Abby.

"Okay, I know this sounds wild, but—" Abby threw off the covers and picked up the lace "—I'm pretty sure I was attacked by a ghost."

Chapter Three

Abby woke to sunlight. She leaned against the oversized satin pillows, admiring the view of snow-covered mountains that filled the windows across the room. In daylight, the room looked less scary and more like a luxury hotel, with its golden walls, ornate desk, and sleek fainting couch. It took her a moment to remember where she was.

And that she had nearly been killed by a ghost.

Abby leaped out of bed, hurried to the nearest mirror, and traced her finger over her neck. Faint pink lines sneered back at her, all that remained of her struggle the night before. She shut her eyes, recalling the sensation of frigid hands against her skin sucking the air from her lungs. What was that, if not a ghost? A bad dream? Shivers shot down her spine despite the blanket draped over her back. The mark on her neck was proof that it was much more than a nightmare.

She turned away from the mirror with a shudder. Maybe the curtain had fallen. Maybe she had been flailing around in her sleep and gotten tied up in it. As she cleaned up and made her way downstairs, excuse after excuse popped into her mind, but they faded as fast as snow on hot coal.

She knew what she'd seen—and what she *hadn't*. There was no doubt. She had been attacked by a ghost.

That meant that ghosts were real, which was something that Abby was *not* ready to process at eight in the morning. Or ever.

Abby stepped into the living room in her borrowed pajamas, a pair of slippers, and an oversized bathrobe that she had found in a closet. A sweet nutty scent of coffee wafted over her—far more deliciously fragrant than the kind they served at work. Lucas and Mina sat silently across from each other on opposite couches, firelight flickering between them. A sketchbook lay open in Lucas's lap, his fingers guiding a pencil in smooth strokes across the worn pages. His tongue rested between his lips, while a calm, concentrated expression wrinkled his brow.

The sight made Abby smile. At least *something* hadn't changed.

Mina lounged on the couch across from him, her dark hair tangled over the throw pillows as she scrolled her phone. She merely grunted in acknowledgment at Abby's presence, before turning back to her screen. Despite the crust in her eyes and the scowl on her face, she gave off a cozy, peaceful vibe.

Ignoring the empty chairs, Abby took a seat on the floor with her back to the fireplace and examined the assortment of berries and pastries on the coffee table in front of her. As she reached for a croissant, she realized Lucas had shut his sketchbook and was now staring at her. "What?"

Lucas cleared his throat. "I think you owe us an apology for last night."

Mina leaned back, folding her arms across her chest. Sunlight gleamed off her studded earrings and her warm brown eyes.

"Oh. Mina, I'm sorry that I brought up that thing about Michelle not wanting you here—"

"Not for that," Lucas said loudly as Mina's eyes narrowed to slits. He looked at Abby expectantly.

Abby couldn't think of anything else she had done wrong, so she shrugged, waiting for him to continue.

"For playing Haunted House at 2 a.m.," Mina supplied.

"I wasn't playing," Abby insisted.

"It wasn't funny," Lucas said.

Mina shoved aside the blankets, revealing her *very* toned arms as she reached for her mug. "You pissed off Michelle."

"Seriously, I wasn't trying to scare anyone."

"Oh?" said Lucas. "What did you think screaming your lungs out at 2 a.m. and smashing vases would accomplish?"

Abby frowned. Lucas was supposed to have her back. That was the number one rule of their unspoken agreement of friendship that had existed for as long as she could remember. She kicked him in hopes it would jog his memory of this.

It didn't work. He just said "ouch" and glared at her.

Mina smirked, wriggling her fingers. "It was the '*ghoooost*' that smashed the vase."

Abby set down her fork and turned slightly sideways, as her back was growing uncomfortably hot. "The ghost didn't smash the vase. And I wasn't the one who screamed! That was the creepy blonde girl."

"Annabelle?" Lucas rolled the sleeves of his navy sweater up to his elbow as he layered butter onto a piece of toast and held it out toward the fire like he was roasting a marshmallow. "What was Annabelle doing in your room?"

"You mean Mrs. Kensington's room," Mina corrected between swigs of coffee.

Abby sighed. "If you let me explain, you won't have so many questions."

Moving to the opposite side of the table, she told them about the attack the previous night, how she woke to being suffocated by lace with an invisible presence looming over her; how she had knocked the vase over as a cry for help; and how Annabelle and Abby had scared each other senseless.

When she finished, Lucas sat stoically, looking thoughtful.

Mina dunked the last piece of her muffin in the bottom of her coffee.

"So?" Abby prompted. "Do you believe me now?"

Mina raised an eyebrow.

Lucas adjusted his hair, folded his hands, and leaned forward. "I believe you *think* you saw a ghost. But ghosts aren't real."

"Okay, then who was the invisible person strangling me with the lace?"

"A hallucination? The lace fell, waking you up, but you had a few seconds of sleep paralysis, which makes it feel like you can't breathe. Your half-awake mind tried to rationalize this by thinking it's a ghost." He patted Abby's arm. "It could happen to anyone."

Abby shrugged away from him. His words made sense, but they were *wrong*. "I wasn't paralyzed. I tried to pull the lace off but something was holding it down."

Mina pushed back her crumb-filled plate and stood, slipping her hands into the pocket of her sweatpants. "Ghost or no ghost, I'm going to see if Michelle needs help cleaning up."

Her slippers pattered softly against the hardwood floor as she walked out.

Abby turned back to Lucas with a sigh. "Come on, man! You know me, I don't make stuff like this up."

"You literally make a living off lying to little kids about magic."

"It's called 'entertaining', okay. It's no worse than when we pretended to believe in Santa Claus at your family Christmas dinners."

"We were kids. We weren't pretending. We actually believed in Santa Claus."

"*You* did. I'm Jewish. I never thought Santa was real."

"You thought he was Jesus's grandfather."

"Yeah, okay." Abby let out a sharp breath of air. They were getting off track. "My point is—I may spin the truth, but in a *good* way. An *uplifting* way. I don't go around causing drama. Why would I stage a ghost attack?"

Lucas dabbed his lips with his napkin and leaned back in his chair. "I don't think you staged it. Like I said, I think the lace fell and it scared you, so you made up an explanation. Maybe even your subconscious made it up."

Abby folded her arms across her chest. "How did the lace fall?"

Lucas scratched his chin. "Maybe the heat came on and blew it over."

"The power's off."

"Maybe it was old. It ripped."

"It was tied on all four sides."

"Whoever tied it could have been bad at tying knots."

Abby's jaw clenched. "Why can't you just admit for a second that it *could* be a ghost?"

"Fine, it could be a ghost." He put his napkin on his plate, collected his sketchbook, and stood. "I'll put that on the list right between tooth fairy and evil witch. Can you get dressed now, so I can have my shirt back?"

Abby shoved her chair back. "No."

"No?"

"No." Abby huffed. "Not until you admit that there is at least a *possibility* ghosts are real."

Lucas tucked his sketchbook under his arm and reached for his reusable water bottle. "You're incorrigible."

Abby rolled her tongue across the roof of her mouth, trying to decide if that was a compliment or an insult.

"It means frustratingly stubborn," Lucas explained.

"I knew that." A feeling of guilt pooled in Abby's stomach. She hated lying to Lucas, even when the lie was as harmless as pretending to know the meaning of a word.

Lucas's eyes flashed with emotion. Since when had his emotions become unreadable to Abby? Her stomach knotted at the thought. She was supposed to be using this opportunity to rekindle their friendship, not extinguish it. "Abby—"

He said her name in a way that reminded Abby too much of the way her mother spoke when disappointed. Not wanting to hear the rest of what he had to say, Abby jumped to her feet and declared, "If you don't believe me, fine. I'll prove it."

THE OLD STAIRCASE creaked as Abby returned upstairs. She understood believing in ghosts was a lot to ask, but a little faith wouldn't kill Lucas. She had hoped he would at least consider the possibility of something attacking her, even if he was not ready to believe it was a ghost. But no, he needed proof.

Chelsea wouldn't have needed proof.

Abby took a deep, shuddering breath and pressed the door to Mrs. Kensington's room open, slowly.

The carpet was spotless. Bed sheets had been stripped and wadded in a pile at the bottom of the mattress, and the lace canopy was returned to the top of the four-poster bed. Michelle's work, no doubt.

Abby stood on the bare mattress and examined it for rips. There were none. She tugged each corner. The knots held.

Green sun-kissed walls surrounded her, adorned with nicely framed oil paintings and a small wooden fireplace. It looked like a normal room, but Abby couldn't shake the feeling that it was hiding something.

She was determined to find out what. If her friends wouldn't help her, she would find help elsewhere.

Chapter Four

"**A** paranormal investigator?" Lucas shook his head as he read the website displayed on Abby's phone below the low battery symbol. "You're really letting this ghost thing go to your head."

Wiping snow cream off her chin, Abby dropped her spoon into an empty bowl and stretched toward the fireplace, savoring the warmth. "I *know* what I saw, Lucas. Or what I didn't see. You know what I mean. This guy can help."

She locked her gaze on his, silently pleading him to go along with her.

He rubbed at the corners of his lips, as if he was trying to clear his frown away. It just made it more prominent. "How?"

"He has all sorts of equipment that allows him to communicate with ghosts. He can tell us if one is stuck here, and help it move on."

Lucas's skepticism radiated through his words: "Over a phone call?"

Abby rubbed her thumb along the hem of her jeans as her stomach churned with nervous excitement. "In person."

"You *didn't*." Lucas gasped. "Abby, tell me you didn't invite him here. Mrs. Kensington would—"

"Relax, I didn't invite him." Abby stood and stretched, trying to act casual like she didn't care about Lucas's reaction, but her eyes never left his face. "We're going to visit him."

His lips tightened. "What?"

"He lives near here. He's fascinated by Kensington Manor. He'll help us."

"He told you this?"

Abby shrugged. Technically, she had inferred it from the past few hours she spent stalking him on the internet. His blog constantly mentioned this place. Along with a restraining order Mrs. Kensington had taken out against him after catching him sneaking inside four years ago. The blog had gone silent shortly after that. "More or less."

Lucas shook his head. "I can't believe this."

"Believe it. It's not far. We'll be back by dinner." Abby moved to the hall and opened the coat closet, studying the luxurious clothes inside. She removed a black fur-lined coat, pulled it over her shoulders, and rolled up the sleeves until they were almost the right length.

"Wait, you want to go now?" Lucas's shadow fell over her, blocking the golden light from the front windows. "The roads are closed—"

"We don't need roads." Abby continued down the winding hall, through a small door, and into a narrow stairwell that led to the six-car garage. Lucas's heavy footsteps behind her heightened her confidence. "He's only a couple miles from here."

Her sneakers squeaked against the polished floor as she hurried past a row of luxury cars to the very end, where a golf cart waited, complete with a snow plow.

Abby unzipped the plastic enclosure and hopped into the driver's seat. She turned, pleased to see Lucas had followed her across the garage. But he wasn't getting into the golf cart.

"I'm not driving that thing out in the cold—" he lowered his voice to an urgent hiss "—and Mrs. Kensington will kill you if she finds out."

"Will you *relax.*" Abby pulled a key from the glove compartment and held it up like a prize. "Mrs. Kensington won't be killing anyone. She could *pay* us, I suppose, but would that really be so bad?"

"Why on earth would she pay us for stealing her golf cart?"

"*Borrowing,*" Abby corrected, slipping on a pair of red gloves that had rested below the key. The fabric was soft and warm. She wondered if they were cashmere or some other luxury wool. "We're doing her a favor. Sandra says they're low on firewood. I offered to get some, and she told me I could take the golf cart."

Lucas shook his head, eyes wide with awe or disbelief—probably both.

"Hop in." Abby grinned as she pressed a button overhead. The garage door slid open, letting in a frigid gust of air.

Shivering, Lucas glanced over his shoulder as if he expected someone to come running after him. "I don't have a jacket."

"Sure you do." Reaching into the backseat of the golfcart, Abby pulled out a puffy blue coat, a hat, and some gloves. She tossed them to a startled Lucas.

"Where did you get these?"

"The closet."

Lucas frowned. "I'm not wearing some stranger's clothes."

"Come on, it's David's. Or his brother's. They're practically family. I wore your shirt last night and you didn't mind."

"Yeah because I know you."

"Just put the jacket on and get in the golf cart."

"Look, Abby, don't you think this is—"

"If you want to stay here, you can stay here. When poor old Sandra is dying of frostbite, I'll just tell her it was too cold for you to go out and get more firewood—"

Lucas stomped over to the passenger seat and crawled inside, stuffing his arms into the jacket. "You're incorrigible."

Abby grinned. "You know it. Now, let's get this sled on the road!"

"Let's get this *show* on the road," Lucas corrected.

Abby sighed as she turned on the ignition and gripped the steering wheel. Even through her gloves, it was unpleasantly cold. "It was a play on words, you know, since we're going out in the snow."

"But we're not in a sled."

Abby slammed her foot on the gas.

The golf cart roared to life, ripping out of the garage and onto the snow-covered road beyond. With a holler from Abby and a groan from Lucas, they sped down the curved driveway. Wind whipped their faces as snow splattered the windshield. Birds flew out of their path in a squawking panic.

Lucas gripped the sidebar as Abby spun the wheel. The cart veered right, lifting the back tire off the snow, sending them skidding off the driveway and onto Mrs. Kensington's front lawn.

Lucas screamed.

"Sorry," Abby said as the back tire slammed to the ground.

"I just need a second to get the hang of this."

She turned the wheel again, softer this time, and they glided gently down the snowy front yard to the salted driveway where icy slush awaited.

Lucas let his hands fall to his lap. "I have no desire to be a ghost when we show up to this ghost hunter's house. Please get us there before that happens."

"Will do." Abby steered the golf cart to where the driveway bled into a deeply wooded stretch of road that wound between alternating patches of bare trees and evergreens.

Nestled on a hill on the outskirts of a mountain range, Kensington Manor loomed over them for quite some time before it faded behind the bend of a forest.

Lucas leaned back in his seat and muttered, "Leave it to Michelle to get married in the creepiest, most remote house ever."

"What's with you two?" Abby asked. "You were close."

Lucas snorted.

Abby frowned. She knew they had gotten along at least until their late teens. When had they started acting like they were nuisances to each other? "What changed?"

Lucas folded his arms across his chest. "She acts like she's so picture-perfect, but she's just a selfish, conniving little spotlight-stealer."

Abby raised an eyebrow. "Spotlight-stealer?"

"Any time I get close to anything good, she snatches it away from me. It's like she can't stand the idea that I could compete with her, so she messes up my chances."

"Like what?"

The cart jostled as they crossed a log bridge over a frozen stream. A pair of birds soared between branches overhead.

"Where should I start? My parents couldn't come to my senior orchestra performance because she had to get her appendix taken out."

"I don't think she could control that."

"When I applied to magnet school, she switched the file on my application—she couldn't stand the idea of me getting into her perfect little magnet school, so she sabotaged my chances at success."

Abby's grip tightened on the wheel. *She* had been the one who switched his application, but she wasn't about to tell him that. The thought of attending high school without her best friend had terrified eighth-grade Abby. She had thought he wouldn't notice. And when he had, she figured he would forget about it once he got into the groove of freshman year. Apparently not.

She cleared her throat. "That was years ago. I think you're pretty successful."

"Because of her, I didn't get into Harvard, Yale, or—"

"Dude, you went to *Oxford*."

"For grad school. I had to do my undergrad at University of Virginia."

Abby sighed. She tried to assuage her guilt with the thought that Lucas's family wouldn't have been able to afford out-of-state schools, even if a more prestigious school had given him an advantage on his application. What worried her more was that he had taken his anger out on Michelle. "What has she done since then?"

"She's vindictive, Abby. She sabotages me."

When the forest opened into a stretch of snow-covered fields, Abby turned off the road, flooring the gas as they wound their way up the side of a hill.

Lucas clutched his seat. "What are you doing?"

"Driving."

"Yeah, but where?"

"The paranormal investigator's. His name is Glen Ashford. He lives back here somewhere—"

"*Somewhere?*"

"Yeah—down in the valley on the other side of the mountain. We're taking a shortcut."

Lucas shut his eyes and muttered a prayer. When he opened them, he turned to Abby and leaned back in his seat.

"Abby," he said in a serious tone. "When did you first start believing in ghosts?"

"Last night," she said in annoyance. "When one tried to kill me."

Lucas studied her. "And why is it *so* important that you prove they're real?"

"So it doesn't kill me—or you—or anyone else."

Lucas nodded with a frown like he wasn't sure if he believed her or not. "And you're sure this has nothing to do with—you know—" He cleared his throat.

"With what?"

"With—someone else's ghost?"

Abby slowed the golf cart and turned to stare at him before his request dawned on her. It felt like a blow to the ribs. The second part of their unspoken rules of friendship was that Lucas never—under any circumstance—mentioned Chelsea. "You think I'm making this up because of what happened to Chelsea?"

"I don't think you're making it up." Lucas rubbed his gloved hands together. "I think you miss her. Such a tragedy can cause some people to believe—"

"No, no," Abby cut him off, revving the engine as she

returned the golf cart to full speed down a winding snowy bank. "I'm not delusional."

"It's not delusional to want to talk to the dead."

Abby's heart clenched with upturned grief as her stomach churned with anger toward her best friend for picking at old wounds. Of course she wanted to talk to Chelsea. She would give anything to hear her laugh again, see her smile. There was so much she wanted to say, so much she wanted to make right. But just because *a* ghost was real, didn't mean *Chelsea's* ghost was real. Or did it?

Her heart fluttered briefly with hope before crashing in a wave of despair. Why was Lucas toying with her emotions like this? Did he seriously think this was some delayed grief response? She had not even thought of Chelsea until he brought her up. That was a two-rule violation. He was on thin ice.

Lucas cleared his throat. "I heard you were in her neighborhood yesterday."

Abby did a double take. "Who told you that?"

"Your mom called."

Abby threw her head back against the driver's seat. She should have known better than to have called her mother. It shouldn't have surprised her that her mother would overreact and repeat the conversation to Lucas—with her own personal spin, no doubt. "Of course she did."

"She's worried about you."

Abby risked a sideways glance at Lucas. He had that pitying, fearful look in his eyes. It was the same look he got when Abby broke down crying at random reminders of Chelsea. Usually, it came with gifts and kind words, or at least a hug. But this time, he made no move to console her. She tapped her gloved thumb against the steering wheel. "Did she tell you *why* I was in her neighborhood?"

Lucas shook his head.

"Of course she didn't." Abby gave a bitter laugh. "I was working a birthday party. It just so happened to be next door."

"Ah." Lucas relaxed a little.

"I'm guessing she left that part out?"

"She did."

Abby clenched the wheel tighter. "You thought—what, that I was going to check up on her ghost?"

Lucas shrugged. "I didn't know what to think."

"And now?"

He leaned forward, folding his arms across his chest. "I still don't know what to think."

Then why don't you trust me? Abby wanted to scream the words at him. Instead, she focused on driving until her anger ebbed enough that she could speak civilly. "This has nothing to do with Chelsea, okay?"

Silence filled the space between them, broken only by the golf cart's dull roar as it churned through snow. In the distance, smoke billowed from the chimney of an old house. A crow landed on a barn with a snow-coated roof.

"Okay," Lucas said at last.

A weight lifted from her shoulders. She was still mad at him, but hopefully this would be the end of his nagging skepticism. She turned on the radio and flipped through static channels and Christmas hymns until she found a soft-rock station from the early 2000s.

Tucking deeper into her jacket, she watched the countryside roll past. As much as she tried to get warm, she couldn't stop the chilling thoughts Lucas's question had unleashed—could the ghost that attacked her have been Chelsea?

She imagined Chelsea standing in Mrs. Kensington's house with an artsy shawl wrapped around her, handmade earrings dangling under her long auburn hair. She tried to imagine her furious, but the Chelsea in her vision just laughed and hopped onto the foot of the bed to admire the patterns in the velvet.

Abby shook her head. If Chelsea was a ghost, she wouldn't hurt her. Lucas was responsible for this pain in her chest, by bringing up Chelsea in the first place. He should know better.

With music blaring and the cool morning breeze brushing her cheeks, she could almost imagine they were back in high school, riding to school together in her old Toyota with its finicky heater and temperature control. Back then, they had traded melodramatic secrets about their lives and dreams— and often, about Chelsea. Abby had complained when she first showed up—how dare Mrs. Perkins assign Abby a seat next to the know-it-all new girl and not her lifelong best friend? But her complaints soon turned to curiosities (Did you know she's in art club? Have you seen her art? Is she any good?) and eventually nervous admiration (She said she's going to home-coming—do you think she has a date? Do you think she wants a date? Do you think she wants *me* as a date?).

Abby had spent days getting up the courage to ask Chelsea to homecoming, only to realize Chelsea already had a date. Or so it had seemed at the time. How was Abby supposed to know that the girl Chelsea mentioned going to homecoming with was her cousin? She just remembered sitting in the bleachers, watching Chelsea fold origami swans and glaring at the girl she gave them to.

Abby snapped back to reality as the golf cart struck a patch of ice. The cart screeched and skidded sideways down a large hill.

Slamming on the breaks, she gripped the wheel, spinning furiously to straighten out.

"Abby!" Lucas shut his eyes and screamed for his life.

A frozen stream glistened ahead. The wheels spun up snow that cascaded down the hill into sharp, jagged jaws of cracked ice.

Gritting her teeth, Abby worked the brakes and the wheel until she managed to slow their descent. The cart teetered and stopped inches from the frozen stream, near a snow-coated mailbox.

Abby's hands trembled. Her fingers ached from gripping the wheel so tight. She lowered them slowly, taking a deep breath. Frigid air stung her lungs as she examined the mailbox. A word gleamed blurrily behind icicles. Brushing a gloved hand across the icy exterior revealed the name 'Ashford.'

"Told you we'd make it." Abby tried to sound confident, but she had a feeling Lucas knew her well enough to pick up on her frazzled state as she parked the golf cart and stepped out, too rattled to drive it the remaining dozen feet to the front door. Besides, the driveway was partially blocked by a fallen tree.

Lucas shook his head disapprovingly, but remained silent as he dusted his gloved hands together and followed her up the snowy bank to a small stone cabin surrounded by pines.

The fallen oak lay across the driveway, coated in layers of snow and ice. Its branches spilled onto the front porch, stopping short of the boarded-up windows. Bits of splintered wood and twisted metal lay scattered in the grass.

"This place is a mess," Lucas said. "That tree is a safety hazard."

Abby agreed, but it wasn't enough to stop her. Determined to speak to Glen Ashford, she scrambled over the fallen tree. Her gloves brushed fresh snow and the scent of pine followed her toward the front porch.

A cardinal perched near the door, pecking at a wreath with shriveled dried fruit. It darted away as they approached.

Abby hesitated on the doorstep. No sound came from inside. She knocked softly, listening for a response.

Receiving none, she knocked again, louder.

"Hello?" she called. "Mr. Ashford?"

"He can't possibly live in this disaster," Lucas muttered.

Abby frowned. Now that Lucas mentioned it, there was no car in the driveway, no smoke in the chimney, and no glow of lights. Maybe Glen had lost power too and ventured to a neighbor's for the day. Or maybe this was his second home, and he had a nice luxurious mansion like Mrs. Kensington's on the other side of the hill.

She was about to express these thoughts aloud when a grizzly old man appeared from the side of the wrap-around porch. Abby grabbed Lucas's arm. She hadn't heard him coming at all.

The man's forehead wrinkled as he sized them up. Short and broad-shouldered, he wore a jacket too light for the weather and a scowl too frightening for comfort. He looked like the kind of man she wouldn't want to run into on a remote hiking trail—or anywhere, for that matter.

"Mr. Ashford?" Abby asked warily. "Glen?"

"Depends on who's asking," the man said, grunting.

Abby cleared her throat. The porch creaked as she shifted

her weight. "I'm Abby. Abby Spector. I was hoping you could tell us about the ghost in Kensington Manor."

"Were you now?" The man's eyes flickered between Abby and Lucas. He folded his arms across his broad chest. "Why do you want to know? You reporters?"

"No, sir—" Lucas began.

"We're staying at Kensington Estate," Abby proclaimed, jumping straight to the point. "And I've seen the ghost."

The man's eyes lit up. "Well, isn't that something? Come on in. Let's talk ghosts before you catch a cold and become one."

Biting back her nerves, Abby opened the front door and stepped into the shabby home of a man who made a living off dead people.

Chapter Five

G len Ashford had a home fit for a ghost.

The dimly lit space was cluttered with stacks of old newspapers, dusty books, and antiques. Mirrors gleamed between the windows, scattering light across built-in shelves and onto a sword and crossbow mounted over the mantle. Cold seeped from the corners as bitter wind thrashed the walls.

Abby sunk deeper into her borrowed coat. The inside of the cabin was hardly warmer than the outside, thanks to the cracked and poorly boarded-up windows. Abby eyed the boards with concern as she reassessed her thoughts on Glen. When she had first seen his picture, she had hoped he was the real deal. His rugged look had helped him then—he did not look suave enough to be a con man—but paired with his old musty house, she started to wonder if he was as reputable as his website had led her to believe.

Lucas made eye contact with her. She interpreted his facial expression as a plea for them to leave, but she shook her head, following Glen deeper inside. She had to at least *hear* the man out first.

"I apologize for the state of things." Glen leaned over the old-fashioned fireplace, bracing his back. "Don't get visitors here much. Either of you want to light this damn thing?"

"Sure." Abby pulled a box of matches from the mantle and struck one, lighting some splinters in the log before dropping it into the kindling below. The brittle logs caught fire, devouring several leaves, bugs, and cobwebs in the process.

Glen took a seat at a round wooden table and gestured for Abby and Lucas to join him.

Abby sat across from him, studying the way his eyes crinkled as he looked around his dismal cabin. Beneath his gruff exterior, she saw a lonely man whose shoulders sagged with decades of fighting the world before resignedly giving in to life's natural course. He was spirited, but he was tired.

"So, you've found yourself a ghost at the Kensington Estate, huh?" Glen leaned back, twirling his mustache. "How'd you kids get in that place anyhow?"

"His sister's marrying into the family," Abby explained.

"Well I'll be damned." He eyed Lucas in appraisal. "Your sister must be something to catch the eye of that family."

Lucas stiffened. He was clearly too afraid to take a seat—or perhaps even move two feet away from the door. Apparently, the only person who was allowed to judge or insult his sister was him. "She is a very talented hardworking business woman."

"I'm sure she is." Glen gave a sleazy grin.

"We're here to talk about the ghosts," Abby said, before Lucas lost oxygen from holding back insults.

Glen rested his hands on his belly. "So, your sister's moving in and wants this ghost taken care of, is that it?"

"My sister doesn't believe in ghosts," Lucas snapped. "And frankly, I'm not sure I do either."

Glen turned his cold eyes to Abby. "So you're the believer, then?"

Abby nodded. She took a deep breath and tried to keep the tremble from her voice as she spoke. "Since last night. Someone attacked me. I felt a *hand* pressing down on my face but there was no one there." Abby shivered at the memory.

She met Lucas's eyes with a challenging gaze. Lucas sucked in a breath, as if steeling himself for whatever horrible thing he feared Abby would say next.

Glen folded his arms across his chest, watching.

Abby gulped. She felt like she was back in kindergarten, turning to her teacher for backup when her friends said they didn't believe that dinosaurs had ever existed. She thought she was right, but with a so-called expert present, she suddenly doubted herself. "Have you ever heard of that before? Of ghosts that want to harm people?"

"Have I?" Glen rapped his fist gently against the table. "My dear, that's like asking if I've come across a dog that bites or a cat that scratches—of course I've come across ghosts that want to harm the living. What do you think all them movies are based off of?"

Abby's shoulders sagged in relief.

Lucas raised an eyebrow. "You're telling me you think *Ghostbusters* is real?"

"I meant them horror movies." Glen leaned back, shadows dancing across his knobby jaw. "Ghosts ain't no joke. They can be dangerous. But they can also be your friend. You see the thing about ghosts is they're just people—people who've lost everything, except for some unfinished business."

Abby hated that her mind jumped straight to Chelsea. Was she out there, wandering the streets without a body, trying to live out a life tragically cut short? Had she haunted Lilly's birthday party? Was she the reason Abby felt chills down her spine every time she looked at 103 Blackthorn Lane?

"Not everyone becomes a ghost, you know," Glen continued, cutting through Abby's thoughts. "In order to become a ghost, a spirit must be under excessive emotional turmoil or have some sort of attachment to something earth-bound they can't let go of—usually, it's a place or an object that symbolizes something deeper—a child, a lover, their life's work, or even a *feeling.*"

Abby ran her thumbs over her bracelet, trying to recall if Chelsea had been under emotional turmoil in her last moments. She doubted trying to make it to a movie on time would make the cut.

"I once sent on a ghost who was so attached to the rush of adrenaline, he was haunting a roller coaster," Glen said grimly. "Scared kids so bad, they died of fright."

Lucas whispered in Abby's ear. "I told you roller coasters were dangerous."

"I thought you didn't believe in ghosts," Abby replied with a hint of amusement.

"I don't, but if I did—if ghosts were real—then how come they're not common knowledge?" He glanced from Abby to Glen. "If all the dead are walking around out there, why aren't they on the news? Why haven't they been scientifically proven?"

"It's not as common as you might think." Glen stroked his beard. "I'd say about one in a hundred become a ghost, and even then, most ghosts don't stick around for long—a quick check in on their loved ones or some unrequited love and poof—they're off to the great beyond or what have you. And that's for one you can see with equipment. A ghost that you can see with the naked eye is a rare sight indeed. One in a million—if that. And even then, they look so real, most people don't even realize they've seen a ghost."

"I didn't see this one," Abby corrected. "I felt it."

Glen nodded. "That's a little more common. Far as I can tell, most ghosts don't know they're ghosts—they just kind of go through the motions they did when they were alive. But now and then, some of them gain awareness. And they can use that awareness to interact with the living—whisper messages, appear for short bursts of time, or even touch you."

Abby ignored the chills returning to her neck, knitted her fingers together, and leaned forward. "Do you know of any ghosts who might be haunting the house?"

"Do I? You bet." He strode across the room to a bookshelf, muttering to himself before pointing to a large leather-bound book. "One of you mind getting that down for me? My back's not what it used to be."

Abby hopped up and hurried to the shelf, stretching onto her tip-toes to reach the book. When she turned around, she caught Lucas peering into the closet with a fearful expression as if he feared it housed weapons or skeletons. All Abby saw was cleaning supplies.

She brought the book to the table, turning page after page of scrawled handwriting in different colored ink. "What am I looking for?"

"You'll know it when you see it."

"Ah," Abby said, stopping on a page. She turned it so Lucas could see.

Kensington Estate Deaths was scrawled over a list of names and dates.

"That's all the people that died on the property," Glen explained.

Lucas's eyebrows pinched together. "There's over a dozen names on here."

"It's an old estate. A lot of people died there. And lived there." Glen pointed to the page across from it titled *Kensington Estate Residents*. This list was much longer. Some names were struck through, others had notes or asterisks beside them. Most were just a name, followed by a set of dates.

"You think all these people haunt the estate?" Lucas asked in surprise.

"Lord no." Glen snorted. "Usually, I'd say it's lucky if a house like this has even one ghost. Ghosts are one in a hundred, remember. But there's something odd about Kensington Estate. That place seems crawling with ghosts. And half these folks seem like they could have a haunting in them—" He rattled his book.

"Who do you think is most likely?" Abby asked.

"Without a proper look, it's hard to say." He stroked his chin. "Mr. Richard Kensington was a stern old man with an attachment to tradition. Didn't like when his granddaughter—the current Mrs. Kensington—was able to have her own bank account. In fact, he wrote her out of his will for doing so. His son, Richard Kensington II, wrote her back in, once he inherited the estate."

Abby wrinkled her nose. Thank goodness times had changed.

Glen ran his hand down the list, as if stroking cards that would predict his future. He stopped on the final name. "Of course, Dean Johnson's death has all the elements of a good haunting—he was a repairman, who recently died on the estate in a terrible storm."

Lucas frowned at the writing. "This says he died in the 90s."

"Guess that has been a while now, hasn't it?" Glen scratched his head. "It had been pretty recent when I first passed through here."

"Do you mind if we take a picture of this?" Abby asked, pulling out her phone.

Glen shook his head. "Take it. Hell, you can take all my ghost-hunting equipment if you want. Not like I get around much these days."

Abby grinned at him like he had announced she had won the lottery. "Are you serious?"

"Dead so." Glen smiled, revealing a row of crooked teeth as he tipped his baseball cap in her direction. "Tell me if you find anything, will you?"

Tenderly, Abby picked up the book and flipped through the pages like it was a prized possession.

Glen cracked his neck. "Hand me that briefcase."

Abby followed his gaze to a briefcase on top of the bookshelf. It was a few inches out of reach for Abby, even if she stood on the tips of her toes. But Lucas reached it easily, although his arms sagged with the weight and he looked like he was about to faint from fright. Somehow, he managed to carry it to the table without dropping it.

"What's in this?" Lucas asked, massaging his arms as he stepped back. "Bricks?"

Glen's eyes sparkled with a mischievous glint. "Skeletons."

Lucas stumbled backward, knocking over a chair as he rushed for the door.

Glen laughed. "Kidding! Keep up, young man—these are my tools."

Lucas froze with his hand on the doorknob, a scowl spreading across his face.

Glen gestured toward the briefcase. "The lock is all threes."

Abby spun the lock until only threes were visible. It clicked. She leaned forward in anticipation, expecting high-tech gadgets or ancient mystical objects. Instead, the contents were surprisingly ordinary.

Dark binoculars rested over a rusty compass, some outdated batteries, and a pocket knife. An antique gun with an absurd number of gears peeked out from behind small wooden boxes labeled 'bullets.' Packets of salt and strips of fabric littered the space between.

Abby and Lucas exchanged glances. Lucas's said this was nonsensical. Abby's said don't be so quick to dismiss it.

Lucas turned to Glen with a sigh. "How much?"

Glen waved his hand dismissively. "No price. Just promise me you'll find that ghost, and let me know who it was once you do, eh?"

"Deal," Abby said, her attention locked on the ghost-hunting equipment. "How does all this work?"

"Pretty self-explanatory." He pointed to the bronze binoculars. "These'll let you see ghosts. And this compass—it'll lead you to them."

"What's the gun for?" Lucas asked warily.

"Why, for the ghost of course. You load it with salt capsules—aim at a ghost if it gets too viscous and it'll dissipate for a while."

"It doesn't kill it?" Lucas asked.

"No, just weakens it for a bit. To vanquish the ghost, you need to do one of two things: help it complete its unfinished business, or destroy its tether—an object it's connected to, that's keeping it here. Usually, this is something that was meaningful to the deceased during life—a diary, a ring, a piece of furniture—but sometimes, it'll surprise you. It could be the murder weapon, or even something that belongs to a rival—something charged with the emotion that's keeping them here."

Glen reached for each supply as he spoke, but pulled his hand back as if remembering that this was not his job anymore. He shook his head and stepped back from the table. "If your ghost is bad enough it's attacking strangers, your best bet is to destroy its tether."

"How do we do that?" Abby asked.

Glen shrugged. "However you can. Fire, water, crushing it with a hammer—whatever the object is, you destroy it, and your ghost won't have anything to keep it here anymore."

"What happens to the ghost then?" Lucas asked.

Abby bit back a grin at his genuine curiosity. Lucas was finally starting to believe in ghosts. Or maybe he was just taking extra precautions, preparing for the existence of ghosts like how he used to keep a map in his car in case of a global power outage or zombie apocalypse.

"Who knows?" Glen said. "It goes wherever the dead go."

Abby shuddered, recalling the funeral home in her hometown where Chelsea had been laid to rest. She wasn't sure why she imagined the ghosts going there, and not to a peaceful afterlife or eternal void. Instead, she imagined the dead floating through the narrow halls of the funeral home as if sleepwalking.

"That's not reassuring," Lucas muttered.

Abby shook herself from her thoughts. She wasn't here to think about the dead—well, not the restful souls anyway. She was here to talk about the ones that were awake, so to speak. With the briefcase laid out on the table, she was pretty sure she had gotten everything she came for.

"Thank you," she said, picking up the briefcase. "For all of this. You've been more helpful than I could've imagined."

"Happy to help a true believer," Glen said with a twinkle in his eye.

Lucas was already holding the door open, gesturing for Abby to hurry outside.

Abby nodded, the briefcase's worn leather handle growing warm in her grip. If all Glen had said was true, she had everything she needed to prove the existence of ghosts.

She would find the one who attacked her and keep it from attacking anyone else.

Chapter Six

A bby and Lucas returned to Kensington Manor half an hour before sunset. Electric light filled the windows with a yellow glow and precious heat welcomed them inside. Lucas hurried upstairs to plug in his laptop.

Abby warmed her hands over the living room fire while her phone charged on a nearby end table. Sandra brought her a mug of hot chocolate and a couple sandwiches left over from lunch.

Lucas returned moments later—lured by the scent of chocolate, no doubt—and they took their usual seats in the living room while their fingers warmed and their stomachs stopped growling.

As soon as Abby's plate was clean and her mug empty, she reached for the briefcase.

"There you are!" Michelle stormed into the room, pointing a finger at Lucas. "I've been looking everywhere for you."

Abby slipped the briefcase from her lap to the floor and

tucked it under the couch, out of view. The last thing she wanted was for Michelle to confiscate or break it.

"I thought you wanted me gone," Lucas grumbled through a mouth full of sandwich.

"Yes, well, that was *before* the snow decided to ruin everything."

"What's wrong?"

"What's *wrong*?" Michelle's delicate slippers pattered against the hardwood as she paced the length of the bar. "Where do I begin? The storm's delayed *everything*. David's stuck in Chicago, I wasn't able to pick up my dress, the fundraiser for the new homeless shelter has been postponed—"

Lucas frowned. "How is that your problem?"

Michelle continued as if he hadn't said anything. "—the tables and chairs aren't being delivered until Wednesday, and just look at the backyard!"

Abby peered past velvet drapes and frosted windows to where snow speckled the shrubs like powdered sugar. Beyond the veranda, white stretched in every direction, coating every tree, rock, and bench in sight. A small pond glistened behind a fountain so white, it resembled a three-tiered cake.

"It's beautiful," Lucas commented.

"Yes, *now*," Michelle moaned, twisting her dolphin stud earring. "But it'll melt by Friday! And then it'll be *soggy*."

"What did you want me to do about it?" Lucas asked.

"You could stop eating and start helping me."

"With what?"

She shoved open a pair of double doors into a bright sitting room that looked out into the garden. Crafting supplies littered the table. Amidst the chaos, Mina sat at the head of the table, hot-gluing seashells to glass jars. Beside her, Annabelle poured sand into the freshly decorated jars and carefully topped each with a tea candle.

"You can start by helping them decorate."

Lucas rubbed the back of his neck. "Aren't your bridesmaids supposed to help you with this?"

"Annabelle is. The rest won't be here for a few days. Now, get to work. I've got to call the caterer."

Lucas chugged the last of his hot chocolate and joined Mina at the table.

"You too, Abby, if you don't mind?"

Abby glanced at the space where the briefcase was obscured from sight. Her mind raced for an excuse, but she couldn't think of one that would include Lucas as well and she didn't want to start using the equipment without him.

"Sure," Abby said at last. If she was going to waste precious time with arts and crafts, at least she would be doing it with Mina.

Satisfied, Michelle left the room.

Abby pulled out a chair, which earned a grumpy *meow* from Marie Antoinette, who blinked lazily from where she was curled on the cushion.

"Sorry, milady." Abby mock bowed as she slipped the chair with the fluffy cat back under the table and sank into the cat-free chair beside it. "What are we working on?"

"Lanterns." Mina dropped a votive candle into a jar of sand to demonstrate. In her baggy skull T-shirt and ripped jeans, she looked like she was better suited for more extreme labor than delicate lanterns.

"Great." Lucas rubbed his eyes. "I'm going to need more tea for this."

"Since when do you drink tea?" Abby asked. "I thought you preferred coffee."

"Coffee hurts my stomach," Lucas said simply.

Abby shrugged, reaching into a large plastic bag of supplies, and pulled out a container of saltwater taffy. "I take it this isn't for the lanterns?"

"Those are for the gift bags." Mina reached for them with amusement. Her ring-coiled fingers brushed against Abby's palm as she took the taffy away. "Michelle said to keep you two away from these."

"Did she?" Lucas smacked his lips together. "She's cruel."

"She left out snacks." Mina gestured to an antique sideboard. A silver platter rested on top, lined with fruit, cheeses, crackers and spreads.

"I take that back, Michelle is amazing!" Lucas began filling his plate with pineapple and crackers before disappearing to the kitchen.

"Grab me a hot chocolate!" Abby called as the doors swung shut behind him.

Annabelle winced as if Abby's shout had been too loud for her delicate ears. Marie Antoinette meowed grumpily. Amusement flickered across Mina's face.

Michelle's voice carried through the walls from where she paced in the hall, explaining to someone on the other end of the phone that she was out of town, but of course she had time to communicate the new date and location of the fundraising event. As if she didn't have enough on her plate already.

Annabelle quietly shut the door, muffling the sounds.

Abby picked up a plastic sandcastle. "What's with the beach aesthetic?"

Mina shrugged. "The wedding is beach themed."

Abby's gaze darted to the snowy mountain venue as she arched an eyebrow. "They didn't want to get married on a beach?"

"Michelle wanted to, but David insisted they marry here."

"It's tradition," Annabelle said softly. "All but one member of the Kensington family has gotten married here, and his marriage ended tragically."

"In death?" Abby asked, an uncomfortable knot forming in her stomach.

Annabelle shook her head. With a shudder, she whispered, "Divorce."

Lucas returned from the kitchen, his mug steaming with hot tea. "Did he see his bride before the ceremony on his wedding day?"

Abby's eyebrow arched up. "Seriously?"

"What?" Lucas asked between sips.

"Where's my drink?" Abby asked.

"In the kitchen. Waiting for you to make it."

Abby pursed her lips. Why was he being so difficult? She shook the thought away and focused on the second thing that bothered her. "You think seeing a bride before a wedding is bad luck, but you don't believe in ghosts?"

"Superstition makes a lot more sense than the supernatural. It's a cultural and societal phenomenon—"

"Okay, okay." Abby threw her hands up. "So, Michelle believes she'll be cursed if she gets married on the beach, but she refuses to believe the house is haunted?"

The hot-glue gun squeaked as Mina forced the last remains of a glue stick onto the back of a seashell. "*Mrs. Kensington* believes in the curse. David wants to please her and Michelle wants to please David so—" she waved the shell toward the window "—we're bringing the beach to the mountains."

"Got it." Abby plugged in an extra glue gun while Lucas began carefully filling jars with sand. She took a peanut butter cracker from his plate and made a face.

"These crackers are awful."

"They're low-sodium," Lucas explained, sliding his plate out of Abby's reach.

"They're gross." Abby leaned back in her chair and watched Mina turn a lantern into something that resembled a heap of trash pulled from the sea. She drummed her fingers on the table. "So how do you know Michelle?"

Mina's silver rings gleamed as she rotated the jar, assessing her work. One of her rings looked like a dragon, while another was shaped like bat wings. "We were friends in high school."

Abby leaned forward, waiting for her to elaborate. As she did, she caught a whiff of a sweet nutty scent, too faint to be cologne. Likely, it came from her shampoo or body wash. It was nice, cozy, reminding Abby of roasting marshmallows on a summer evening.

"My husband is David's brother," Annabelle replied, steering the conversation away from Mina.

Abby tried to hide her disappointment as Mina's lips remained shut, her fingers methodically arranging a bow.

"Ah, so you got married here too, then?" Abby reluctantly turned her attention to the blonde woman. She wondered why she hadn't seen any pictures of Annabelle in the living room.

Annabelle's shoulders fell as she nodded solemnly. "Nine years ago."

"Nine?" Abby stared at Annabelle in surprise. She didn't look much older than Abby. Nine years felt like a lifetime ago.

Nine years ago, Abby was still in high school. Chelsea was still alive. "You must have been young."

"We were," Annabelle admitted sheepishly. "I was twenty, Robert was twenty-four."

Abby stared at Annabelle's wide blue eyes. She couldn't imagine getting married so young. Of course, when she was eighteen she had planned on getting married by the time she was twenty-five, but now that she was twenty-six she felt way too young to even think about marriage.

Lucas cleared his throat. "Hey well, when you know, you know, right?"

"How did you meet?" Mina asked.

Annabelle tucked a strand of hair behind her ear. "I grew up a few miles from here. We must have driven past this house a hundred times—my mother and I. I always loved the way it looked at Christmas. One day, when I was fourteen, my mother made me wear my nicest dress and brought me here to sing Christmas carols. I was *mortified*. And that was *before* Mrs. Kensington slammed the door in my face."

Mina snorted. "What a jerk."

"She can be callous," Annabelle agreed. "But deep down, she's a kind woman. She probably thought we were trying to scam her out of her money. She was always accusing my mother of such things."

Mina's lips pursed. "You're defending her over your own mother?"

"My mother was not entirely without fault," Annabelle said with a sour expression. "Though I hate to speak ill of the dead."

Mina, who had looked as if she was about to say more, fell silent, her shoulders growing tense and her face hardening into the unreadable mask of someone trying to hold back a flood of emotions. She caught Abby watching her and her mask turned into a scowl.

Abby turned her attention back to Annabelle. "Your mother was trying to scam her?"

"Of course not," said Annabelle. "My mother was a great woman. But she cared more about social status than Robert or I ever did. Ever since I met him that day, when he saw me crying on the front lawn and invited me in for hot chocolate— he's been nothing but the perfect gentleman. We didn't start dating for a few years, but from that day on, Mom was always *pushing* me to ask him out. 'Play nice with the Kensington boys,' she always said, 'and you'll be set for life.' I finally gave in the summer after graduation, just to get her to stop pestering me. He took me to dinner and *The Nutcracker* ballet, which I'd been dying to see for years. It was a beautiful night. So what can I say? I fell for Prince Charming." She said the words fondly, with a touch of sadness that made Abby wonder if there was something she was holding back. Did she regret marrying into the Kensington family? Was Robert hiding a secret that was too much for Annabelle? Perhaps a family secret involving ghosts?

"And was marrying into the Kensington family everything you thought it'd be?" Abby pressed.

Lucas leaned forward and rubbed his hands together, as if excited to hear the dirt on his sister's new family.

Annabelle hesitated, twisting her delicate wedding ring. "Yes, and no. Robert and David are wonderful. But their father never approved of me. He died a few months into our relationship and I can't help but wonder if he would have approved of our wedding."

"So what?" Mina said. "The only approval you need is yours. And, I suppose, your husband's."

"Amen," said Lucas.

Annabelle's eyes remained downcast as she nodded solemnly.

"And what was your theme?" Abby asked, attempting to lighten the mood.

"Royalty," Annabelle responded, lifting her chin. The setting sun gleamed off her ruby necklace. With her petite jaw and elegant long neck framed by a chic designer dress, she looked like royalty. A silver clip in her hair even sparkled like a tiara.

"It suits you," Abby replied.

Lucas kicked her under the table.

"I meant it as a compliment," Abby hissed. He must have thought she was implying that Annabelle was rich. But that was so obvious, Abby didn't need to imply it. Her jewelry alone cost more than Abby's monthly rent. She had only meant that Annabelle looked sophisticated.

Clearing her throat, Abby turned back to Annabelle. "When you were married, did anything weird happen?"

"What do you mean?"

"Did you ever hear weird sounds at night, feel unexplainable presences, or see—"

Marie Antoinette chose that moment to growl at the legs of the table, fur rising along her spine.

"Ghosts," Annabelle finished in a whisper.

"Yes," Abby said excitedly. "Did you?"

Mina rolled her eyes. "Don't encourage her."

Annabelle's face paled. Her dress rustled in a way that reminded Abby of a winter breeze as she stood and tiptoed to the hall door, cracking it open just enough so that Marie Antoinette could slip out.

"Sometimes, I'd get a strange feeling," she said softly, returning to her seat. "Like I was being watched. I thought I was just being paranoid about the wedding, meeting so many new people and attending so many formal events but…" Shivering, she pulled her shawl from the back of her chair and draped it over her shoulders.

"But what?" Abby prompted. "Did you see something?"

Annabelle shook her head. "Not then. But last Christmas, Mrs. Kensington had this big party. Robert and I stayed late to help clean up. When we were alone, one of the tents started to collapse on top of us—we made it out just in time."

Chills spread down Abby's spine. "You think a ghost knocked over the tent?"

Annabelle shook her head. "No."

"What, then?"

"I can't explain it," Annabelle said, smoothing out the skirt of her dress. "*Something* happened. All I remember was the tent falling toward us, the horrible sound of metal scraping against metal—I thought I was going to die! And then—the strangest thing happened—a breeze swept through with a hint of fog. Somehow, it held the tent up long enough for Robert and me to scramble out."

Abby's eyes widened. "The ghost *saved* you?"

Annabelle shook her head. "It wasn't a ghost."

Abby blinked in surprise. "No?"

"It was a guardian angel."

Abby stared at her blankly. She couldn't tell if she was joking or not. Judging by Lucas's face, he couldn't decipher it either.

"Ever since that day, I've felt a presence—" Annabelle twisted her necklace as if it were a religious relic "—as if someone or *something* is looking out for me. I haven't seen it since that day in the garden, but I know it's there, watching over me."

Abby chewed her lip. Is this how the others had seen her when she mentioned seeing a ghost? She was starting to understand their hard refusal to believe her. Annabelle sounded like a church recruitment video. There was no way an *angel* was living in Mrs. Kensington's bedroom. It certainly wouldn't go around strangling people.

Abby shook her head. "But if it's an angel, why would it attack me?"

"If an angel wanted you dead, you'd be dead," Lucas pointed out.

Abby frowned at him. He wasn't helping.

Annabelle's lips pinched together. She slipped her chair from the table and tucked her hands into pockets hidden in her dress. "I should be going now. I have a terrible headache. You don't think Michelle will be offended if I don't make it to dinner, do you?"

"If she is, that'd be on her." Mina picked up the lantern Annabelle had cutely adorned with seashells and fake kelp. She added netting, which made it a lot creepier—not to mention a fire hazard. "She better understand. And she better thank us for our help."

With a polite nod, Annabelle slipped from the room.

Lucas elbowed Abby.

"Ouch! What was that for?"

"You upset her."

"I didn't," Abby protested. "She had a headache."

"So she *said*. Maybe she just didn't like you making fun of her beliefs."

"I wasn't making fun!" Abby insisted. "I'm trying to figure out what happened. Maybe *you* upset her when you made fun of her angel theory."

"I did not. I have a lot more faith in angels than I do in ghosts. As long as they aren't like the ones in *Good Omens*."

"Will you two give it a rest?" Mina set her lantern down so forcibly the table shook. Her dark eyes narrowed, her thick eyebrows knitting together. "There are no angels or ghosts in this house, but there's a very real wedding to prepare for. So if you two could stop this nonsense and help——"

Mina gasped as the table trembled and lurched, as if struck from underneath. A recently decorated jar teetered and fell, plummeting toward the wooden floor. Mina caught it before it could shatter.

"What was that?" she asked, breathless.

"Maybe the house is settling?" Lucas ventured.

Abby shook her head, a grin creeping over her lips. "A ghost!"

Mina's grip tightened around the jar, her dark purple nails scratching the lace. Her jaw locked like she was holding back a stream of curses. "Why do you always say that?"

"I know what I saw," Abby said stubbornly. "Why are you so adamant ghosts don't exist?"

"I never said ghosts don't exist," Mina said coldly.

Abby blinked. Hadn't she? Abby could have sworn she was alone in her ghost theory. Maybe that was just because Michelle and Lucas were so loud about it. But hadn't Mina teased her about it at breakfast? She frowned. "You didn't?"

Mina set the lantern down gently, her shoulders sagging as a soft sigh escaped her lips. "I believe ghosts are for the living—something for us to hold on to when we lose people we love. Maybe they're figments of our imagination, or messages from the beyond. They aren't evil—they don't lurk the halls waiting to *kill* people."

Abby felt a tug on her heart, like a ship jerked back by a rusted anchor. If ghosts were real, then that meant the dead were sticking around long after the living had moved on. Did that mean that her past was sticking around to haunt her as well?

Abby's bracelet suddenly felt too hot, too warm against her wrist. She fidgeted with it, sliding her finger under the string, revealing the extremely pale strip of skin behind it. Glen Ashford had said that ghosts could linger when attached to a sentimental object. Could her bracelet hold that kind of sentiment? Abby's heart clenched with desire, fear, and grief all writhing together, struggling for control. Some ghosts were easier to face than others.

Abby glanced back at Mina. Maybe she was right. Maybe ghosts were just memories blurred with imagination. But maybe they were something more. Meeting Mina's gaze, she was surprised to find warmth there. She forced a smile. "Let's find out."

Leaving the others staring in surprise, she bolted from the room and sprinted to the couch. She reached underneath to pull out her briefcase of ghost-hunting supplies. It came easily, with only a slight spotting of dust.

She dropped it on the tablecloth between Mina and Lucas, where it stuck out like a trick card slipped into the wrong deck, its worn leather dark against the crisp lace cloth.

"What's that?" Mina leaned forward, warily poking the side.

Abby opened the briefcase, exposing odd tools and gadgets. She grabbed the pair of bronze binoculars and held them up by a faded strap for the others to inspect. In the crisp lamp light, black scuff marks and dark stains made the binoculars look ancient and rugged, like they were stolen from the set of a steampunk Indiana Jones remake. "This is what's going to help us find out the truth about ghosts."

"Please tell me you didn't pay for that," Mina scoffed.

Abby shivered at the thought the dead could be watching her. But there was no turning back now. Not unless she wanted to be plagued by her own curiosity for the rest of her life. She glanced at her best friend. "Ready, Lucas?"

He shook his head. "I'm still not convinced that's anything more than a con man's pile of junk. You better clean that thing before you put it up to your eye."

Abby sucked in a deep breath and lifted the binoculars. Through the lenses, the room looked the same, except dimmer, with a blue-gray hue of twilight. Mina still sat at the head of the table, but her usual vibrance was gone, as if she were a photograph faded with age. Lucas lacked his usual warmth as well.

"Well?" Lucas asked, unable to keep the curiosity from his tone. "What do you see?"

Abby frowned. It occurred to her that she should have asked Glen what exactly she should be looking for—a hazy blur or a radar reading? She began to adjust the binoculars, expecting to zoom in and out. Instead, the color faded from her friends even more, until they were partially transparent. At the foot of the table, a dark bloodhound stared up at her.

It appeared so suddenly, she nearly dropped the binoculars as she tore them from her face, staring at the legs of the table. The dog was gone.

Abby laughed.

"What?" Lucas and Mina asked simultaneously.

Abby checked once more, just to reassure herself that she had in fact seen what she thought she had. Sure enough, the ghost of the dog appeared each time with the binoculars—wagging its tail and pawing at the table leg—only to fade out of existence as she removed them.

A thrill tickled the back of Abby's spine. All this time, she had been right. There *was* a ghost in Kensington Manor.

Which meant, ghosts were real.

The weight of it struck her so hard she leaned against the table to keep from collapsing.

Hands trembling, she passed the binoculars to Lucas. "See for yourself."

Lucas grimaced as he wiped the eyepieces with the sleeve of his shirt, then lifted them toward his eyes, careful to keep the metal from touching his face. He swept his gaze slowly across the room.

"Look down," Abby directed. "Right about…here." She pointed to where the dog had been.

Lucas looked. He jerked back, swearing.

"What is it?" Mina asked.

Lucas composed himself as he lowered the binoculars. "It must be a trick," he said, standing slowly, eyes darting to the empty space under the table where the dog had been.

"You saw something?" Mina asked, her voice neutral, although her fingers clenched tight around her wrist.

Abby handed her the binoculars.

Mina took them hesitantly, her thick eyelashes disappearing behind the bronze device. She gasped. "It's…a dog?"

Lucas wrung his trembling hands together. "It must be a hologram. Or a computer program—something designed to project images over your surroundings."

"Maybe." Mina inspected the binoculars with caution, as if

she expected them to shoot slime or sound an alarm.

"Or maybe there's really a ghost here."

"Of a dog?" Lucas raised an eyebrow. "What kind of unfinished business could a dog have?"

"Beats me." Abby dropped to a low squat and reached out a hand toward the table, near where the dog had appeared in the binoculars. "Hey, buddy. What are you doing here?"

"Don't talk to it," Lucas said.

"Why not?"

"It could bite."

"Oh so *now* you believe it's real?"

Lucas blinked. He shot a cautious look at the binoculars. "I don't know. All I know for sure is that you shouldn't go sticking your hands near a potential ghost-dog's mouth."

"This better not be a prank." Mina dropped the binoculars to the table, eyeing the walls as if searching for hidden cameras.

Abby tapped two fingers against her chin as her mind raced. How could she prove with absolute certainty that this ghost was real and not a mere projection? If it were human, she could try speaking with it, but a dog…she had a hard enough time communicating with living dogs, much less the ghost of one.

Abby scanned the supplies laid out on the white tablecloth. The compass wasn't helpful since they already knew where the ghost was. She didn't want to hurt the ghost-dog, so the salt gun and pocket knife were out. She reached for a packet of salt that had fallen beside Lucas's plate. Her eyes lit up as she snapped her fingers.

Instead of grabbing the salt, Abby swiped a low-sodium cracker from Lucas's plate.

"Hey, I was going to eat that!"

Ignoring Lucas's protest, Abby dropped to her knees and held the cracker out to the dog.

"Come here, buddy." Abby tapped her knees, then whistled in the way she called her cousin's dog. "You want a treat?"

Everyone stared as the cracker slipped from Abby's hands to the floor, where it skidded back and forth.

Lucas tugged at his collar as his face broke out in a nervous sweat. "Please tell me this is a magic trick."

"It's no magic trick," Abby whispered back.

"It's a ghost," Mina said with a voice steeped in shock. She stiffly passed the binoculars back to Abby.

As she peered through the lenses, she saw the dog had moved from under the table and was now happily shoving his ghost tongue into the cracker, sending it darting across the floor.

Abby passed the binoculars to Lucas.

He lifted them to his eyes, gulped, and lowered them slowly. "I think I'm going to faint. That's a ghost! A *real* ghost."

Grinning with triumph, Abby took the binoculars from him and attempted to pet the dog. He shoved his head through her hand, more interested in the cracker.

"Who's a good doggie?"

"This is a lot to take in." Mina leaned against the table to steady herself. Her eyes glistened with the faintest hint of tears, like frost over an already frozen lake. Her shoulders stiffened, her grip growing tighter.

"Are you okay?" Abby asked.

Mina kicked the table, turned, and stormed out of the room, the jars and various decorative supplies still rattling in her wake.

Abby took that as a no.

She started to go after her, but Lucas stopped her with a gentle hand on her arm. "Give her a minute. This is a lot to process."

Abby chewed her lip. She longed to run after Mina, to comfort her, to *know* her. But it was clear those actions wouldn't be welcomed. If a few years ago someone had unexpectedly proven to her that ghosts existed, she would have drowned in her own tears and desperation, begging to talk to Chelsea.

She had to give it to Lucas—he was handling this well.

He merely rubbed his eyes, as if expecting to wake up from a dream. "So, this house really is haunted, and our ghost is a dog. Why would a dog try to kill you?"

"I don't think he did." Abby looked back to the skittering cracker. The ghost of a dog was one thing, but if dogs could be ghosts, that meant people could be ghosts. And if people could be ghosts— Abby sucked in a sharp breath of air. That meant *anyone* could be a ghost, even Chelsea.

Trembling, Abby returned the binoculars to her eyes and gritted her teeth as if preparing to dive into a winter lake. She swept her gaze over ghosts as easily as cobwebs. In the living room, a thin man in a waistcoat stared into the fire, adjusting his wiry glasses. On the veranda, an elegant woman with high cheekbones and a blue bustle dress leaned against a dark-haired man in a fancy silver vest, swaying gently to a sound Abby couldn't hear. A blond middle-aged woman watched them from the hall, her hands knotted over a more modern floral dress.

But of all the ghosts in sight, there was not a familiar face. Chelsea was not among them.

With a sigh of relief and a twinge of disappointment, Abby lowered the binoculars and the inhabitants vanished. She wouldn't have to face her past. At least, not today.

"There are a lot of ghosts in this house," she declared, turning her attention back to Lucas. "It's up to us to figure out which one tried to kill me. And why."

"And how to stop it before it hurts anyone else, right?" Lucas squeaked.

"That too," said Abby. She had a feeling that would be the hardest part.

Chapter Seven

Lucas draped a blanket protectively around his shoulders, shivering despite the steaming mug of tea in his hands and the pleasant fire across the room. "I was just starting to enjoy this place, and you had to go stirring up ghosts."

"I didn't stir them up," Abby protested, flipping through an old photo album. The photos consisted primarily of David as a child, cuddling a dog that looked suspiciously like the ghost dog. "I just noticed them. Would it have been better if I'd let you live in blissful ignorance until you woke up strangled?"

Lucas made a sound of disapproval and sank back in his chair. "All I know is, I'm *not* sleeping tonight."

"This guy looks like the skinny guy with glasses, don't you think?" Abby asked, pointing to a sepia-toned picture of two men shaking hands. One had friendly round features and a fancy jacket, while the other was a thin man in simple attire who resembled the ghost Abby had noted as 'skinny guy with glasses.'

Lucas set down his tea and leaned forward in the oversized armchair, rubbing his thumb across the album's glossy page protector. "I think so. Who's that?"

"No idea. The back of the photo just says 'George and Archie.'"

Mina returned then, dressed in a different flannel shirt and well-fitted jeans. Even her fresh coat of makeup couldn't hide the puffiness of her eyes.

Abby opened her mouth to ask how she was feeling, but Mina rushed forward and snatched the binoculars from beside Abby. Holding them to her eyes, she moved around the living room.

Abby held her breath in anticipation. For what, she couldn't say. Perhaps one of the ghosts she had seen earlier was Mina's loved one. Surely, most of them seemed too old? Judging by the fashion, the woman in the floral dress was the only one who may have died this decade, but she bore no familial resemblance to Mina, and she was too old to have been a close friend or lover.

"There's another ghost out in the garden," Mina said simply, turning from the window. "A middle-aged man in overalls. He's stomping through the rosebushes."

So this is how Mina wanted to proceed—by keeping her emotions to herself. Wanting to respect her wishes, Abby bit back her curiosity. She crossed the room to stand beside Mina, and held out her hand.

Mina passed her the binoculars and Abby pulled them to her eyes. They were warm and smelled faintly of almonds. Abby tried not to think about how—mere seconds ago—Mina's face was pressed against the same metal now pressed against hers. That felt too intimate.

"Someone's upset," Abby said, watching the ghost of a man scowl as he drifted through the bushes. A simple T-shirt and overalls marked him as more modern than the other ghosts. Perhaps he was a former gardener or the repairman who had died on the property. Of course, he could also be the former owner of any number of objects the Kensington family had procured over the years. Identifying the ghosts inhabiting the manor was turning out to be tougher than she'd thought.

Rubbing the back of her neck, Abby turned back to her notebook. "That makes ten ghosts we've seen so far, plus the dog."

"So what do we do now?" Mina slipped her thumbs into her jeans' pockets. "Call a ghost exterminator or something?"

Abby bit back a smile. "Who you gonna call?"

Mina shrugged. "I don't know. There must be someone——"

Lucas and Abby both shouted "Ghostbusters!" and burst into laughter.

Mina glowered in disapproval.

As the laughter died down, Abby cleared her throat and took a seat on the side of an armchair. "Glen said there are two ways to get rid of ghosts—help them move on, or destroy what's keeping them here."

"An object that was close to them," Lucas elaborated. "Something that's tied into their unfinished business."

"Easy," Mina said sarcastically.

Abby tapped her fingers against the notebook she had borrowed from Lucas. "First we have to figure out which ghost is our wannabe murderer, then we have to find a way to send it on."

Mina frowned. "Before it murders someone?"

"Preferably, yes."

"How do we figure out which ghost is the culprit?" Lucas asked.

"The same way you determine a culprit in any investigation," Abby said with a shrug. "We interrogate them."

Mina stared at her blankly.

Lucas gulped. "We interrogate *ghosts?*"

"*Murderous* ghosts," Mina amended.

"Come on," Abby pleaded. "Only one of them is murderous, and they're obviously not very good at it since a little light scared them away. Besides, we've got a salt gun to protect us, and none of our suspects can go very far. I'd say this is pretty straightforward detective work."

Lucas shifted his weight, letting the blanket fall down his back. "But none of us are detectives."

"I have some experience," said Abby.

"Watching TV where people solve murders doesn't count."

"I took a criminal justice class."

"In high school."

"I've helped Dad with cases."

"He's a criminology professor. His cases went cold years ago. By the time they got to his desk, none of the suspects were living."

"Neither are ours," said Abby triumphantly, clapping Lucas on the back. "Trust me, we've got this. How hard can it be to get a few ghosts in a room and ask a few questions? They're probably *dying* to talk to someone new. I bet we'll have our culprit by midnight."

THEY DID NOT have their culprit by midnight.

After hours of chasing ghosts and failed attempts at communicating, midnight found them shivering in a kids' room, with two twin beds and an air mattress pulled together in a circle of salt.

"I told you I wasn't getting any sleep tonight," Lucas grumbled from one of the twin beds. He rolled up the sleeves of his superhero pajamas and took out a flashlight and a book.

On the other twin bed, Mina rolled over to face the wall, grunted, and buried her face in a pillow.

Abby sat on the floor, attempting to communicate with the ghosts via a cardboard spirit board she had rushed together after dinner. It remained as motionless as it had all night—as stoic as a marble coffin.

Scrolling through her phone, she read off various incantations that would supposedly allow her to communicate with the dead. So far, the closest any had gotten to working was when the temperature dropped a few degrees, but that could have simply been because the radiator shut off.

Abby scrolled through various forums, searching for something she hadn't tried yet. She found a spell that claimed to summon the dead. It was written in Latin and came with instructions to read aloud, three times.

She had barely made it through the first verse when Lucas leaped from his bed and snatched her phone.

"Hey!" Abby protested. "What was that for?"

"Do you know what you were reading?"

"A ghost invitation?"

"*Incantation*," Lucas corrected. "And no, you weren't. That spell was for possession. You were inviting the ghosts to *possess* you."

"So?"

"So?" Lucas's voice hitched. "Have you seen a horror movie? Possession is *bad*, Abby. Bad! First there's creepy music and all this suspense, then people are crawling around upside down and throwing themselves all over the place, then there's vomiting, and priests, and blood and murder—"

"That's all film stuff." Abby waved her hand dismissively. "That industry's built on lies."

"That's my career you're talking about," Mina said, grunting.

"You work in film?" Abby asked, impressed. She had a hard time picturing Mina as an actress considering the way her emotions radiated off her at all times. But she could picture her toiling away in a dark writers' room or editing studio.

"I'm a stunt double," Mina said casually, as if she were talking about a mundane career in finance and not being strung up in wires, jumping off buildings.

"That's so cool! I wanted to be an actress but—" Abby fell silent at the reminder of what had steered her dreams off course. How she had spent the summer after high school crying over Chelsea's death instead of looking for an apartment in LA. How she had spent all her savings on grief counseling and yoga and concert tickets—anything she could get her hands on that promised to lessen the ache of loss.

"—it's so expensive," she finished in what wasn't a lie, but wasn't the entire truth. She cleared her throat. "What films have you worked on? No wait, what's the coolest stunt you've pulled?"

"Listen, Abby," Lucas said, rifling through the briefcase of ghost supplies, pulling out fistfuls of wrinkled newspaper clippings and fabric scraps used for padding. "How do you know what's real and what isn't? This morning, we didn't even know ghosts were real—"

"I did," Abby corrected. She wanted to ask Mina more questions about her awesome career, but Lucas didn't give her the opportunity and Mina shoved a pillow over her ears.

"Okay, fine. *Two days ago*, we didn't even know ghosts were real. Now that we do, we can't just make assumptions about what parts of the lore are real and what parts aren't. Until we can find a rule book or something, we should assume anything's real—" Lucas clutched both sides of his head like he'd stepped off a ride that had spun him around so much he couldn't see straight. His eyes widened. "What if *I'm* a ghost?"

Abby shoved his elbow. "You're not a ghost."

"I've seen the movies, Abby." Lucas shuddered. "Most ghosts don't even know they're ghosts. What if we're all ghosts?"

"We're not ghosts."

Mina let out a heated breath and sat up, her baggy nightshirt slipping down one shoulder. She frowned at Abby. "I thought the point of you keeping watch was so we could sleep."

Abby pulled a metal rod coiled in spring from the case. "What's this? A fishing pole?"

"I think it's an antenna," Lucas said, snapping out of his 'what-if-we're-all-ghosts?' daze. He took the metal from Abby, rolling it in his wide palms. "Maybe this is how we communicate with them. I need a phone."

Abby handed him her phone.

He shook his head. "Something old-fashioned. Something with an antenna."

Abby sighed in exasperation. "Where are we supposed to get one of those?"

"There might be one in the attic," Mina suggested.

"The attic?" Lucas croaked in terror as if she had just

suggested checking a dungeon.

Mina rolled her eyes. "Michelle and I were up there the other day, looking for outdoor heaters. There was a box of old office supplies and electronics—I think I saw a phone."

"It's worth a shot." Abby scrambled to her feet and picked up a flashlight.

"You aren't thinking of going *now*?" Lucas cried.

"Of course I am," said Abby. "Who's coming with me?"

Mina slipped a flannel shirt over her sleeping shirt and sweatpants, put on a thick pair of socks, and tiptoed into the hall. Abby followed.

Moonlight filtered through the windows, dimly illuminating the hall. Abby stepped carefully, the floorboards creaking under each step. She felt like a teenager sneaking out of the house—especially as they passed the room Michelle slept in. She was painfully aware of her own breathing, which sounded loud against the soft creaks of the house settling in for the night.

Mina stopped. She turned on her phone's flashlight and aimed it at the ceiling. Its pale rays slid across the wood, revealing a thin rope. After placing her phone on the ground, Mina gave the rope a sharp tug. Creaking and groaning, it spilled a wooden ladder toward Mina, who guided it to the floor.

The ladder landed against the polished wood with a loud *snap*. Abby froze, exchanging a frightened glance with Mina as the sound echoed down the hall.

A door creaked open. Abby's gaze darted to Michelle's door. It remained closed.

Glancing further down the hall, she saw Lucas tiptoeing out of the nursery, a blanket draped over his pajamas.

"I'll keep watch," he whispered as he drew closer. He glanced from side to side, squinting in the shadows. Without his contacts in or his glasses on, Abby was surprised he hadn't tripped over himself. She wondered if he was still worried about his whole 'we're all ghosts' theory, or if he was afraid to be alone now that he knew the house was haunted.

Either way, Abby didn't argue. She climbed toward the attic, relieved to hear Mina climbing behind her.

Abby loved attics. They reminded her of treehouses—high up, creaky, and wooden. They were the perfect place to hide secrets. Or old memories. Secrets and memories were often intertwined. Scents of aged wood and parchment washed over her as she climbed. But when she reached the top, she was not surrounded with the familiar cramped space and smooth floorboards—the attic was cold, silent, and dark. Shadows lurked at the edges of her flashlight, spilling out of bags and hiding behind boxes. Floorboards creaked and wobbled. She stumbled, clutching a dusty beam to steady herself. Her palm came away with a splinter.

"It's somewhere around here." Mina maneuvered gracefully around the clutter as if she were a dancer on a balance beam. The floor barely creaked, and she didn't lose her footing, not once.

She sidestepped an old bike and, kneeling under an exposed beam, pulled a large cardboard box out from behind a sewing mannequin. "This is it."

Abby stumbled to her side, shining the flashlight into the contents. CDs, cassette tapes, and old files gathered dust.

In the middle of the retro collectibles, there was an old flip phone. Mina reached for it. Abby frowned. "Does it have an antenna?"

Mina flipped it open and closed, shaking her head.

"Maybe there will be a better phone," Abby said, trying her best to keep her hopes from crashing as she plunged her hand into the collectables.

After some fumbling through cords and cassette tapes, she felt something metallic and phone-like. She pulled it out only to discover that it wasn't a phone, but a walkie-talkie.

At least it had an antenna.

Abby extended the antenna and slipped the springy ghost-hunting antique over the top. It fit well enough.

"Hello?" Abby whispered into the walkie-talkie. "Ghosts? Can you hear me?"

The attic creaked. Wind moaned against the shutters, begging to get in. Not a voice spoke.

"It's out of power," Mina pointed out, rummaging through the box. "Maybe we need to charge it. Does this look like the charger to you? Or maybe this one?"

After several minutes of debate, they decided to carry the entire box back to the former nursery. It proved a more dangerous endeavor than either of them had anticipated, considering the box nearly ripped in half outside Michelle's bedroom. They managed to hurry the rest of the way to the nursery with only a few wires dragging on the floor.

Abby tried charger after charger until she found one that fit. Relieved, she plugged it into the socket and sat back on her heels to wait.

The minutes passed slowly. She played a game on her phone and remembered to text her boss at the coffee shop to say she wouldn't be in on Tuesday. She then texted her coworkers, asking them to take over her shifts for the rest of the week. The pay cut would hurt, but spending time with Lucas was worth it.

When the walkie-talkie finally powered on, Abby pressed

every button. It beeped in response.

"Lucas!" Abby hissed. "Mina?"

Gentle snoring was the only response.

Feeling less confident now that her companions were asleep, Abby hesitated. She flipped the walkie-talkie back and forth from one hand to another. Twisting the braided bracelet on her wrist, she recalled the summer evening years ago when Chelsea had braided those strands on her back porch. Her hair had been pulled back, held in place by a rainbow hair tie. She had been wearing a green shirt—or was it blue? Abby hated that she couldn't remember. Was that how talking to Chelsea would be now? Would her ghost have forgotten aspects of her living self? Or would she be completely preserved, as if she had traveled through time?

Abby shook the thoughts. Chelsea wasn't here. Her ghost might not exist at all, anywhere. She was not trying to communicate with a ghost from her past, but with a potentially dangerous spirit that had recently tried to kill her.

After taking a deep breath, she held down the talk button and whispered, "Hello? Is anyone there?"

The walkie-talkie let out a quiet sound of static. Beneath the static came soft, fragmented notes of a song. Abby lifted it to her ear and whispered once more, "Hello?"

A jumble of words came spilling out, as numerous voices spoke at once:

"—it's my turn!"

"Shh, not yet!"

"Ask her about the magic box—"

"—hasn't heard me yet—"

"One at a time!" A voice shouted over the others. "She can't hear us *all*."

Abby lifted the binoculars to her eyes and slowly scanned the room until she came across three ghosts. A boy with a plaid vest and corduroy slacks leaned against the wall with his arms crossed. A slightly younger girl in a frock sat on the edge of the nightstand, just outside the circle of salt, kicking her feet excitedly. An older girl, perhaps eleven or twelve, glared at both of them before turning toward Abby.

Her words crackled across the walkie-talkie. "Can you see us? Can you hear us?"

"Yes," Abby breathed in wonder. "Yes, I can."

"Ask her about the blue dog," the boy said, at the same time as the girl said, "Ask her for animal crackers."

"Shh!" said the older girl. She composed herself with a sigh. "Forgive us, it's been a while since we've spoken with the living. I'll admit, I didn't think it was possible."

"I told you it was," the younger girl exclaimed with a hint of a British accent. "You and Nan'y were wrong!"

"Have you come to play with us?" the boy asked.

"I've come to ask you some questions," Abby said, relaxing when none of these children seemed interested in strangling her. Not wanting to wake her friends, she tiptoed out into the hall and shut the door behind her before speaking into the walkie-talkie. "Someone attacked me the other night. I think they wanted me dead. Do you know who that was?"

She returned her binoculars to her eyes as the three ghost children emerged from the walls, glanced at each other, and shook their heads.

"We aren't strong enough," the oldest girl said. She reached for the pull switch of a nearby lamp, but her fingers went through it.

"We can't even start the magic box," the youngest girl said sadly.

The boy pointed through the wall and asked, with a note of hopefulness, "Can you?"

Abby chewed her lip. The 'magic box,' she assumed, was some kind of radio or television. The way they spoke, she was inclined to believe them.

Abby tapped her fingers against the walkie-talkie. She had too many questions to decide where to begin and her eyes were starting to droop shut. "I'll tell you what. I'll turn the magic box on for you in the morning, and I'll get animal crackers, if you keep watch tonight. If any ghost comes in trying to hurt anyone, you scream. And chase them out if you can. Deal?"

All three nodded enthusiastically.

"Oh thank you," the oldest girl said with a curtsy.

The air around her took on a sepia-colored haze. Abby lowered the binoculars and saw the hall light was on.

"What do you think you're doing?" a voice snapped.

Abby turned to find Michelle standing in a silk bathrobe, arms folded across her chest, a scowl on her face.

"Where's Lucas?"

"Asleep."

"Don't cover for him. I heard him talking to you."

Abby held up the walkie-talkie. "Actually, what you heard was a ghost."

Michelle rolled her eyes. "Enough of this ghost nonsense. Get back to bed. Lucas, that goes for you too. If I—" Michelle's eyes widened. Abby followed her gaze to the attic, where the folded ladder stuck out a few inches. "Did you get those from the *attic*?"

"I can explain," Abby said.

Michelle shook her head. "I don't want to know. But I'll be taking this—" Michelle plucked the walkie-talkie and binoculars from Abby's hands "—and this."

Abby gaped after her. "But that's mine!"

"Somehow, I doubt that." Scowling, Michelle retreated to her room. She paused in the doorway, shut off the hall light, and turned to face Abby. "Get some sleep. You better be on the road by sunrise."

The door slammed shut behind her.

Chapter Eight

Abby had never been good at following directions. Instead of going to bed like Michelle had asked, she grabbed a blanket and tucked herself into a corner of the hall to wait. She figured an hour would be enough time for Michelle to fall asleep; Abby could then sneak in to retrieve her equipment. She would sit patiently and wait.

SOMEONE WAS SHAKING her.

Abby yawned, finding herself spread out across the ornate rug. She shuffled into a seated position. The portrait across from her glowed eerily with moonlight.

"Are you alright?" Mina knelt beside her, her face scrunched into a panicked look.

"Fine," Abby whispered, cracking her neck. "What time is it?"

"What are you doing passed out in the hall?" The concern in Mina's voice made her sound stern and frightened all at once.

"Michelle took the binoculars," Abby grumbled. "And the walkie-talkie. I was going to wait until she fell asleep to sneak in and get them back—"

"That's a terrible plan." Mina choked back a laugh and gently punched Abby's shoulder.

"Ouch!" Abby glared at her. "What was that for?"

"For scaring me to death!" She gestured to the floor. "When I saw you lying there, I didn't know what to think—that the ghost had come back and strangled you, or possessed you to strangle someone else. But no, you just *fell asleep*."

Mina combed her fingers through her thick hair, shaking her head like she couldn't believe it.

"Oh," said Abby, feeling guilty for worrying Mina, and a little touched that Mina cared enough to be so shaken. "I'm fine. Do you think Michelle is asleep yet?"

"I think she's about to wake up." Mina glanced warily toward Michelle's door. "But if you want your equipment back, it's better to wait until later."

"Why?"

"Did you see where she put them?"

Abby shook her head.

"And how did you expect to search her room in the dark?"

Abby snuggled deeper into the blanket. Mina had a point. She had been so intent on getting her equipment back as soon as possible that she hadn't exactly formulated the best plan. Or any plan. "But when Michelle wakes up, she'll kick me out. Even if I do get everything back, I won't have time to track down the evil ghost, much less vanquish it."

Mina pursed her lips. "She's not going to kick you out if you stay out of her way. Or better yet, *help* her. Look how much she's warmed up to me in the past twenty-four hours, just because I glued some seashells on some jars."

Abby wondered once again why Mina had chosen to come, if she and Michelle had ended their friendship years ago.

Abby studied her face, trying to see if any answers were written there. But her questions were too detailed, too specific. Mina's wrinkled brow and open posture only conveyed that she was tired and earnest.

"What happened between you two?" Abby asked.

Mina shook her head, scattering moonlight. She rubbed her hand across her wrist, her gaze flickering briefly to the floor and back to Abby. "I made a bad decision."

Another earnest response. Abby nodded, encouraging Mina to elaborate.

Before she could, a bed creaked. Michelle's bed. Footsteps pattered across the floor. Mina grabbed Abby's arm and pulled her to her feet as they hurried into the nursery and shut the door behind them.

A dim sunrise streaked the east-facing window, filling the room with lavender light. Mina's hand lingered on Abby's shoulder, gripping the T-shirt she had borrowed from Lucas. Her brown eyes sparkled under her dark eyelashes. A strand of hair fell across her face, sticking to her lips. Before Abby realized what she was doing, she had raised her thumb to Mina's lips and was brushing the strand away.

Mina's eyes widened. She opened her mouth, but before any words came out, Lucas snored in his sleep.

Mina moved away from Abby, folding her arms across her chest. When she turned back around, she was out of reach, her face hardened. "Did it work?"

"Did what work?" Abby asked, thinking about how warm Mina's hand had been against her shoulder.

"The antenna. Were you able to speak with them?" Mina whispered. "With the dead?"

Abby nodded.

Mina stiffened. "What did they say? Did they—did anyone have a message for me?"

"For you?" Abby raised an eyebrow. When Mina didn't elaborate, she continued. "No, I just talked to a few kids."

"Kids?" Mina looked horrified.

"I mean they're ancient," Abby said, trying not to think about the sad fact that these kids had died so young. "Pre-internet era. And they seem happy enough. I don't think they attacked me. I'm supposed to turn on a magic box for them. What do you think that is?"

Mina shook her head and took a deep breath. "Beats me." She sat on the trunk at the foot of the bed. "I'll get the binoculars and walkie-talkie back, if you let me borrow them for a minute."

"You've lost someone?" Abby pressed. "And you want to see if you can reach them?"

Mina's eyes narrowed, implying that Abby was correct, but that she didn't want to speak about it. "Just, trust me. And try not to get kicked out in the meantime."

Before Abby could respond, Mina was walking away.

ABBY SPENT THE next hour cleaning snow off her car and carefully removing the cap to the valve stem on her front driver's side tire. She tucked the cap into the front pocket of her jeans. In case she needed a reason to stall, a flat tire would suffice. She hid the air pump she had seen in the garage behind a stack of boxes and wiped her hands of the matter—both literally and figuratively—as she cleaned up in the kitchen sink.

Sandra was kind enough not to ask about the dark smears on her hands. Instead, she obliged Abby's suggestion of making two breakfast sandwiches 'to go,' which Abby carried upstairs to Lucas.

"Rise and shine," she called, turning on the lights in the former nursery. "Your bacon and egg sandwich awaits."

Lucas responded by yawning as he leaned against his headboard and rubbed at his eyes.

Abby set his sandwich down on the nightstand, sliding his sketchbook to the side. It was open to a sketch of a rather intimate embrace between two superheroes Abby had never seen before. "Who are they?"

"No one." Lucas snatched his sketchbook and shut it, reaching for the plate with his other hand. "Mmm, smells delicious! Did you make this?"

Abby tried to hide her pain at being shut out of Lucas's life. She missed spending hours on his living room floor while he shared the plotlines for his comics—now he wouldn't even tell her about a pair of characters. "Sandra did."

"Thanks for bringing it up." Lucas made a sound of delight as he took a large bite. "But you know what? It could use some hot sauce."

"I'll get it," Abby said quickly.

Lucas placed the dish back on the nightstand and stood, draping a blanket over his pajamas like a cape. "No need. I was going to get a cup of tea anyway—"

"No," Abby said quickly. She didn't want Lucas to run into

Michelle, who was expecting them to be on the road by now. The more time she could buy them, the better—both for her tire to deflate and for her to come up with a plan to get Michelle to let them stay. She tried to think of an excuse. "The kitchen is a mess."

Lucas frowned. "What did you do?"

"Why do you think *I* did something? There's just…" Abby floundered for a reasonable excuse. "Mice."

"Mice?" Lucas looked horrified.

Thankfully, the door opened before Abby had to explain more. Mina slipped in, shutting the door behind her.

"Any luck?" Abby asked. Turning her back to Lucas, she made circles with her fingers and brought them to her eyes.

A mischievous smirk played across Mina's face, accentuated by her golden eyeshadow. Her bracelets clattered as she held up the binoculars, then the walkie-talkie, setting them both down on the nightstand by Lucas's breakfast.

Abby grinned, impressed. She had spent most of the morning thinking of ways to keep Michelle distracted from her room, but apparently wedding preparations were enough.

"Thanks." Abby picked up the walkie-talkie and noticed it was dead. Returning it to the charger, she asked hesitantly, "Were you able to talk to—whoever it was you wanted to?"

Mina's eyebrows pinched together. She shook her head, tucking her hair behind her ear, revealing several golden earrings.

Abby wanted to ask more about this mysterious ghost that Mina was so interested in meeting. She opened her mouth to do so, then thought about Chelsea, and shut it again. If Mina wanted to talk about the dead, Abby would let her bring it up in her own time.

Mina drummed her nails against the edge of the nightstand. "I saw your ghost kids, though. Turns out the 'magic box' they wanted was the TV."

"I knew it," Abby said, feeling pleased with herself.

"They'll answer any questions you want, as long as you put cartoons on for them."

"Sweet." Abby snatched the binoculars and turned on the old-fashioned TV. "Bring them in."

"Ooh, can I ask the questions?" Lucas pulled a spiral notebook from his suitcase. "I took an investigative journalism class in college."

His enthusiasm made Abby grin. Here was the eager and supportive friend she remembered.

"Have at it," Mina said, heading toward the door.

Abby felt a jolt of sadness as Mina reached for the brass doorknob. "Don't you want to stay?"

"Hell yeah! But I think my skills are better suited to hanging greenery and getting on Michelle's good side. You two have fun. Good luck saving the day." She mock-saluted Abby on her way out.

"Alright, alright." Lucas rubbed his hands together and reached for the walkie-talkie. "So they can hear me if I talk through this?"

Abby nodded. "Leave it charging, though."

Lucas peered through the binoculars and pressed the walkie-talkie button with a grin. "Hello?"

Static cracked in return. Then the ghost boy spoke: "You look ridiculous with those things, you know."

Screaming in alarm, Lucas dropped the binoculars.

Abby laughed. "What did you expect?"

"He was right up in my face," Lucas stammered. "Just

popped up through the floor."

"They're ghosts. They do that."

Lucas handed Abby the binoculars. "That's it. You watch them. I'll take the notes."

"What happened to Mr. 'I took an investigative journalism class'?"

"I've seen enough, okay. *Enough.* Besides, the dog keeps walking through my legs."

"He just wants you to pet him."

"Can I go back to the moving pictures?" the boy asked, his voice crackling through the walkie-talkie.

Abby nodded.

As the boy gleefully ran back to join the other ghosts in front of the TV, Abby pushed her notepad toward Lucas.

He frowned. "This is all you have?"

Abby shrugged at her scribbled words of various sizes slanted in different directions and her half-finished poor attempt at drawing the dog. "They're kids."

"So?"

"So, kids aren't suspects."

Lucas stared at her with a look of disbelief. "You heard of Damien Thorn? Joffrey Baratheon? Jack from *Lord of the Flies*?"

"You heard of the word '*fiction*'?" Abby shook her head. He had seen too many scary movies. "Those guys are made up. These ghosts are *real*."

"I'm still getting used to that." Lucas scratched his neck and lowered his voice, as if he was uncertain where the ghosts were and what they could understand. Abby didn't blame him for that. She was starting to suspect that the ghosts could hear them without the walkie-talkie, but they needed the walkie-talkie to hear the ghosts. It was unsettling, the way the

kids had seemingly followed Mina to her and been waiting
for the TV to turn on.

"But shouldn't we interview them anyway?" Lucas asked.

"They aren't strong enough to do anything. The oldest girl
couldn't even turn on the light, much less attack someone."

"She could have been faking."

Abby shook her head. "I know people. Remember how I
always knew which teachers would lie about grading tough?"

"I remember you failing your Chemistry exam because you
thought Mr. Simmons liked you."

"That was one time," Abby protested. "And he did like me.
I just forgot to study. He let me make it up with extra credit."

Lucas rubbed his chin. "What about the circus guy?"

"That was eighth grade. How was I supposed to know he
was a con artist?"

"I lost two weeks of lunch money because of your poor
judgement. Which you still owe me, by the way."

"Okay, fine. It's like ninety-nine percent accurate," Abby
admitted, releasing a heated breath. She frowned at Lucas.
He used to admire her intuition. So why was he fighting her
on it now? The lack of trust was disheartening, so she shoved
it aside. She needed to focus on catching a murderous ghost
before Michelle caught on to her. She didn't have time to waste
questioning her best friend. These kids were innocent; she
could sense it.

"She wasn't lying," Abby insisted. "Trust me on this."

"Okay." Lucas pinched the bridge of his nose. "Then, who
do we question?"

Abby picked up the remote and turned off the TV. All three
ghost children let out cries of protest.

"I'll turn it back on," Abby said, raising the binoculars to her eyes, "as soon as you bring me my next witness."

"Suspects," Lucas corrected.

"You really think one of us attacked you?" Elizabeth slumped forward, her eyes wide and innocent.

Well, that proved Abby's theory alright. The ghosts could hear them without the walkie-talkie. They would need to be careful, especially around the other ghosts. They could never know who was listening in.

"I thought you were our friend," said the youngest girl, on the verge of tears.

Abby glared at Lucas and gestured as if to say this was what she was hoping to avoid by referring to them as witnesses. "We don't think that. But maybe one of you—or someone you know—saw what happened?"

The children looked at each other, their frowns deepening. It was disconcerting, looking at them through the binoculars, where they looked so real she could see the seams of their clothes. Meanwhile, Lucas faded to a pale and ghostly vision behind them.

"We could ask Nan'y," Tommy said. "She knows lots of things. Like how to turn on the television."

"Nanny?" Lucas asked. "Who is Nanny?"

"Our friend," said Elizabeth. "But she isn't here right now."

"Why not?"

Elizabeth shrugged. "She goes away sometimes."

"Where?"

"Just away." The cold, vacant tone of her voice made Abby shiver. Was it possible that ghosts could move through the land of the living and whatever came beyond?

Abby shook the thought—she'd rather not know. "Well, is there anyone here now that we *can* question?"

The littlest ghost got to her feet and floated to the door. She returned a moment later with another ghost.

A brunette woman waited politely in the doorway, hands clasped in front of her, a confused expression on her face. Her hair was elegantly styled over a ruffled blue dress with a large bustle. Abby recognized her as the woman who had been dancing on the veranda, who she had written in her notebook as 'dancing woman.'

"Who's this?" Abby asked. "She looks like someone from the set of *Bridgerton*."

"The costumes in that show were completely inauthentic," Lucas commented. He took the binoculars and peered hesitantly through them. "She looks like someone from a Jane Austen novel."

Abby snatched them back. "Oh and the costumes in her novels are so much more authentic."

"Yeah." Lucas blinked. "Because she wrote them in that actual time period."

"But the movies are *so* boring," Abby complained.

"Did I just hear you refer to one of the greatest literary authors of all time as *boring*?"

The walkie-talkie crackled and Tommy's voice came through with a whine. "What's boring is this conversation. Mary brought you Miss Sarah. May we have the dog back now?"

Abby turned the TV on and ushered Sarah and Lucas into the room across the hall, where they could speak without the sounds of *Blue's Clues*.

The room they stepped into had lavender walls, comfy sofas, and large mirrors. A box of wedding signs sat on a table between two armchairs. Some portraits had been taken down, replaced with modern mirrors and studio lights. Abby suspected this was Michelle's doing, and this was the room she intended to use to get ready on her wedding day.

Abby peered through the binoculars and addressed the fancy woman. "Miss Sarah, is it? I'm Abby and this is Lucas. Thank you for joining us. I know it must be a little odd, speaking with the living—"

"Honestly, I forgot you all even exist." Sarah chuckled. "You just look like bits of smoke unless I really focus on you. Heavens! Is that what the women are wearing these days?"

Abby pulled on the sleeve of her oversized sweater. "And men. And nonbinary folk. Pretty much everyone loves a good sweater these days. Did they not have them in your time?"

"They look like men's sleepwear," Sarah said with a note of disapproval.

Abby turned to Lucas curiously. "Did you know sweaters were a modern invention?"

"Knitted tunics have been around since at least the 15th century, but they were usually worn by working men."

"What were they called before 'sweaters'?"

"Guernsey," said Lucas.

"*Faux pas*," said Sarah.

Abby ignored Sarah and asked Lucas, "How do you know this? *Why* do you know this?"

Lucas nudged her and pointed to the space where Sarah had been, reminding her to focus.

"Right," Abby said, raising the binoculars back to her eyes. Despite her pristine dress, a simple gold wedding band circled her finger. Strands of dark brown hair slipped from her bun and calluses lined her fingers. Abby suspected her interest in fashion had begun later in life—after she was married. Perhaps that's when she had become wealthy enough. "Did you attempt to strangle me the other night and if so— Ouch."

Abby rubbed her arm where Lucas had elbowed her too firmly, then continued, "Why?"

"You're not supposed to be that direct," Lucas hissed.

"Strangle?" Sarah's voice went higher. "How awful! I wouldn't dream of it, much less understand how to do it. Strangling the living, can you imagine? Well, it'd be like strangling a ghost."

"Do you know of anyone strong enough to do that?" Abby asked, moving a bridal magazine out of an armchair to take a seat.

"Or evil enough," Lucas added.

"We are a good, kind family, in life and after," Sarah said sternly. "I can't imagine any member of the family wanting to bring harm to anyone. And that goes for the Gardners too."

"The Gardners?" Lucas asked.

"Mr. Gardner was our groundskeeper," Sarah explained. "He and his wife live in the carriage house behind the garden."

"They're still alive?" Lucas asked.

"Oh, I suppose they're ghosts now, aren't they? Funny, when you've been dead so long, you forget you're dead."

She laughed. Abby and Lucas exchanged worried glances. Lucas started to point a finger at himself but Abby shoved it down, shooting him a look of concern.

"How long have you been dead?" she asked Sarah, keeping her attention on Lucas.

He attempted to elbow her in the side—likely for asking a question he thought was insensitive—but she sidestepped it.

"Who knows," Sarah said. "A dozen years? A hundred? A thousand? Who keeps track of time these days?"

"Sarah," Abby mused. "Sarah Kensington. Where have I heard that name before?"

"Are you *the* Sarah Kensington?" Lucas asked, checking his notes. "Married to George Kensington?"

"Yes." Sarah smiled. "George is my husband."

"George was the original owner of the house," Lucas explained. "He built this house for his wife, Sarah."

Ah, so George must have been the man in the expensive suit who had been dancing with Sarah on the veranda. "He built this whole thing by himself? Is he a ghost too? Were you dancing with him the other day?"

Sarah's eyebrows pinched together. Something about Abby's questions appeared to bother her. Abby needed to slow down, so she could figure out which part. She wondered if this was merely a lack of tact on her part, asking about her dead husband, or if there was something more there.

"He funded it," Lucas explained, looking up from his notes. "As a wedding present to his bride-to-be. It took him six years just to design the floorplans."

"He spent way too much time with that architect," Sarah muttered in agreement.

Abby turned to Lucas. "Seriously, how do you know all this?"

"You asked me to research the house, so I researched the house."

"You can learn all this from research?" Abby knew Lucas was smart, but she was impressed. That was a lot of digging to do in only a few hours.

Lucas raised an eyebrow as if he thought little of his accomplishments.

"It is wonderful, isn't it?" Sarah said airily. "The house. I love sitting there at the piano and looking out at the garden."

Lucas glanced around the room. "What piano?"

Sarah's face fell. "I forgot. That darned woman sold it."

"What woman?"

"The mean woman. We call her the hurricane. She comes in here and gets rid of our stuff, like we're nobody. Like we don't exist."

Abby frowned. It sounded like she was describing Michelle, but surely Michelle hadn't sold a piano? That would more likely be one of the Kensingtons. "Mrs. Kensington?"

"Yes?" Sarah replied.

"No, I meant, the current Mrs. Kensington—wait—" Abby frowned. She turned to Lucas and wondered aloud, "If the current Mrs. Kensington was born into the family and had a husband, why didn't she take his last name?"

Lucas shrugged. "Maybe she wanted to keep ties to her own family."

"Or maybe they got divorced," Abby speculated. "And she changed it back."

Lucas shook his head. "I looked up his obituary. Mr. Mason Turner—the late husband of Mrs. Kensington, David and Robert's father—was still married to the family when he died."

"You found his obituary?" Abby stared at him, impressed. She wouldn't even know how to find that information, much less think about looking it up. One thing clearly hadn't changed about Lucas—he never did anything halfway.

She turned back to Sarah. "Were you perhaps acquainted with the former man of the house, Mr. Turner?"

Lucas glanced at her. "Why are you talking so stilted?"

"I'm speaking old-timey English."

"They didn't speak that way."

"Then why are all old-fashioned books written like that?"

Lucas gave Abby a look of exasperation and took the walkie-talkie. "Does the woman you call the hurricane look like this?"

He moved across the room, his slippers pattering against the hardwood with a soft crunching sound like hail on autumn leaves. He opened the door and pointed across the hall, to where a portrait of the current Mrs. Kensington hung over a console table.

They both glanced at the walkie-talkie, but there was no response.

Abby put the binoculars back to her face, her lips pulling into a frown.

Sarah Kensington was gone.

Chapter Nine

Abby was good at many things: speeches, magic tricks, lateral-thinking puzzles, and the occasional video game. But one thing she was terrible at was being patient.

She had imagined ghost hunting would have her sneaking down secret passageways, finding hidden notes, or digging up lost treasure—not wandering around the house with a pair of binoculars, listening to restless spirits ramble about 'the good old days.'

For hours, she and Lucas had questioned ghost after ghost, and yet they were nowhere near shrinking their list of suspects. Abby had waited in the stuffy library while George Kensington paced the shelves, ranting about loud guests. Then she kicked up snow while Mr. and Mrs. Gardner inconsiderately strolled the garden and pointed out where their favorite rose bushes used to be. Lastly, she had stormed out during Sarah Kensington's blatant criticism of her 'unbecoming' clothes and 'boyish' hair.

Huddled by the fire with an oversized mug of hot chocolate, Abby found it difficult to concentrate on their latest suspect, who was prattling on about the design of the windows in the drawing room.

"Who are you again?" Abby asked, plucking a candy cane off the Christmas tree. She stuck it in her mug and swirled the chocolate around, then cut to the chase. "Do you want to kill anyone?"

Lucas gave Abby a look of annoyance while the ghost gasped with offense, muttering about manners. Abby glanced back through the binoculars in time to see him shoving his hands into his pockets.

"Why is it that women's clothes have changed so much and men's haven't?" Abby asked. "This guy is wearing your prom outfit."

Lucas snatched the binoculars from her. He frowned as he peered through them. "I didn't wear a collar like that. And he just said his name is Archie Hall—that means he's the guy who designed this place."

"Seriously? Archie Hall?"

Lucas lowered the binoculars. "What about it?"

"He's an architect. That's like a sailor named 'pointy sail.'"

"Stick to the point," Lucas warned.

Abby took back the binoculars and sipped her hot chocolate, studying the ghost before her. He was unmistakably the 'Archie' she had seen in the photograph—thin with a brown mustache and a loose-fitting suit that looked like something she would find in Lucas's closet—which was to say that it was dull, brown, and weathered. The only speck of color came from his piercing blue eyes, capable of hiding deep secrets.

That was about the only thing he seemed capable of. His arms were so scraggly, Abby wondered if he was strong enough to smother her. In life, probably not. But in death—who knew what supernatural powers might come with lingering around after someone's expiration date. "Archie, do you know of anyone in the house who would wish to harm me?"

Archie frowned. "Did you insult anyone else's name so blatantly?"

"He has a point," Abby said, stifling a yawn. In all her time questioning ghosts, she hadn't found a single one who seemed vengeful or jealous. She couldn't see any reason why someone would want to attack her.

If she couldn't figure out the motive, at least she could try to figure out who each of her suspects were. And when they were alive. "Are you acquainted with any of the other ghosts in the house?"

"A few. I don't like to be bothered."

"And you don't think any of them are dangerous?"

"Not that I'm aware of," he said stiffly. "Although, as I've mentioned, I don't particularly seek out their company."

"What about Mrs. Kensington's late husband?"

"George would never harm anyone!" Archie's voice boomed through the walkie-talkie with such intensity, Abby winced. This guy was defensive of George.

"So you know him, then?" Abby turned the volume on the walkie-talkie down. "Do you know Mrs. Kensington too, or did you meet her husband after he died?"

"Uh, George is the *original* Mr. Kensington," Lucas corrected. "The one Archie here designed this house for is Mrs. Kensington's great-great grandfather."

"Oh." Abby scratched her head. "I meant the, uh, *current* Mrs. Kensington—the living one—" She looked to Lucas for help.

"Paige," Lucas supplied. "Paige Marie Kensington."

"And her late husband was Mason Turner?"

Lucas nodded.

"Well that explains why she didn't take her husband's last name."

"How?"

"Well, she wouldn't want to be Mrs. Paige Turner now, would she? Not when she's a member of high society."

Lucas stared at Abby as if she defied logic. He shook his head and tapped his notebook, turning back to the empty seat across from him, clearly thinking Archie's ghost was there and not pacing in front of the windows. "Mrs. Paige Kensington is the current owner of the house."

"Ah, so she's to blame for the erroneous additions to my masterpiece," said Archie.

Abby held up her hands. "Hey, man, you do you, but we don't need to hear about what turns you on, okay."

"Erroneous doesn't mean what you think it means," said Lucas. "It means flawed."

"Oh," said Abby. "That makes more sense. So you don't like her renovations?"

"I most certainly do not," said Archie. "Nor do I like the thought of being interrogated by a pair of adolescents like I'm some kind of miscreant."

"See," Abby whispered to Lucas. "Big words."

Lucas tapped his pen against his notebook. "Abby believes she was attacked by a ghost—"

"What's this 'Abby believes' nonsense?" Abby looked at him with a mixture of surprise and accusation. "I *know* I was attacked. You can't tell me after all this—after we spent all day conversing with ghosts—that you still think I imagined it."

"Abby was attacked," Lucas amended, clearing his throat.

He had avoided using the word 'ghost,' but his amended phrasing was an improvement to his original, so she hesitated to call him out.

In her hesitation, Archie spoke, "And you want to know if I did it, eh?"

Lucas leaned forward, his elbows digging into his notebook. "Well, did you?"

"Of course not," Archie said matter-of-factly. "I like my peace and quiet. A murder in the house would not bring peace or quiet. With the investigation and the funeral, there would be dozens—if not hundreds—of visitors. It would be a nightmare."

Abby felt an involuntary shiver at the word *funeral*. The word stirred up memories of a lily-scented room with too-large wooden portraits of Chelsea's face grinning over a casket and the feeling as if the ground were falling out from under her. She remembered running out in the middle of the service, turning her back on family and friends, missing the final moments that the world remembered Chelsea.

"He does have a point." Lucas's words cut through her memories as he scratched at his chin. It was still weird to see the hint of a beard on it.

Abby shoved down her memories and the discomfort that came with them. She set her empty mug on the coffee table and gestured in the direction she had last seen Archie. "Can you move this?"

"I'm not your servant," he scoffed.

"But can you move it?"

"I do not have to tell you what I can and can't do," he snarled. A quick glance through the binoculars found him pacing the length of a bookcase with a menacing gleam in his eyes. For the first time since meeting him, Abby thought the willowy man might actually be capable of hurting someone. "In fact, I don't have to tell you anything at all."

He walked straight through Abby, sending chills down her spine, and disappeared through the wall behind her.

Shivering, Abby brushed her arms, attempting to wipe his touch off even though he had left nothing behind. The couch groaned as she sank deeper into it. "Well, that went well."

"How did that go well?" Lucas asked. "He gave us nothing. I've got more questions than answers."

"That's good. Questions are the first step to finding answers."

"Except we're still on the first of who-knows-how-many steps to identifying the ghost who attacked you. And even if we identify that ghost, we have no clue how to send it on. And Mrs. Kensington will be home any second."

"That's great."

"How is that great?" Lucas's voice rose an octave. "She'll kick us out! That's like finishing the first question of a timed test with mere seconds left!"

Abby checked the room to make sure it was free of ghosts, then whispered conspiratorially, "When Mrs. Kensington gets home, we can question her, see what she knows about the ghosts."

Lucas gulped. "What if they try to kill us first?"

"Then we'll know who our culprit is."

"What if they succeed?"

Abby picked up the old-fashioned salt gun. "We won't let it come to that."

Lucas's face went slack. "I don't want to use that thing."

"Relax." Abby opened the chamber, where several worn cylindrical packets leaked salt onto her lap. "It's just salt."

"It's a gun."

"With *salt*. Like paintball."

"I don't play paintball."

"What do you mean, you don't play paintball? We used to have so much fun at that little place behind your cousin's house—"

"Until I got a black eye and vowed never to go near one of those things again."

"Excuse me," the walkie-talkie crackled.

Abby pulled the binoculars to her eyes and saw a blonde middle-aged woman in a floral sundress and cardigan poking her head around the corner. She had a stern expression that reminded Abby of her seventh-grade English teacher. "The kids told me you were looking for me?"

"Ah, you must be the nanny," Abby said, extending her hand.

The ghost blinked in confusion.

Realizing that ghosts probably couldn't shake hands, Abby wiped her empty palm along her jeans sheepishly. "I'm still getting used to this talking to ghosts thing."

The ghost frowned at the gun leaking salt onto the couch, before asking, in a polite though wary tone, "What can I do for you?"

Abby cut straight to the point. "We're trying to figure out who attacked me the other day. Do you have any idea who would want to hurt someone?"

"How awful." The nanny moved deeper into the room, peering out the window at the garden beyond. Her pale hair was pinned at her nape—not a strand out of place—revealing a long dainty neck with a delicate necklace that matched a pair of round ruby earrings. Everything from her stance to her manicure was polished and screamed perfection. She seemed like the kind of person who wouldn't leave the house without makeup, who had high expectations for the children under her care, and who would do anything to help a young lady find a proper husband. "I can't think of anyone who would do such a thing."

Abby sighed. "That's what everyone's saying."

The nanny pursed her lips. "Well…"

"Well what?" Abby prompted.

The ghost smoothed out the thin straps of her dress. It's a good thing she couldn't feel the cold, otherwise she would be freezing for all eternity. Abby's teeth jittered just looking at her.

"Well," the nanny repeated with her chin held high. She glanced over her shoulder as if to check if anyone was listening. "I don't like to talk ill of anyone. But there was a repairman who died here. He can be…a force to be reckoned with."

"Dean Johnson," Lucas offered.

"He has quite the temper," said the nanny. "And I just saw you talking to Archie. He gets very upset when it comes to his designs. When they re-modeled a bathroom, he attempted to explode the toilet. Who knows what he'd do if someone were to propose bigger changes."

"But there aren't any big renovations planned, are there?" Abby asked. "*I'm* certainly not planning them."

"Beats me," said the nanny. "I don't keep up with the living."

"What about the dead?" Abby asked. "Have you ever met Mr. Turner, Mrs. Kensington's late husband?"

"Yes," the nanny replied shrewdly. "Unfortunately."

"You don't like him?"

"He is a stuck-up man with an awful temper."

"Do you think he would want to hurt anyone?" Abby asked.

"No, but—" the nanny composed herself and lowered her voice to a whisper "—I wouldn't put it past him. Maybe he saw you and felt his family was being threatened."

"I'm not threatening," said Abby.

"Of course not," said the nanny. "But you *were* in Mrs. Kensington's room."

Abby considered that response. Perhaps Mrs. Kensington's late husband had come to check on his wife, expecting to find her sleeping peacefully, and panicked when he had realized it was someone else entirely. It was plausible.

"How did you know Abby was attacked in Mrs. Kensington's room?" Lucas asked.

"The kids told me."

"You don't think *they* have any reason to harm anyone?" Lucas asked warily.

Abby gave Lucas a shrewd look. "When did—"

She fell silent as the front door slammed open. Boots clamored stiffly across the hardwood.

A stern feminine voice shouted from the main hall. "Sandra! What the devil happened in here? Did someone let the storm inside? It's freezing!"

Abby peered over the balcony as a frail old woman in a black fur coat and feathered hat strutted into the living room, tossing her gloves onto a table.

Marie Antoinette ran to her, leaping into her arms. The old woman knelt down to catch her, making loud smooching sounds as she covered the cat's forehead with kisses.

That could only be Mrs. Kensington.

Abby saw her chance to introduce herself. She seized it by

racing down the stairs, ignoring Lucas's stuttered protests.

Abby slowed as she neared the first floor, calling over the banister, "Mrs. Kensington, you have a lovely home."

"Who are you?" Mrs. Kensington asked, still cradling a purring Marie Antoinette, who was shedding all over her dark sweater.

"I'm Abby, Lucas's friend."

"Lucas?" Mrs. Kensington raised a questioning eyebrow.

Lucas waved over Abby's shoulder, unusually tense.

"Oh, you." Mrs. Kensington finally set Marie Antoinette down and strolled further into the living room, where she made herself comfortable in a cozy armchair. The cat immediately jumped into her lap, headbutting her arm for more attention. Mrs. Kensington pet her absently, her gaze on Lucas. "You're still here? I thought your sister told you to leave."

"We got snowed in," Abby explained, following Mrs. Kensington into the living room.

Mrs. Kensington pursed her lips. "The roads are clear now."

"Yeah, but unfortunately my car had some trouble—"

"Trouble?" Lucas's eyebrows shot up. He hurried to the window and looked outside to where her car remained at the edge of the circle driveway. "What kind of trouble?"

Abby shrugged, slipping her thumb into her pocket where the valve stem cap pressed snug against her skin. "Flat tire. Roadside Assistance said they were too busy to make it today."

Lucas clenched his fists. "And you were going to tell me this when?"

"At the right time." Abby didn't meet his eyes, hoping he couldn't see through her lie as she shrugged.

Lucas groaned. "Michelle is going to *kill* me."

Abby patted his arm as she turned to Mrs. Kensington. "I

hope it won't be too much trouble if we stay one more night?"

Mrs. Kensington frowned, stroking her long fingers down Marie Antoinette's fluffy back. "Visitors are always *trouble*."

Marie Antoinette peered back at Abby and meowed. Hesitantly, Abby stepped forward and reached out her hand, cautiously patting Marie Antoinette on her forehead.

"Huh," Mrs. Kensington said with a weary sigh. "She likes you."

Abby bit back a grin. "Does this mean we can stay?"

"Don't keep me up past nine," Mrs. Kensington snapped.

"A.m. or p.m.?"

Lucas elbowed her, then turned to Mrs. Kensington and spoke using his polite customer service voice, which he had perfected during his high school job serving ice cream. "Where are the others? Were they able to fly home this morning?"

"No," she said simply. "Now there's a storm on their end."

"I hope they're alright," said Lucas.

"Oh yes, how tragic to be forced to spend an extra couple days at a luxury resort." Mrs. Kensington removed her hat and patted her stiff gray hair. "I'm sure they're fine."

Abby took a piece of candy from a crystal bowl on the wet bar and drummed her fingers against the wood.

If Chelsea were here, she would find something nice to say to Mrs. Kensington. She could make anyone feel at ease. She was the kind of person who daydreamed her way through life, assuming the best of people without letting their moods, thoughts, or opinions disturb her own. Winning second place in the artist showcase made her no more happy than when she showcased without winning at all. "No one loses in art," she had said when Abby questioned the authenticity of her excitement after the award ceremony. "It's subjective. It's expression. How can you win or lose at expression? Just having my work on display, watching people's expressions change as they view each piece, that's winning."

Abby's gaze drifted to the oil paintings that lined the walls. "I love your art. Are these paintings all originals?"

"Most of them." Mrs. Kensington grunted. "Don't ask me who the artist was. They've been in the family for generations."

"Well, they are lovely. As is the house—it's gorgeous. Is this a family home?" Abby asked, slipping back into interrogation mode. She already knew the answer, but wanted a believable segue into her more pressing questions. And a little flattery couldn't hurt.

Mrs. Kensington grunted affirmatively in response.

"How old is this place, anyway?"

"It was built in the 1870s," Mrs. Kensington said proudly. "By my great-great-grandparents."

"Impressive. A house this old, several generations of families growing up here, getting married, having kids, dying—makes you wonder if it's haunted, doesn't it?"

To Abby's disappointment, Mrs. Kensington didn't respond. She merely diverted her attention to a book of poems she'd picked up from the coffee table during Abby's lead up to her question.

"Let's go," Lucas whispered to Abby. "Before she changes her mind about letting us stay."

Abby watched the old woman. "Have you ever seen a ghost, Mrs. Kensington?"

Mrs. Kensington raised an eyebrow over the top of her book. "Yes. Several."

Abby's jaw nearly dropped. The certainty of her response had caught her off guard. Her heart pounded with excitement.

Maybe Mrs. Kensington knew something about who had attacked her. Maybe Mrs. Kensington had faced the malicious ghost before. "In this house?"

Mrs. Kensington nodded, her gaze still lingering on her book.

"Where?" Abby asked, unable to contain her anticipation.

Mrs. Kensington pointed across the living room, to where the blank TV reflected sunlight onto the ornate rug.

"They do like to watch TV," Abby mused.

"I think she means she saw them *on* TV," Lucas said. "In movies."

"Exactly," said Mrs. Kensington.

Abby's excitement deflated. Mrs. Kensington had been toying with her.

"If you're looking for ghosts," Mrs. Kensington continued, "I suggest *The Haunting of Hill House.*"

Lucas whistled in amazement. "She's seen *The Haunting of Hill House?*"

"I know, right?" Abby shivered. "That creeped me out."

"The book was good," said Lucas. "But I couldn't make it through the show. The special effects were scary."

"In case you haven't noticed, I'm trying to *read*," Mrs. Kensington said sharply. "I trust you can see yourselves out? Or do I need to call someone to escort you?"

"I'm happy to escort them to their car." Michelle's stern tone carried across the room, stiffening the mood as effectively as if lightning had struck.

She glared at Lucas as she stepped into the foyer, then forced a smile and turned to Mrs. Kensington, smoothing out the wrinkles in her dress. "Welcome home, Mrs. Kensington."

Mrs. Kensington shut her book and folded her hands across

the cover. "David's not back, if that's what you want to know. His flight's delayed another day or two."

Her tone was as casual as if she were announcing that they might postpone their trip to the state fair a few hours, but Michelle looked pained by the response.

"If I was him, I'd stay away as long as I can," Mrs. Kensington continued. "He's making a big mistake, getting married."

A pained expression crossed Michelle's face. No, not pain, *anger*. Hot anger flashed behind her eyes as her nostrils flared and her eyebrows pinched together. She let out a deep breath and the expression dulled to a mere grimace.

The back door opened. Mina and Annabelle entered, shivering in their coats. They wiped their boots, covering the welcome mat in snow like confetti.

Marie Antoinette glared at them, her fur bristling. She growled in their direction.

"Careful," Mrs. Kensington snapped. "You're scaring poor Marie, letting that blizzard inside. You should know better, Annabelle."

Annabelle hung her head apologetically as she began carefully unlacing her boots.

Mina held on to a column by the doorway as she popped off one boot, then the other, spraying bits of snow against the floor that melted into minuscule puddles.

Mrs. Kensington shook her head, making a face as if she had tasted something sour. "I told both my boys they'd be better off bachelors. But look at where we are now. One locked in a marriage, the other doomed to the same fate in less than a week."

Michelle's fists clenched. "Didn't you love your husband?"

"I suppose. Although, I never would have married him if

I could have lived on my own. But times were different back then. I'm just lucky he kicked the bucket while I'm still hearty."

Abby shook her head, unable to imagine such 'times.' Had Mrs. Kensington's husband known she felt this way about him? She swept her gaze along the shadowy floorboards, wondering if Mrs. Kensington's late husband was drifting between the walls, listening. She wished she hadn't left the binoculars upstairs.

Annabelle silently reached for Michelle's shoulder and nudged her toward the kitchen.

Mrs. Kensington glowered at them. "It's good to see you have competition now, Annabelle."

Annabelle blinked, her face pale as her hands fidgeted at her side. "Competition?"

"For my money. For this place." Mrs. Kensington waved her hands dismissively at the ceiling. "Annabelle's always trying to get her hands on it, just like Nancy."

"Who's Nancy?" Abby asked.

Michelle frowned at Abby, waving her hand in a shooing motion.

"Her mother." Mrs. Kensington's lips twitched in disapproval. "I caught her trying to steal one of my candlesticks, you know."

"That's not true," Annabelle said quietly, but heatedly. "I don't want your money, Mrs. Kensington. My mother never stole from you."

"You say that now." Mrs. Kensington cocked a finger toward Michelle. "But she'll be fighting you for my candlesticks over my dead body."

Abby would have laughed at the notion of frail Annabelle attempting to fight former track-star Michelle, but coming from Mrs. Kensington, it sounded like an omen. Abby gulped, trying to reassure herself it wouldn't come to that. Annabelle didn't appear to have a mean bone in her body. And Michelle wasn't the kind of person to start drama. Mrs. Kensington clearly didn't know her daughters-in-law very well.

Lucas cleared his throat. "Mrs. Kensington, could I get you anything to drink?"

"You don't think I'm capable of getting a drink myself?" Mrs. Kensington snapped. "What am I, too old?"

"N-no, that's not what—"

"What happened to your stocking, child?" Mrs. Kensington barked, pointing a knobby finger at Michelle's left knee, where her tights had ripped. "You weren't getting up to trouble, were you? I won't find any missing jewelry in my bedroom or missing china in my cabinets, will I?"

Michelle shut her eyes. It looked like she was using all her self-control not to snap back at Mrs. Kensington. Whatever she was doing to keep her mouth shut, it was working. If that insult had been hurled at Abby, she'd have brushed it off with some witty remark by now and be slamming the door in Mrs. Kensington's face.

Michelle stood stoically, breathing in the dry air.

Mina, however, lunged at Mrs. Kensington. She looked as if she was going to grab the old woman, but stopped inches from her face and spat, "How *dare* you speak to her that way? Michelle isn't a thief. She's one of the kindest, most hardworking people I've ever met. She is honorable and intelligent and your son is *lucky* she agreed to be his bride. If you can't see that, then you don't deserve to be her mother-in-law."

Mina's words lingered in the air as Mrs. Kensington stared wide-eyed in surprise. Marie Antoinette leaped from her lap, wisely removing herself from between the two of them. Holding her tail high, she slunk past the crackling fire and disappeared around the corner.

Lucas tugged on Abby's sleeve and jerked his elbow toward the door. Abby was pretty sure this was none of her business, but she didn't budge. She stared at Mina in awe and fascination.

Mrs. Kensington pursed her lips. "You dare speak to me that way in *my* home?"

Mina folded her arms across her chest. "You dare speak to *the bride* this way before her wedding?"

"It's okay, Mina," Michelle said, stepping forward.

"No, it's not okay!" Mina snapped. "She should apologize to you."

Michelle's brow furrowed in concentration, while her gaze darted from Mina to Mrs. Kensington like a moth trapped between a cage and a flame. She said diplomatically, "We're all tired. Let's let Mrs. Kensington get some rest."

She gently—though insistently—ushered Mina out the door and into the main hall. Abby, Lucas, and Annabelle followed, fleeing Mrs. Kensington's gaze as if it carried the sting of a blizzard. Abby instantly felt warmer as Michelle pulled the wooden doors shut behind them.

Abby turned to Mina with a triumphant grin. "You sure put her in her place!"

Mina frowned, folding her arms across her chest and leaning against a nearby pillar. "Not really. Michelle, I don't get why you don't stand up to her."

"She's about to be my *mother-in-law*," Michelle whispered heatedly. "And it's not personal. She's just…a little paranoid."

"It's true," Annabelle said, twisting her thumb around her necklace. "She accuses everyone of trying to steal from her.

Last time I was here, she even called the police."

"On you?" Lucas asked, eyes wide with horror.

Annabelle shook her head. "She thought it was a stranger. Said she heard someone in her room. But no one was there."

"Unless it was a ghost," Abby whispered ominously.

Lucas elbowed her to keep quiet.

Letting out a heavy sigh, Michelle leaned against the faded floral wallpaper. "I just want this wedding to be over with."

Abby felt a flicker of pity for Michelle. She couldn't imagine what it would be like to have a woman like Mrs. Kensington for a mother-in-law. Chelsea's mother had been nothing but kind to Abby, even kinder than Abby's own mother, on many occasions. Michelle must really love David.

"Don't say that." Mina took her hands. "I meant what I said back there. You're awesome. You deserve an amazing wedding day. Don't let Mrs. Stuck-Up take that away from you."

Michelle smiled.

Mina embraced her. "Send me pictures. I bet you'll look fantastic."

When they pulled away, Mina dragged her bare feet across the polished floor. "Well, I guess I should get going before the roads freeze over again."

Oh right. Since Mina was not an actual bridesmaid, she was no longer needed at the estate. She hadn't even been invited to the wedding. With a twinge of disappointment, Abby realized this could be the last time she would ever see Mina. She considered faking a flat tire in Mina's car too.

"I forgive you, you know," Michelle said softly.

Mina cocked her head. "For what?"

Michelle wrung her hands together. "For what happened back in college. I know you were going through a hard time.

But—"

"But I shouldn't have showed up to your dorm drunk and slept with your roommate," Mina finished for her.

"Wait, that's what all this is about?" Lucas asked. "All this over a guy?"

"A girl," Michelle corrected.

Abby glanced at Mina with renewed interest, finding her expression genuinely apologetic.

"And it wasn't so much the act of them getting together as it was the showing up unannounced and trashing my place," Michelle continued.

"To be fair, she did most of the trashing," Mina said, scratching the back of her head. "But I'm sorry I dragged her into my mess. And I'm sorry I ruined your camera."

"It was the library's." Michelle folded her arms. "I spent a whole semester paying that off."

Mina winced. "Again, I'm sorry. With everything going on, I was upset. I'd come to talk to you, but then your roommate was there, and I got drunk and one thing led to another and—"

"I'm glad you found her instead," Michelle said with a laugh. "I wouldn't have slept with you."

Now it was Mina's turn to laugh.

"Do you think—" Michelle chewed her lip. "If you're free the rest of the week, would you want to stay for the wedding?"

Abby held her breath, pleading for Mina to say yes.

Mina grinned. "I'd love to."

Tears glistened in Michelle's eyes. She dabbed them away, trying her best not to ruin her mascara, and turned to the others. "What are you all standing around for? We've got decorating to do." She shooed Mina and Annabelle away. "And what are you still doing here?" she added to Lucas. "I thought you were heading out this morning?"

"Car trouble," Abby said. "Lucky for you, we're sticking around for a few days."

Michelle picked up a garland dotted with electric lights and shoved the end through the banister. She hissed as she jammed her finger, dropping the garland.

Abby caught it before it reached the floor. Ignoring the itch of prickly plastic, she wove the greenery over the wooden banister.

Michelle shook out her hand, studying her. "How is that lucky for me?"

Abby shrugged. "Now you have an extra set of hands. Two extra sets, if you count Lucas's sticky fingers."

"Excuse me? I'm an outstanding citizen. I've never stolen in my life."

"I didn't say you did."

"You said I have sticky fingers."

"Yeah because you spilled hot chocolate on them."

"That was yesterday. I cleaned them right after."

"Okay, you have two pairs of unsticky hands."

"Kids." Michelle snapped her fingers between them as she had many times when they were actual kids, and she had acted as if her mere three years' seniority made her an adult. "If you want to help, you can help Mina and Annabelle clean out the basement."

Abby and Lucas exchanged glances.

"Why do you need to clean out the basement?" Abby asked.

"It's our backup reception area, in case of bad weather."

Abby and Lucas looked horrified.

"What?" Michelle asked in exasperation.

"Why not in the living room?" Lucas asked. "You have this nice big house and you're going to lock people in the *basement*?"

"I'm not *locking* anyone anywhere—"

A crash shook the house. Abby grabbed the railing, waiting for the sound of thunder or the lights to flicker, but the house remained the same as before, except Michelle was wincing and Lucas was screaming.

"What was that?" Lucas said shakily. "It sounded like a wall fell inward."

"I have my suspicions." Abby dropped the rest of the lights and raced back down the stairs shouting, "Mrs. Kensington! Mrs. Kensington, are you alright?"

The halls remained eerily silent as she approached the ground floor. She craned her neck, hoping to find Mrs. Kensington seated in the armchair turning her book of poems as if nothing was wrong, and fearing to find her crushed by a fallen bookshelf.

Mrs. Kensington was standing in the corner—thankfully, uninjured—dusting off her sleeves. Marie Antoinette circled her heels, hackles raised. She glared at the center of the room, where the chandelier lay in a heap of broken shards and twisted metal.

"What happened?" Abby asked, rushing breathlessly into the living room.

Michelle and Lucas hurried in behind her, surveying the disaster.

"Just a fallen chandelier," Mrs. Kensington said in a way that would have been better suited to a minor form of inconvenience, such as a wobbly drawer, and not the disastrous demolition of an expensive antique, which had mauled her former chair with the strength of a wild animal.

"Oh no, are you hurt?" Sandra asked, rushing in from the kitchen. She reached for Mrs. Kensington's elbow, but Mrs.

Kensington pulled it away.

"I'm fine," she snapped, taking a small step back. She glared toward the kitchen doorway, where Mina stood with her jaw open, Annabelle clinging to her side.

Marie Antoinette hissed at them, daring them to step closer.

"Although I can't say the same for the room." Mrs. Kensington flicked a shard of crystal from her hair.

"I'll get this cleaned up," Sandra announced.

"The boys can do it."

"Who knows when they'll be home. We don't want Marie Antoinette stepping on a shard and hurting her paw now, do we? Why don't you take her upstairs and let me clean this up?"

Mrs. Kensington seemed to ponder her suggestion a moment before nodding. "As you wish."

"That means she loves her," Abby said.

"This is not the time to make *Princess Bride* references," Lucas hissed.

"Inconceivable."

Michelle flashed Abby a warning look as Mrs. Kensington stepped gingerly around the fallen crystal and scooped up Marie Antoinette, who made a small mew of protest before flopping against her shoulder as she was carried upstairs, Mrs. Kensington's black shawl sweeping behind them.

Sandra retreated to the kitchen.

The others took slow steps toward the chandelier.

"How did this happen?" Annabelle whispered.

"Sabotage?" Abby speculated.

Michelle glared at Abby like she was an opponent in a boxing match. "Will you give it a break? It's old. A screw must have been loose."

"Or it could be a ghost," Abby said, holding out her

binoculars. "See for yourself."

"I don't have time for one of your games."

"It's not a game! This house is haunted!"

"She's telling the truth," Lucas piped up, gesturing to the fallen chandelier. "How else would you explain this?"

"Loose screws, like I *just said*!"

"That happened to give way at exactly the time Mrs. Kensington sat under it?" Abby countered.

"It's her house." Michelle gave a tense shrug. "She spends every afternoon under it. It was a matter of time before it fell."

"Just like it was a matter of time before the lace attacked me?"

"Yes!" Michelle brought a hand to her forehead and took a deep breath. "I don't have time for this nonsense. Believe what you want, just stay out of my way with the decorating. And don't break anything."

She turned and stomped out of the room, calling Mina to follow her.

"Coming," Mina called back. On her way out, she met Abby's eyes with a look that Abby interpreted as 'I believe you, but she needs me right now.'

Abby nodded in understanding before turning back to her remaining audience—Lucas and Annabelle. She reached for the fallen chain. Firelight flickered in the reflection of the dark metal. She examined the dusty links and the hook that they had once been suspended from. It all added up to support one conclusion.

"The chain didn't break," she announced. "It was pulled from its hook. Someone tried to kill Mrs. Kensington."

Chapter Ten

Abby chewed her thumbnail as she stared at the fallen chandelier. This was the aftermath of attempted murder. Until now, her investigation had felt more like touring a museum or solving a video-game puzzle. She had forgotten the ghosts posed a *real* threat. They had provided entertainment and stimulation for a while before disappearing behind closed curtains or shut computers. They weren't supposed to go around dropping chandeliers on people or attacking them in their sleep.

But these ghosts—one of them, at least—clearly did.

Abby's skin prickled as she inched away from the shattered glass, recalling the cold invisible hands that had smothered her with lace. She glanced over her shoulder, suddenly fearful the ghosts were pressing in all around, waiting in the shadows, preparing to strike.

Annabelle inched forward to inspect the chain, her dress rustling softly like wind through daffodils. "How can you tell it was sabotage? Are you like Sherlock Holmes or something?"

"Yes," said Abby.

"No," said Lucas.

"Come on, you stopped watching *Psych* with me because I kept figuring out the bad guy ten minutes in."

"That's TV! This is completely different. This is *murder*."

"Technically, it's *attempted* murder."

"Technically, you didn't figure out *every* bad guy," Lucas muttered, moving closer to Abby. "Why did it go after Mrs. Kensington? Do you think she knows something?"

"Maybe." Abby chewed the inside of her cheek, her mind racing. The first attack had happened two days ago, in Mrs. Kensington's bedroom. Then, there had been no attack for over twenty-four hours. And now, as soon as Mrs. Kensington returned, a chandelier had nearly crushed her to death. Had the ghost been planning on killing all of them, but timed it poorly? Or was it after Mrs. Kensington now? Her eyes widened. "Or maybe it's been after Mrs. Kensington all along."

Lucas frowned. "What do you mean?"

"Think about it. I was attacked in Mrs. Kensington's room. What if the ghost wasn't after me at all, but Mrs. Kensington?"

Lucas looked at her like she had chocolate smeared across her face. "You don't look alike at all."

"I know. But it was dark. As soon as the light turned on, the ghost left me alone."

"You think it mistook you for Mrs. Kensington?" he asked skeptically.

Abby shrugged. "It's possible." A theory she wasn't ready to rule out. It made a lot more sense that someone would want to harm Mrs. Kensington than *her*. Practically every ghost they had talked to was upset with Mrs. Kensington for one reason or another. Had it been a mistake on the ghost's part? Or was the ghost going around after everyone now? Abby shuddered. They would all need to be careful.

She turned to Annabelle and asked, "What do you know about this estate and the family who lives here? Or more importantly, those who died here."

"Not much." Annabelle fidgeted with the sleeve of her lavender cardigan as she backed away from the broken chandelier. "It was built over a hundred years ago. All the Kensingtons I've met are still alive. For all their eccentricities, they're a kind family."

"What do you mean by eccentricities?" Abby asked.

"Oh, you know, all the big elaborate parties, the old-fashioned taste in clothes, business. Everything, really." She gestured around the Victorian-style room to emphasize her point.

"Do you know of anyone, dead or alive—preferably dead— who would want to harm Mrs. Kensington?"

Lucas leaned forward, careful not to step any closer. "Are you *sure* the ghost is after Mrs. Kensington?"

Abby pointed at the broken chandelier. "I thought we'd just established that."

Lucas shook his head. "Maybe. Or maybe the ghost did it to throw you off so it can attack you unsuspectingly in your sleep tonight."

"Why would the ghost want to kill me?"

Lucas shrugged. "Maybe you've annoyed it with all your questions."

Abby playfully swatted his arm. "Very funny."

Annabelle looked between them, her face pale. "Do you really think the ghost wants to hurt Mrs. Kensington?"

"It's a theory," Abby admitted. "That or the ghost is attacking people at random, which sounds a lot scarier to me, don't you think?"

"Well, she's not the most popular woman," Annabelle said, pulling her cardigan tighter around her paisley dress. "I know a dozen people who would intentionally 'forget' to invite her to their galas or what have you, but I can't think of anyone who would go as far as to want her dead."

"Not even her late husband?" Abby asked.

Annabelle's face tightened. "Of course not!"

Abby held her hands up. "I thought you said he was difficult to get along with."

Annabelle sighed. "He was stern, but he wasn't violent. They may never have truly loved each other, but they got along. They seemed to enjoy each other's company, when they were actually around each other."

"They spent a lot of time apart?"

Annabelle nodded. "Mrs. Kensington liked to travel. Without a job, she was free to go anywhere she wanted, anytime she wanted. Sometimes she'd head over to Europe for months at a time. Her husband didn't have that luxury."

"Do you think he's resentful of that?"

Annabelle shook her head. "Not that I've seen. He cared for her and he loved his sons until the very end. But there was one thing—"

Abby perked up. "What?"

"A repairman died here about twenty years ago. His wife was furious. She blamed Mrs. Kensington for his death, saying it was her fault for demanding he work in such severe weather conditions. She threatened to sue. Mr. Turner wanted to pay off the wife, but Mrs. Kensington insisted that she had told the repairman *not* to work that day and that he'd chosen to anyway."

Abby nodded. The repairman was a likely suspect. They would have to interrogate him soon enough. She wasn't looking forward to that, considering he looked awfully disgruntled stomping through the garden earlier.

"But she didn't end up suing?" Lucas asked.

"I don't know," Annabelle said. "Mrs. Kensington never talks about it."

"It must have been substantial if Robert thought it worth mentioning after all these years," Lucas pointed out, rubbing his chin in a thoughtful motion.

Annabelle shook her head. "Robert didn't tell me. I was here."

Abby and Lucas stared blankly. She was here in the 1990s? Wasn't she like ten back then?

"Do you have a DeLorean with some fancy flux capacitor that lets you travel back in time?" Abby asked. Lucas shot her a look that said this was not the time to be making *Back to the Future* references. Abby disagreed. It was *always* a good time to make *Back to the Future* references.

Annabelle clasped her pale hands together. "I lived down the road. I met the Kensingtons a few years after it happened, but there was still some fallout. The adults tried to keep us away from the drama, but I overheard some bits about the lawsuit, and I saw Mrs. Johnson storming up the front steps, threatening to sue the life out of Mrs. Kensington."

The kitchen door swung open. Lucas jumped, his hand flying to protect his face as if he expected a ghost to charge at him. But it was only Sandra returning with a broom. Abby stepped aside as she began to sweep shards of crystal and glass.

Annabelle leaned toward Abby and whispered, "Do you think the ghost is Mrs. Johnson coming to carry through on that threat?"

Abby and Lucas exchanged glances.

"Anything is possible," Abby admitted, moving into the kitchen and toward the open supply closet. "I think we better go see what Mr. Johnson can tell us."

Lucas followed. "Why don't *you* talk to him?"

Abby gave him an incredulous look. "Are you afraid?"

"No. I just don't want to go back out in the cold and question yet another ghost who could potentially draw us in closer to a murder-in-the-making."

"Fine." Abby tossed him some plastic gloves and a duster.

"What are these for?"

"For cleaning out the basement."

"I'm not cleaning out the basement. There are cobwebs."

"So?"

"When there are cobwebs, there are spiders. You know I don't do spiders. Where there are spiders, there's pain."

"And wriggling and screaming," Abby said. "I'll never forget that day you crawled under the deck."

"You mean when you locked me in there?"

"We were ten," said Abby. "It was the dungeon. Prisoners get locked in the dungeon. How was I supposed to know that you needed a special combination to unlock the lock?"

"You used a combination lock on your bike," Lucas countered, before shaking his head and dropping the cleaning supplies with a grand declaration that echoed off the walls:

"I'm *not* cleaning the basement."

"You will be if Michelle finds you." Abby gestured to the ceiling where the faint patter of footsteps and creaking floorboards gave way to Michelle and Mina's voices.

"What'll it be?" Abby asked. "Spiders or ghosts?"

Abby could see Lucas checking every corner of his mind for a third option, but as Michelle's voice grew closer, he reached for the back door.

Grinning, Abby led him outside. They had a ghost to interrogate.

Chapter Eleven

The problem was Dean Johnson's ghost was nowhere to be found, and none of the other ghosts knew much about him.

"He's a recluse," said Archie.

"I don't recall him," said Sarah.

"He never comes inside," said the nanny.

It wasn't until Abby and Lucas were shivering with cold, considering heading back to the fireside, that they stumbled across Mrs. Gardner, a kind, elderly ghost, who showed them a bench Mr. Johnson liked to sit on to watch the stars.

Of course, it was far too cold and cloudy for stargazing, but Abby reckoned a ghost wouldn't be bothered by the weather when performing a habit that lingered beyond death.

So they waited a few feet from the bench, tucked into their borrowed coats. Abby was thankful for the pair of fur earmuffs she had found in one of the closets and the scarf Mina had let her borrow. While the scarf was a bit thin for freezing weather, it carried a pleasant earthy scent that reminded her of Mina, making it feel warmer than it was.

Abby twisted the frayed ends as she watched the bench with bored anticipation. It was a pretty bench, with wooden panels peeking out from a blanket of snow that thinned every time the breeze picked up, dusting the twisted iron armrests. Eventually, Abby noticed the top panel was engraved with the phrase '*In Loving Memory of*—the name had been scratched out. Beneath it, a single pair of initials had been carved by a shaky hand, encased in a heart.

Abby tried not to think about the time Chelsea had carved their initials on the picnic table behind their high school cafeteria. Or maybe she had drawn it. The details were hazy, they came in fragments—a warm breeze carrying the scent of ice cream, the fluid strokes of Chelsea's fingers as she scribbled with such *certainty*, their initials gleaming with sunlight in a manner that felt so monumental, so *permanent*.

With a shaky breath, she burrowed deeper into Mina's scarf and grounded herself, moving the binoculars to focus on the pinkening horizon as she waited for Dean Johnson to reveal himself.

When the sky grew dark and Abby's fingers ached from clutching the binoculars to her face, he finally appeared.

It was a gradual appearance, murky and granular, like powdered lemonade dissolving in water, only instead of a delicious drink at the end there was a pale outline of a man seated against the bench staring into the horizon.

He looked so peaceful, Abby's first instinct told her not to disturb him. Then she remembered he could have been the one to strangle her and her jaw locked. She slid out the antenna on the antique walkie-talkie.

"Mr. Johnson?" she asked, cautiously. She felt like she was

poking a sleeping snake without knowing if it was venomous or not.

The ghost continued to stare at the horizon, where snow-laden evergreens bled into the dark. He grew a bit more solid. Through the binoculars, Abby could see the wrinkles in his overalls and the stubble on his chin. While he was definitely the ghost that had been stomping through the rose bushes the other day, he looked much more peaceful now. There wasn't a trace of anger, nor recognition that he had even heard them.

The walkie-talkie beeped as Lucas pressed it multiple times, repeating, "Mr. Johnson?"

Abby tried his first name. "Dean?"

The ghost turned to them slowly, dazed. He widened and squeezed his eyes as if he was attempting to blink, but had forgotten how.

"Can you see us?" Abby asked, flailing her arms both to attract attention and to send warmth back into her fingers.

Dean gave the world's smallest nod. His voice came through the crackling walkie-talkie, faded and soft. "Do I know you?"

"No," Abby said. "You died before we were born. But we were hoping—"

"*Died?*" The walkie-talkie hissed, making a harsh electric sound like the crack of thunder.

"Oh. Is that, uh, news to you?" Abby felt a pang of guilt as she shifted her weight and glanced to Lucas for help.

He shook his head, backing away behind a rose bush—one of the very bushes Dean had stomped through the day before. Abby gulped, recalling how angry he had looked. She didn't want to unleash his temper.

"When?" Dean Johnson looked around in confusion. "How?"

"Ah, it's best not to go into details," Abby said, not wanting a hysterical ghost on her hands. But this news was unexpected. If Dean Johnson didn't know he was dead, what motive would he have for attacking her and Mrs. Kensington?

"I'm guessing you haven't seen your wife around here lately either?" Abby asked as she mentally moved the Johnsons back to the bottom of her list and tried to visualize who that left at the top.

"Meredith?" His face darkened. "Is she dead too?"

Abby glanced at Lucas for the answer, but he shrugged and gave her a 'beats me' expression. They probably should have checked up on that.

"We're not sure," she said, trying to be as diplomatic as she could manage, "but either way, she lived a lot longer than you did."

"Thank God," said Dean, turning back toward the horizon with a blissful smile.

Abby let out a breath, relieved she hadn't upset him more. She pressed on, a little more cautiously. "What do you know about the Kensingtons?"

"Who?" Dean asked.

"The owners of the estate." Abby gestured to the manor behind her.

Dean folded his arms across his overalls. "Not much. Just that they're loaded and have old wiring. Well, guess I better get back to it." He stood and stretched, grabbed a ghost wrench that appeared midair, and headed toward the side of the house, trudging through the hedges.

Abby scratched her head. Maybe he hadn't been stomping Mrs. Kensington's rose bushes in an attempt to ruin them, but merely didn't see them. Was it possible he didn't see anything that had been added after his death? "Where are you going?"

"To finish my repairs," the ghost said.

"Uh, I think those were finished like twenty years ago," Abby pointed out.

"Twenty-one," Lucas corrected.

Abby stared at him.

"What?" said Lucas. "I was being precise."

"I was also precise. Twenty-one is precisely 'like twenty.' Besides, what difference does a year make to a ghost, right?"

Abby turned to Dean Johnson, but he was no longer in sight. A quick scan through the binoculars found him across the yard, climbing onto the roof, where he removed his hat, tucked it into his pocket, and reached for the ghost of a satellite that no longer existed.

"He's…working," Abby mused.

No sooner had the words left her mouth than his ghost went rigid. He collapsed, convulsing against the shingles, sliding dangerously toward the edge of the roof. His overalls tore as he toppled over the edge and fell, disappearing out of sight.

Abby shouted in alarm. She threw her hand to her chest, attempting to massage away the dread that was spreading through her veins. Every bone in her body wanted to run forward and check on him, call a paramedic, do everything she could to save him—but she was twenty-one years too late.

"What's wrong?" Lucas asked.

"I think he just died."

"He's already dead," Lucas reminded her.

"Can ghosts die twice?" Abby asked, attempting to steady her shaky voice. She dropped the binoculars, letting them hang loose by the strap around her neck, and turned away from the house. "Or survive a thirty—possibly twenty-nine, possibly twenty-eight—foot fall?"

Lucas glared at her.

Abby feigned innocence. "What? I'm being precise."

"That's not precise, that's annoying. And no, I don't think he fell again—"

"He did!" Abby insisted. "I saw him."

"I know," said Lucas. "I think you saw him reliving his initial fall. He's reliving his death."

Abby scraped some snow with the heel of her boot as she thought about it. "Can a ghost relive things when they're dead?"

"I don't know," Lucas mused. "He's re*death*ing."

Abby shuddered. "That poor guy is stuck reliving his death night after night."

Forming fists around the binoculars, Abby strolled hastily toward the warmth of the house, her mind churning while her muscles warmed, fueled by determination. How awful it must be, experiencing your own death over and over again. Had Dean broken out of his death-loop long enough to go after Mrs. Kensington? Or was he too wrapped up in reliving his last moments that it hadn't even occurred to him to blame her for his death?

"What now?" Lucas asked, breaking her train of thought. "If Mr. Johnson doesn't even remember Mrs. Kensington, he couldn't have attacked her."

"He could have remembered momentarily," Abby countered. "Or he may not have been aware of what he was doing."

"That's a lot of speculation. Should we run it by Nancy Ghost and the Hardy Ghouls? You think they've had enough Blue's Clues yet?"

But Abby was shaking her head. "New plan," she announced, as they stepped into the warmth of the manor. "We're going to send Dean Johnson on."

Chapter Twelve

Abby spent the rest of the afternoon trying to shake the memory of Dean reliving his death. But if two cups of hot chocolate, half a dozen freshly baked cookies, and a soak in a hot tub couldn't do it, she was pretty sure nothing would.

"I don't get it," Lucas called over the gentle roar of the Jacuzzi jets. "Why are you so convinced Dean is our guy?"

Abby picked at the straps of the modest blue swimsuit Annabelle had loaned her. She shut her eyes and leaned back, savoring the warmth as chlorinated steam tickled her nose. "I just am."

Lucas deserved a better answer, but Abby wasn't ready to give it. How could she explain that everywhere she looked, she saw a ghost locked in their final moments? Sometimes that ghost was Dean, but sometimes it was Chelsea. Sweet, innocent Chelsea in her green sweater and handmade jewelry crying out for help as she was crushed by a storm of broken glass.

Chelsea had never dealt with the harsher side of life well. She had avoided stress as much as possible, skipping school on the days they had to dissect anything. She turned off sad movies before the end. She refused to drive on highways during storms, and after dark. By avoiding risky activities, she thought she was eliminating the potential to introduce negativity into her life. Imagining her death was painful enough—the thought that she could be reliving it was torture.

"What about the architect?" Lucas asked. "He seemed pretty upset about the renovations. You might not have anything to do with that, but Mrs. Kensington does."

Abby sighed. "We can question him." She reached for the walkie-talkie.

"Don't get it wet!" Lucas jumped out of the water, grabbed a towel, and used it to snatch the walkie-talkie. Wrapping a plush robe over his swim trunks, he looked around for something—likely the binoculars.

Abby wiped her hands on a towel and held an open palm toward Lucas, indicating she wanted the walkie-talkie.

He shook his head. "We can't just call up every ghost on a whim."

"It's not a whim. You made a good point about the renovations."

"I know," said Lucas. "But that doesn't change the fact we can't jump up and follow every idea that crosses our minds."

"Why not?"

"Because—" Lucas flailed his arms. "That never gets us anywhere. We need to think this through. Make a list, check the facts, narrow it down to our top two or three suspects. A second ago, you were convinced it was Dean. All it took was a few words and you're chasing after Archie."

"I still think it's Dean. I was humoring you."

"Humor me with a list." Lucas picked up his phone from a

nearby table and began typing on it. "Our top three suspects—Dean, Archie, and…?"

He turned to Abby expectantly.

Abby leaned back in the hot tub with a sigh. She rubbed her forehead in an effort to clear the memory of Dean Johnson reliving his death, but it didn't work. She shut her eyes and pinched the bridge of her nose. When she opened them, Lucas was staring at her and frowning.

"What?"

Lucas set his phone down and moved closer. "What aren't you telling me?"

"Nothing."

His eyes narrowed. "It's not nothing."

"Let's call Archie," Abby declared, waving her hand dismissively.

"I'm not going to call a murderous ghost without a plan." Crossing his arms, Lucas settled into a nearby chair. His stubbornness was infuriating.

Abby sank so deep into the hot tub, only her neck and face were exposed. "You can ask him about the renovations, and I'll ask him what he knows about Dean reliving his death."

The walkie-talkie crackled. Archie's disembodied voice filled the room. "I'm not just a being that can be summoned."

Lucas jumped up, the walkie-talkie flying from his hands. Abby reached for it, but she was too far away. Her heart pounded as their only means of communicating with the dead fell toward the ground.

Lucas caught it with his foot, inches from the floor.

"Talk about being careful!" Abby's hand flew to her heart. "I'm revoking your rights to the equipment."

"They aren't yours to revoke." Lucas gingerly cradled the

walkie-talkie and backed away from the hot tub, as if he feared Abby might spray it with water.

"Aren't you going to question me?" Archie's voice crackled smugly through the walkie-talkie.

Abby turned down the jets so she could better hear the ghost, and sank back into a comfortable position, folding her arms over the edge of the hot tub.

She exchanged a hesitant glance with Lucas that conveyed he thought it was just as suspicious as she did that a ghost *wanted* to be questioned.

"Did you drop that chandelier on Mrs. Kensington?" Abby asked as calmly as she could manage despite the chill creeping down her spine. Her gaze flickered to the salt gun lying on a table across the room. It was at least a dozen yards away, and she speculated her ability to run was rather limited by her soaking wet state and the soon-to-be slippery floor.

"Of course not," Archie scoffed.

Abby's shoulders relaxed at his words, her immediate sense of danger dimming.

"Did you see who did?" Lucas asked, tying his robe tighter around him.

"No," Archie said, as if the question was an inconvenience. "I wish I had. I quite liked that chandelier."

A shadow flickered near the doorway, despite the overhead lights glowing strong. It was an odd shadow, attached to nothing and no one that Abby could see, in the outline of Archie's willowy frame. Abby blinked and it disappeared.

"But what about her renovations?" Lucas paced the room. He drew nearer and nearer to the salt gun.

"I don't care for them, it's true. But I would not benefit from her death."

Abby opened her mouth to speak the contrary, but the ghost beat her to it.

"It may stop the renovations for a bit, as you pointed out, but there'd be an extra ghost around here, and we're packed as is. Some new kid would take over the estate, and that's sure to be a disaster—whenever it changes hands, there's always heaps of changes—walls knocked down, doors replaced, facades switched—much larger than the garden improvements Mrs. Kensington has in store. At least she cares about basic historic preservation. The longer she lives, the *happier* I am."

There came a thumping as if the ghost had knocked on the wood. A table skirt fluttered near the doorway, where the flickering shadow had returned. Despite the hot water enveloping her, Abby shivered.

"Although, now that you mention it, Sarah has been quite upset that the old woman gave away her piano." Either he had incriminating information about Sarah that he was reluctant to share, or he held a grudge against her and wanted Abby to doubt her innocence.

"Abby was wondering about the repairman who died here," Lucas chimed in, steering the conversation back on track. "Can you tell us anything about him?"

"He was after my time," said Archie.

"He's reliving his death," Abby explained. "Have you seen that before?"

"I have," came Archie's grim response. "Though I haven't experienced it myself. At least, not that I know of. I've seen it happen to a few of the others, once or twice, but never as often as that poor man."

Abby shuddered, making a mental note to call Glen and ask

him if he had ever seen that, and if there was anything they could do to stop it.

"How often does it happen?" Lucas asked.

"Don't ask me questions about time, I can't keep track of it. But it's a lot. In fact, I don't think I've ever seen him when he wasn't stuck in those last moments."

Abby gulped. She dropped a hand into the water and swirled the bubbles into a spiral around her waist. Even if Dean had attacked her, she had compassion for him. No one deserved to be locked in such an emotionally vicious cycle.

"When he's stuck like that, is it dangerous?" Lucas asked. "Do you think he could have accidentally hurt Mrs. Kensington?"

"It's possible," Archie said. "If she got in his way, there's no telling what a ghost like that could do."

It was easy to imagine a frightened Dean lashing out in a confused rage, storming into Mrs. Kensington's bedroom and attacking her in her sleep, only to come back to his senses when the lights turned on and he found a stranger between his hands.

Abby nodded at Lucas, indicating her suspicions had been confirmed.

"Thank you for your help," said Lucas.

Archie grunted. "Anything to get you out of this place faster."

"Is there anyone else you can think of who would want to harm us?" Lucas asked.

The static crackled in response.

"Archie?"

"He's gone," Mary's voice crackled instead. "Can you turn the magic box on again? That grouchy old woman turned it off."

"In a minute," Lucas said, before powering off the walkie-talkie and resting it on top of his folded sweater. He turned the knob on the hot tub, making the jets roar as the bubbles surged to the surface. "What do you think?"

"Why are we whisper-shouting?"

"So the ghosts don't hear."

Abby was pretty sure any ghost that lurked close enough could hear them just fine, but she didn't express the thought. Instead, she thought about Dean trapped in that horrid death-loop. "We have to send him on."

"Archie?"

"Dean."

Lucas's brow furrowed. "You think he's the one that strangled you?"

"Yes. Maybe the snow storm or the power being out snapped him out of his death-loop, and he went to seek vengeance."

"He went to Mrs. Kensington's room, assumed you were her, and tried to kill you. But when he realized he had the wrong person, he stopped." Lucas considered this for a moment. "It's a theory."

"The best one we have."

Lucas stroked his chin. "But we don't have any evidence."

"They're ghosts. We're not going to find evidence."

"But don't you think we should wait until we consider—"

"Consider what?" Abby threw her hands up in exasperation, splashing water across the tile. "Let's send Dean on and see if the attacks stop. If they do, we pat ourselves on the back for a job well done."

Lucas's water bottle squeaked as he popped the top open, then shut. "And if they don't?"

Abby shrugged. "Then we put a suffering spirit out of its misery and bought ourselves some time. It's a win-win."

Lucas continued to fidget with his water bottle. "I don't know about this."

Abby clambered out of the hot tub. The cool air made her skin prickle until she wrapped herself in an oversized towel. "Then I'll do it on my own."

ABBY KNEW LUCAS couldn't stay away. At least, as she pulled on a pair of borrowed sweatpants and a T-shirt, she *hoped* he couldn't stay away.

She called Glen Ashford with a phone number she had found on his website. It went straight to voicemail.

Leaving a brief message about the day's events, she gave her phone number and asked Glen to call her back with any tips he had for sending a ghost on. Or breaking them out of a death-loop. Or ghost hunting in general.

The phone cut her off before she finished.

He would get the point.

She returned to the old nursery, leaving the door open to help cut the stuffy creepy vibe of its faded blue walls and dinosaur trim, while the ghost children helped her sort through boxes.

Her eyes started to droop shut. She glanced at the clock. It was broken, but she reckoned it was around nine. She wasn't sure how long she could keep this up. Questioning ghosts all day had taken its toll on her. Tossing a stack of old car magazines out of one box and into another, she leaned back with a sigh.

"So many strange things." Elizabeth's voice cackled through the walkie-talkie as she drifted over a box of what appeared to be souvenirs from a 90s college dorm room. "What do people need with all these trinkets?"

"To remember fond memories, I guess." Abby shrugged as she pulled out a can of Silly String and attempted to spray it. It was so old, it merely made a hissing sound and sputtered a few gooey strands onto the rug.

"Strange," said Elizabeth. "I remember my past perfectly without trinkets. In fact, I hardly remember my things at all."

Abby's breath caught as she thought of Chelsea's memories slipping away. Her own memories burned so bright, as if their magnitude could counteract any effect on Chelsea. She remembered the first time she noticed Chelsea like it was yesterday—in her green sweater rolled up to her elbows and her messy side-ponytail, she had looked like she was cosplaying someone from the Baby-Sitters Club. She slipped into the seat beside Abby with such grace and confidence, Abby instantly disliked her. That was Lucas's seat. It didn't matter that Mrs. Perkins had split them up for talking too many times and a new seating chart was on the board. Abby blamed Chelsea. Not only had Chelsea taken her best friend's seat, but she also then had the nerve to call Abby out for reading a comic book in class (Abby still thought it was unfair to get detention for *reading* in English class—wasn't that the point of the class?). But then they were paired up for an assignment and, after several sessions over sodas, Abby got to see that underneath Chelsea's know-it-all facade was a rebel spirit bursting at the seams with creativity and unadulterated ideas. She loved her cats and collected seashells and wanted to be a marine biologist. She was an amazing artist, a decent actress, and had a knack for restyling vintage clothes. She took her work seriously, although she had a tendency to daydream and doodle in the margins of her notebooks.

By the time they turned in their assignment, they were inseparable. Chelsea talked to Abby every day—before class, after class, at lunch on B-days when their lunch schedule overlapped. It wasn't the talking that drew Abby to Chelsea; it was that she listened, really *listened*, without interrupting or arguing or worrying about the consequences of Abby's words. And when Abby finished speaking, Chelsea offered words of assurance and encouragement that made Abby feel like she could achieve her wildest dreams. When Abby wanted to take musical theater instead of Latin, Chelsea helped her write a three-page essay to present to her parents on how acting could help prepare her for academia by advancing her level of communication and public speaking. When Abby decided to try out for the lead in her school play, Chelsea helped her practice for weeks (and when Hannah Brown got the part and Abby didn't, Chelsea took her for ice cream and karaoke, reminding Abby that other people's opinions should never impact her confidence).

If Chelsea's spirit was out there, did she remember those things? Or was Abby the only one left with those memories? If they were Abby's, and Abby's alone, what made them more than dreams? Abby shook the thought. This wasn't the time to think about Chelsea. She needed to focus.

"What do you remember?" Abby asked.

"My life," Elizabeth said fondly. "My family."

Abby's heart warmed a bit. If Chelsea was still out there, maybe she would remember Abby. "What else?"

"My cat. Sunrises and sunsets. Reading by candlelight. My room. A clearing in the woods. I visit it sometimes, when I miss it most."

Abby imagined the room of her cramped apartment, with its unpainted walls, small TV, and old twin mattress. Would she remember that place for eternity? She hoped not. She hated the thought of spending eternity there, literally or figuratively. At the very least, she would be redecorating when she got home.

"That's it." Abby jumped to her feet. "Maybe it's not an object we need to find, but a place! And we already know what place is important to Dean Johnson, don't we?"

"Who?" Elizabeth asked.

Abby frowned, wishing Lucas were with her. She had hoped he would have come to his senses and joined her by now. "The repairman."

"Oh. What place?"

"His bench. The Gardners said he sits there often to look at the stars, but what if there's a different reason? If he wanted a view of the sky, why did he choose *that* bench? Why not the gazebo?"

"It's more comfortable?" Elizabeth suggested.

"More comfortable than the cushioned porch chairs?" Abby shook her head and grabbed an old photo album. She flipped through the pages absentmindedly. "There are numerous places to sit out back. But he went to *this* bench. Why?"

The walkie-talkie crackled in response. Either Elizabeth didn't have an answer or she had gotten bored with the conversation and wandered off.

Abby shut the photo album. She had a hunch Dean was returning to that particular bench for a reason. She wanted to know why.

Abby pulled out her phone and attempted to research the Kensington gardens. She scrolled through pictures until she found one of a pretty teenage girl sitting on the bench, staring into the distant sunset. The girl was a travel blogger who apparently visited the estate in 2015, over a decade after Dean

Johnson died. But there was something about the bench that made Abby's mind churn. A small carving to the right of the girl's hand. She zoomed in until she could see a pair of initials, MB & DJ, encased by a heart.

A soft knock on the door startled her.

She looked up to find Lucas standing in the doorway, leaning awkwardly against the wooden frame.

"Hey," he said, as if their last conversation hadn't ended with him abandoning her. Even if she had been the one to walk away, he was *supposed* to follow.

"Took you long enough," Abby grumbled, folding her arms across her chest.

Lucas stepped into the room, shutting the door behind him. He paced before taking a seat at the edge of a bed that squeaked with his movements. "Find anything?"

Abby shrugged. "Everything."

Lucas's eyes narrowed as if he was suspicious. Abby eagerly awaited his request to elaborate, but instead he said, "Listen, Abby. I want to help you, but I need to know you have a solid plan. You're sure Dean's the ghost that attacked you?"

"Yes," she said defensively. "He has a temper, he's unpredictable. If you experienced your death over and over again, night after night for years, wouldn't you blame the woman who hired you for the job that killed you?"

"It is a pretty good motive," Lucas admitted. "But what if he's innocent?"

Abby fidgeted with her bracelet. "Then sending him on is the least we can do."

Lucas followed the motions of her hands. His eyes widened. "Are you thinking of Chelsea?"

Abby dropped her hands to her side with a shrug. "How

can I not? If she's out there somewhere, reliving her last moments—"

"She's not Dean."

"But she could be *like* him."

"Sending Dean on won't help her."

"I know. But if someone like us were in a position to help her, I'd want them to. Don't you think Dean's loved ones would want us to?"

Lucas sucked in a deep breath. "So what's our plan? Do we know what his unfinished business is or what object is keeping him here?"

Abby's shoulders sagged in relief. "I'm getting close."

She moved to sit beside Lucas, pulling up Dean Johnson's obituary on her phone. "Dean's wife, Meredith, is the one with the grudge against Mrs. Kensington. Her maiden name was Bloom."

"Okay? Is she related to Orlando?"

"No," said Abby dismissively. "Although she might have had a better career if she had been, especially if he'd gotten her work on *Pirates of the Caribbean*. The money from that franchise alone would be more than what she was asking for from Mrs. Kensington."

"She didn't win the lawsuit?" Lucas gathered.

"No," said Abby. "Mrs. Kensington must have paid her a settlement fee. Is that what it's called when you pay someone not to go to court, or is that only in divorce cases?"

"Paying someone not to go to court is bribery," said Lucas. "Settling is when opposing parties come to an agreement outside of court to officially end a dispute."

"Sounds like the same thing to me," Abby said with a shrug. "Anyway, Mrs. Kensington's aunt married a Walker Bloom.

Three guesses what they named their daughter."

"Meredith?"

"Actually, their first daughter was named Claire. But yes, their second was Meredith."

Lucas ran his finger through the air, as if attempting to draw the family tree in his mind. "So, she's Mrs. Kensington's cousin?"

"Looks like it."

"And she didn't get anything—not the Kensington name, not the estate, not even the court case she wanted." He leaped to his feet and began to pace. "It all makes sense! She's haunting Mrs. Kensington because she wants the house!"

"Not exactly." Abby bit back a grin, attempting to hide her amusement. It was great to have Lucas at her side again. He was going *all* in on this. It almost made up for the fact it took him so long to listen to her.

"Because she wants her to pay?" he speculated. "Because she's jealous of the wealth that was so nearly hers?"

"No. The ghost isn't Meredith."

Lucas's forehead wrinkled. "How do you know? We haven't seen our culprit in action. It could be any ghost at this point."

"Meredith Bloom isn't dead." Abby showed him her latest blog post on a gardening website that showed she was alive and well two days ago, on a peaceful farmhouse in Virginia.

As Lucas's theory evaporated, he sank to his knees. "What's so important about Meredith, then, if she's not our culprit?"

"She's not." Abby navigated to another tab on her phone, to the picture of the girl sitting on the bench at sunset. She zoomed in on over the girl's shoulder before handing it to Lucas. "Her name is."

Lucas stared at the blurry image of an engraving on the

bench. "MB+DJ," he read aloud. "Meredith Bloom and Dean Johnson!"

"Exactly." Abby's eyes gleamed with excitement.

"Hold on, hold on." Lucas threw his hands up. "If it is the bench that's keeping him here, what are we going to do about it? We can't destroy it."

"No," Abby agreed. "But I bet we could burn off the carving."

Lucas rubbed his chin. "What if he tries to stop us?"

Abby tossed him a bag of saltwater taffy she'd taken from Michelle's gift bags. They fit almost perfectly into the salt gun. "We'll be quick. Besides, he doesn't even know he's dead."

"So he says. What if he's lying? He could be the murderer."

"First of all, there is no murderer since Mrs. Kensington is still alive."

"You don't know that."

"I just saw her walking out of the bathroom like ten minutes ago."

"I mean you don't know that there are no murderers," said Lucas. "Any one of these ghosts could have killed before."

"Fair point." Abby chewed her lip. "In that case…" She grabbed the salt gun from where the briefcase lay open on the floor. She picked it up, hoping she wouldn't have to use it.

Chapter Thirteen

Abby shut her eyes and prayed that she was as good at winging ghost mysteries as she was at video games and oral history exams. There was a lot more than a bad grade on the line.

With the thrilling anticipation of vanquishing an anguished ghost, she slipped on her borrowed coat and led Lucas downstairs. They crept through the garage, looking for anything that might create a strong flame. After thirty minutes with no luck, Lucas said he remembered seeing a blowtorch in the kitchen pantry. They waited until Sandra was hunched over the stove, the air heavy with sautéed herbs and garlic, before they darted into the pantry, grabbed the blowtorch, and slid out the back door.

Abby's breath lingered in the air. The binoculars hung around her neck, tucked into her coat, as her flashlight swept across snow until it reached the wooden bench.

After clamping the flashlight under her arm, Abby rubbed

her hands together. Cautiously she brushed icy snow off the top of the bench. The cold stung. Her light momentarily dimmed as she warmed her hand against the flashlight and shivered.

"This is why you wear gloves." Raising his own gloved hands to demonstrate, Lucas stepped forward and cleared a larger portion of the bench before kneeling down to inspect the wood.

Blurred by a thin layer of ice, the initials glistened in the flashlight's yellow glow.

"MB and DJ," Lucas read. He added, "Meredith Bloom and Dean Johnson. Forever in love."

"Till death do they part." Abby tossed Lucas the flashlight and pulled the binoculars from her coat. "Keep lookout."

"Why do I have to keep lookout?"

"Would you rather deface property?"

Wrinkling his nose and shooting her an annoyed look, Lucas snatched the binoculars and raised them to his eyes.

Abby swapped places with him and raised the blowtorch to the bench.

"I feel like I'm in one of those old video games," Lucas said, sweeping his gaze, through the binoculars, across the estate grounds.

The blowtorch hissed to life in Abby's hands, spreading a small but bright flame against the bench. She adjusted it so it fell directly on the carving. "Like Pajama Sam?"

"Have you not played a video game in the past decade?"

"Not one as fun as the ones we used to play."

The flame continued to lick the bench, melting nearby ice and darkening the wood between the two initials. She hoped she was doing this right. A quick glance at her phone showed a single missed call—from her mother, not Glen.

Her mother would be no use against ghosts. She could wait.

"I meant I feel like I'm in a scary game," Lucas continued, as if they were on a casual stroll to dinner and not defacing property to send on a potentially murderous ghost. "One of those old-fashioned explore and reveal games, where everything's dark until—bam, there's a skeleton blocking your path or there's evil green poison seeping into your shoes."

Abby held the blowtorch steady, letting the flame do its work. "How does poison seep into your shoes?"

"It's acidic."

"I never got those games. Wouldn't you sense that before you stepped? Wouldn't there be a stench or something?"

Lucas cleared his throat. "We've got an audience."

Abby surveyed the garden, as if she strained hard enough she could see the ghost. "Dean?"

Lucas shook his head, binoculars still raised to his eyes, pointing at the house.

"Who?" Abby asked.

Lucas's expression was hidden in shadow, but his voice was grim as he replied, "Everyone else."

"Be specific. Who's where and what are they doing?"

"Sarah Kensington is in the drawing room, acting like she's playing piano."

Abby nodded. Sarah posed no immediate threat, and she doubted Lucas would have started with her if someone was looming over them with a murderous look in their eyes. This was a good vantage point.

"The ghost kids are playing hide-and-seek in Annabelle's room," Lucas continued. "The nanny's watching over them. God, does Annabelle know her room is so crowded? Maybe I should text her—"

"Who else?" Abby asked. And Lucas said *she* was bad at staying focused.

"Archie. He's in the drawing room, watching us."

"Ah, I always did love an audience." Abby turned her attention back to the blowtorch, where the initials were slowly darkening from the heat. Although the flame licked the wood, it made little difference. All she seemed to be doing was glazing the initials like caramelizing sugar on top of a crème brûlée.

"Wait—that's my sketchbook!" Lucas shouted, turning to Abby with a panicked expression. "Archie's looking at my sketchbook!"

"Great, the guy's 200 years old, he needs some form of entertainment."

"Those are my *private* sketches, Abby."

"Oh no, he might steal your ideas. It's not like he can get them published—"

"That's not the point! Hold the torch still, you're moving it too much."

"I'm not a statue," Abby replied, drawing tiny circles over the initials with the blowtorch. "I can't hold still that long. And besides, I've got to get the whole thing."

"It's not hot enough."

"You worry about the ghosts, okay? I've got this."

Lucas returned the binoculars to his eyes. Yelping, he staggered back, kicking up snow, and dropped the binoculars.

"What is it?" Abby brandished the blowtorch around her, searching for a threat.

Without the binoculars, the night was calm. But Abby's heart thudded like she had woken from a nightmare.

Lucas pointed to a shadowy patch of snow, directly behind the bench. "Dean."

Abby's stomach knotted. Dean was here. Would he even be aware of their presence or would he be locked in that awful loop re-experiencing his death?

The suspense was killing Abby. "Where is he? What does he want?"

"I don't know." Lucas kicked the binoculars toward Abby. "Ask him."

"You have the walkie-talkie," Abby countered.

"I don't want to see him again," Lucas said, gasping for breath. "My heart can't take it. I think I have ghost-induced asthma."

"You don't need to see him to talk to him. Ask him what he wants."

"What if he wants to kill us?"

"Don't let him."

"He's a ghost!" Lucas cried.

"Yeah, so he should be a pretty easy opponent. It's not like he's going to pull out a knife."

At Abby's words, the blowtorch flew out of her hands, wrenched by an invisible foe—Dean Johnson, no doubt. Abby gasped. A scream tore from Lucas's throat. The blowtorch soared through the air. The flame disappeared, hissing as it landed in a pile of snow.

"Get the gun!" Abby shouted, reaching for the binoculars.

Lucas fumbled for the salt gun and flung it toward Abby. It landed out of reach, sliding through the snow inches from her feet.

Abby lunged for it, her fingers closing around the cold barrel. In her entire life, she'd shot a single gun, and regretted it to this day. Her cousin had set up cans for her to aim at, and she had missed terribly, the bullet landing instead on a neighbor's glass table, which shattered, ruining her summer and her pride. When her parents returned, she had been grounded for a month.

"Abby!" Lucas cried, snatching up the fallen binoculars. He stumbled back and held tight as the ghost tried to pull them out of his hands. "What are you waiting for?"

With trembling fingers, Abby pointed the gun over Lucas's head, shut her eyes, and pulled the trigger. She braced for impact. She braced for destruction. The gun felt no different. It was as cool and light as before.

In fact, it was suspiciously light. Rather than shooting a bullet, it sprayed salt through the nozzle like a hose. She held the trigger, inching toward Lucas as the salt sprinkled the snow between them. As she neared him, the spray died down, dripping salt at her feet. Pressing the trigger didn't help. Flipping the gun over, she realized that what she'd taken for a sleek metal exterior was, in fact, plastic.

And the bullet chamber was empty.

Her breath left in a shudder. "It needs more salt."

"Tell me you have some!" Lucas shouted back, clutching the binoculars to his side like a football as he played keep away from the ghost.

"I gave them to you!"

"No, you didn't!" Lucas dropped to his knees, then huddled in a ball over the binoculars. "I'm pretty sure I'd remember that!"

"I did!" Abby insisted while pressing her pointer finger against the trigger over and over again. The most it did was send a cloud of salt inches from the nozzle. "Right before we came out here."

"Is that what the saltwater taffy was for?"

"Yes! Why do you sound so angry?"

Lucas's knees buckled. "I ate it!"

"All of it?"

"Yes! You know I like saltwater taffy. Why didn't you give me salt packets?"

"Where am I supposed to get salt packets?"

"The same place we got a blowtorch," Lucas snapped.

Abby didn't have time for this. The ghost was practically dragging Lucas away from the bench. She had to think fast. If only she had a knife, she could chip away the final trace of the carving. She didn't have a knife, but she had the next best thing.

Lucas screamed, swatting and kicking in every direction as the ghost dragged him deeper into the snow.

Pulling out her wallet, she waded to the bench and fumbled for her plastic rewards card for the arcade that had gone out of business two years ago. Her mother was always telling her to clean out her wallet, but she was certain her old cards might come in handy one day. It looked like today was that day. She hurriedly scraped the card against the bench. Now that the wood was warm, it wasn't hard to chip away. Within seconds, a large chunk of the 'M' fell out. Soon after, the 'J.'

Lucas scrambled to his feet, running toward Abby with his fists raised, his body tense.

Abby picked up the binoculars and scanned her surroundings. The wispy outline of Dean Johnson flickered. He wore a serene expression, his eyes shut as he faded like a sand sculpture in a storm. There was nothing left but darkness.

Abby lowered the binoculars. She had only seen a quick glimpse of his face before he disappeared, but she thought he had been smiling. "He's gone."

Lucas collapsed against the bench.

Abby picked up the plastic gun and sat down beside him. A single star twinkled between heavy clouds.

"Do you think we did the right thing?" Lucas asked.

"Yes," Abby said, though her heart hammered with nervous energy. Dean needed to move on, that much was clear. But, now that the adrenaline of the fight was starting to wear off, she wondered if it would have been better to have had a conversation with Dean before they vanquished him. Maybe they could have worked a confession out of him, or passed a message on to his wife.

The front door slammed open.

"Lucas Michael Clark!" Michelle stormed outside, her bare feet kicking up snow. Moonlight gleamed off her silver sweater and jewel-encrusted jeans. As she approached the bench, she looked royal, commanding as a queen, complete with her chin held high. All that was missing was a crown.

"What's going on?" Her eyes went wide, taking in the blowtorch, Lucas's damp clothes, and the singed bench. Her voice rose an octave. "What have you *done*?"

Chapter Fourteen

Abby was used to getting in trouble. There wasn't a year
through grade school where the teacher hadn't given her
a pink slip with the word 'detention' written across the top or
threatened to call her parents. But in all her years of trouble-
making, she had never been punished with a visit to the florist.

Apparently, the bench they had 'destroyed' was expensive,
and since Abby didn't have the money to pay for it, Michelle
was having her run errands. So at the crack of dawn, Abby
found herself tucked in the back of a fancy sedan with a
grouchy, under-caffeinated Mina on one side and the ever-
quiet Annabelle on the other, rolling into the parking lot of a
lavish florist.

It was strange, sitting so close to Mina. Abby was excep-
tionally aware of how close their knees were, of every time
Mina's jacket touched Abby's coat and every time Mina's thigh
brushed Abby's hands. Was she doing that intentionally? Abby
didn't think so. But the idea that it was happening at all, and

that she was aware of it, felt as prickly as dipping a toe into a freshly thawed lake.

"I'll be back in three hours," Michelle called from the driver's seat, attempting to unlock the back doors. This was clearly not her car, but one Mrs. Kensington had let her borrow to fill with wedding supplies. That explained the old-lady smell. "Text me if you need more time."

"I like your ring," Abby whispered to Mina as the doors finally opened, and Mina stepped into the cold glow of the street lamp.

Abby followed, ice crunching under her shoes, and she slipped. "Is that a dragon?"

Mina grunted in response, but reached out a hand to steady her.

"Thanks."

Mina grunted once more, pulling open the door to the flower shop. Bright lights spilled over them. She held her hand up to her face like she was a vampire that would turn to dust, but it only illuminated her soft skin.

Abby got the feeling she was *not* a morning person.

The next hour was spent painstakingly selecting and trimming flowers to create centerpiece after centerpiece. Abby's hands ached and her mind was unequivocally *bored*. Her gaze kept wandering to the coffee shop across the street, which lit up like a beacon begging for her patronage.

All it took was someone walking out carrying a festive to-go cup for Abby to throw down a fist full of flowers and declare, "I'm getting a snack. Anyone want anything?"

Annabelle shook her head, her attention directed to placing even-stemmed flowers into a golden pineapple-shaped vase. Her work made Abby's look childish: while Annabelle's centerpieces were smooth and even, with balanced colors, worthy of a bridal photoshoot, Abby's exploded with flowers of all shapes and sizes, looking like something suitable to shoot out of a cannon for a Lucky Charms commercial.

"I'll come," Mina offered, setting down a simple floral arrangement that was neither award-winning nor painful to look at. She stretched her arms overhead and slipped into her leather jacket. "I don't think I've sat still this long since the set of some superhero movie."

Abby's jaw dropped. "You were in a superhero movie?"

Mina smirked. "I'm a stunt double, remember?"

"That's so cool!" Abby pulled the front door open and zipped up her hoodie as she stepped onto a slush-filled sidewalk. "Which movie?"

"No idea," Mina said with a shrug.

"What character did you play?"

"Some chick in too much pleather."

"A hero or a villain?" Abby asked. "Marvel or DC?"

"I don't know," Mina said. "Marvel, I think."

Abby stared at her. "You *think*?"

"I haven't seen a superhero movie in years." Mina shrugged as she stepped into the coffee shop and wiped her boots on the welcome mat. "Not that I don't like them. There are just so many these days, I wouldn't know where to start."

Abby glanced around the quaint cafe, taking in its white walls, matching tables, and low-key hipster vibes. Acoustic music drifted through old speakers and various machines roared under the tantalizingly sweet aroma of mocha and freshly baked pastries. It was more polished than the shop she currently worked at, but it had a similar cozy charm.

"You start with *Iron Man*," Abby said, moving around an

old woman who was sipping coffee while flipping through a gardening magazine. "Or *Captain America*, if you want to do in-universe chronological. We're having a movie night tonight. Prepare to be amazed."

"Don't get your hopes up," Mina said, surveying the chalkboard menus before she decided on a cappuccino.

Abby ordered a peppermint hot chocolate and a rainbow cookie, which earned her an amused glance from the barista, who returned with a cookie larger than Abby's palm.

"So, what *really* happened last night?" Mina asked, lowering her voice as they moved to an empty corner to wait for their drinks. "You and Lucas don't strike me as the kind who go around vandalizing things for the hell of it."

Abby grimaced, taking a bite of the cookie. It was soft and gooey, melting on her tongue. She took another bite, savoring the flavor.

"Was it the ghosts?" Mina whispered.

Abby nodded. Michelle might think she was some sort of miscreant, but at least Mina would believe her. "Dean—the repairman—and his wife carved their initials on that bench. We burned them off." Her voice picked up speed and volume with each word until Mina was shushing her.

She continued in a slow whisper, "We thought we'd send him on, so he could stop reliving his death, but when we tried to, he attacked us. He was strong. He threw the blowtorch out of my hands and attempted to pry the binoculars from Lucas."

Mina's eyes widened in horror. "Did you stop him?"

Abby leaned closer to her. "We managed to scrape off the carving, severing his tie to the living. Wherever he is, he's no longer a threat."

"So he was behind the attacks?"

Abby shrugged, chewing her lip. Last night, she was pretty sure he had had the temper and the power to hurt someone, but the more she thought about it, the more she realized he could have seriously hurt her and Lucas if he had wanted to, but he had merely tossed their weapons aside. That didn't seem very killer like. "Yeah. Probably."

Mina raised an eyebrow, but didn't question her. Instead, she strode to the counter to pick up their drinks, and returned with to-go cups decorated with complementary winter patterns. She handed Abby her hot chocolate and sipped from the other.

Abby set her drink down, distracted by a black and white flier by the front door advertising ghost tours. She pointed a thumb toward it. "I wonder if Kensington Manor is a stop."

Mina studied it, shaking her head. "No, but it claims this coffee shop is haunted by—get this—Mr. Beans, the cat."

Her smirk made Abby's heart flutter with warmth.

"Oh? Let's see if we can see Mr. Beans, shall we?" Abby playfully slid the binoculars out of her messenger bag and surveyed the room. "I don't see him."

She circled the entire storefront to be sure, but there wasn't a sign of a single ghost. Coffee-drinkers faded to a dull gray, their laptops turning to little more than a cobwebbed image over the shop, which had its own ghostly footprint of decades past, resulting in kaleidoscope walls of mismatched wallpaper and brick.

Mina leaned casually against the wall as if posing for a picture. Her smile radiated through the binoculars, but her distorted appearance made Abby's stomach knot. Instead of the vibrant woman she had spent the morning with, she saw a ghost of a woman, faded and trapped in a dark in-between. *Just like Chelsea.*

Abby fumbled with the binoculars as panic rose in her throat. Jerking her view away from Mina, she focused instead on the window, where the bright lights of the flower shop illuminated Annabelle as she braided ribbon around flower stems. Someone in full color paced in front of her—a ghost. With blonde hair tied back and a long, flared floral dress, she resembled a modern housewife. Her back toward Abby, she loomed ominously over Annabelle's shoulder, reaching a hand toward the unsuspecting girl. For a moment, Abby thought she was going to shove her and she cried in alarm. But the ghost moved past Annabelle, reaching to the centerpiece beside her and beginning to rearrange it.

"What is it?" Mina asked, concern seeping through her voice.

"That's my centerpiece!" Abby exclaimed. "That ghost is rearranging my flowers!"

Mina laughed. The sound was so warm and full of life, it filled Abby with relief. She lowered the binoculars and gazed into Mina's vivid eyes, which gleamed with fierce amusement. Abby wanted to throw her arms around her broad shoulders or take Mina's hand—anything to keep her close. But her heart hammered against her ribs, reminding her to think of Chelsea and all the pain that came from getting close to someone so fragile.

Mina stepped forward, her fingers brushing Abby's as she reached for the binoculars.

And there was that hyper-awareness again, surging through Abby's arm as Mina's palm covered her knuckles. With a heavy breath, she shoved the binoculars into Mina's hand, pulling away. "See for yourself."

Whatever sparks had or hadn't just passed between them were too much for Abby's frantically beating heart. She stared at her smeared reflection in the window, simultaneously wishing she could let go of Chelsea and wishing she had never had someone she needed to let go of in the first place.

After some time, Mina spoke with a tone full of wonder. "Wow, you weren't kidding."

Abby risked glancing back and saw Mina peering through the binoculars, a cuff of her flannel shirt brushing a lens.

Abby turned back to the window, before she did something foolish—like reach for Mina's hand or voice aloud the complicated feelings brewing in her veins. She cleared her throat. "If that ghost ruins my flowers…"

Abby trailed off, unable to think of a threat. Her mind was still on Mina, and the lingering goosebumps where their fingers had touched moments ago. She picked up her drink, cupped both hands around the warm paper cup, and took a big sip, letting the scent of peppermint clear her mind.

"I think she's fixing them," Mina said, returning the binoculars to Abby.

As Abby took another look, she watched the ghost replace a few brightly colored flowers with white roses, adjusting the stems so the flowers lay at an equal height. The ghost reminded Abby of something—or someone—but she couldn't quite place *who*. With her slender frame, pale hair, and angular features, she bore a striking resemblance to Annabelle. But there was something *more* than that. Abby felt as if she had seen her somewhere before.

Perhaps she had been in one of the portraits at Kensington Manor. But it was her dress that stood out the most. Perhaps it was a common style, similar to the floral wallpaper that coated the guestrooms at Mrs. Kensington's house. Or perhaps she simply had spent too much of the day staring at flowers.

"What do you know," she said in amazement. "That ghost is helping me out. You don't think I need to tip her, do you? I'm out of cash."

With a hint of a smile, Mina picked up her coffee and headed toward the front door.

Abby followed, the wind nipping at her skin. Her breath cast white swirls in the streetlights before dissipating. Tucking her free hand into her pocket, she sipped her hot chocolate as they passed a storefront overflowing with Christmas decorations, complete with dancing nutcrackers and singing bears.

"It was my mother," Mina said softly. So soft Abby barely heard her over the muffled Christmas tunes.

"What?" Abby asked, pulling her attention from the storefront to Mina, who stood with pinched brows and taut lips.

She clenched her coffee with her right hand, her left tucked into the pocket of her leather jacket. Mina gazed fiercely ahead, as if locked on an invisible opponent. "You asked me before who died. It was my mother."

Abby blinked, surprised by the directness of the gaze and the sharp turn in conversation. It took her a second to remember that she *had* asked who Mina had lost, that first night in the snowstorm, when she had seen that hollow look in Mina's eyes that was undeniably grief. Abby nodded in a manner she hoped was encouraging, signaling she wanted Mina to continue.

"It was cancer," Mina said, rubbing her thumb along the lip of her coffee cup. "She was diagnosed when I was twelve. The treatment was rough, but we thought she'd beaten it. Until it came back, when I was in college."

They passed the flower shop, but Abby didn't point it out. Instead, she said, "I'm sorry."

She knew the pain of death couldn't be cured by any words, but she was sorry all the same.

Mina's silence lasted painfully long. After three sips of hot chocolate without any more information, Abby prompted, "Is that why you and Michelle were fighting?"

Mina frowned. "Mostly. I didn't handle it well. Do you think—" Mina slowed, glancing at Abby, her lips pressed into a thin line. "Is there a chance, after the wedding, that I could borrow your binoculars again to see if her spirit is still around?"

"Of course," Abby said tenderly. "Just, don't get your hopes too high. It's possible she's already moved on."

Mina nodded, the fur lining of her coat rustling against the back of her neck. "Usually, when people say that, I'm rooting for the person to have moved on. But usually we're talking about dating new people, not leaving this plane of existence."

"But you're hoping she's still around?"

Mina stroked her fingers through the ends of her hair, eyes downcast, in a manner that was unusually timid of her. It was kind of cute. "No. Maybe. It's selfish, I know."

"It's not selfish to want to speak to the dead. Especially not to someone you love."

"It is in my case. I'm not even thinking about what would be best for her, just how to ease my own damn sense of guilt." She sighed, a self-deprecating smile flickering across her lips as she added, "Imagine how much it would suck to have all your affairs in order, and then get stuck here because your loved ones have a hard time letting go."

"I'm not sure it works like that."

Mina shrugged. "Sometimes I think we're the ones that have the hardest time moving on." She turned abruptly, heading back toward the florist.

Abby ran to catch up. From the sharp motion Mina made as she opened the door, and the overenthusiastic greeting to Annabelle, Abby sensed the conversation was over. The florist's warm interior provided a welcome relief to both the physical and psychological chill that had gnawed at Abby since Mina last spoke. She spared a glance at Mina, wondering if she also felt chilled by the weight of her recent words. She seemed unbothered, as she slid into her chair, set down her coffee, and began absentmindedly twisting a rose between her smooth fingers. In fact, she seemed almost happy, as if she had left the weight of the dead behind—as if by merely stating her desire to move on, she had somehow accomplished that.

Abby wished she could move on as quickly.

She returned to flower arranging, letting her arrangements get sloppier and sloppier as she pretended to ignore the ghost that fixed them. They packed three dozen floral arrangements, grabbed some sandwiches, and spent all afternoon riding around town picking up various wedding supplies.

By the time they returned to Kensington Manor, it was four o'clock and Abby was starving. Her plans to go straight to the kitchen were delayed by the arrival of the Kensington men—Annabelle's husband, Robert; and Michelle's fiancé, David.

In their dress pants and pale polo shirts, both men looked like they could be auditioning for the role of a modern-day prince at Disney World. They stood just over six feet tall, with warm smiles that revealed perfectly straight teeth. David's sandy blond hair accentuated his sea-green eyes, while Robert's wavy locks matched his brown eyes perfectly. The way they stepped forward to greet Abby and Mina in unison would have been the perfect lead into a song and dance.

But the moment their hands clasped in greeting, their words

were cut short by Michelle rushing into the room. She threw her arms around David and kissed him with such passion Abby blushed and looked away. Annabelle, meanwhile, greeted Robert with a subtle nod. They were clearly saving their passion for a more private moment, or years of marriage had taken its toll on their relationship. Either way, this provided an opportunity to question Robert about the ghosts who lived here.

"Why don't we give them some privacy?" Abby said to Mina, as Michelle and David's kissing grew more frantic.

"Good idea." Mina led the way into the hall. Abby, Annabelle, and Robert followed.

They moved down a hall lined with sea-shelled wreaths and sconces wrapped in blue bows. Michelle had really amped up the beach theme. There was even a gingerbread sand castle.

"What a great place to get married," Abby exclaimed, glancing at Robert as she stepped over pale poinsettias topped with faux starfish. "Annabelle said you got hitched here too, huh?"

Robert tugged at the collar of his sleeves. "Many years ago."

"And now your brother is getting married—you must be excited." Abby paused, waiting for a response. When she didn't get one, she prompted, "Will you be in the wedding?"

"Naturally."

Abby waited for more, but he poured himself a glass of scotch. She got the impression he was a man of few words. She had hoped to lure him into conversation that would take a natural course to ghosts, but it was now clear that she would have to be more forward with her questions.

"It must be tough for David, getting married without his father around."

Robert raised an eyebrow.

Mina shot Abby an incredulous look, as if wondering where she was going with the statement. Abby shrugged, since she wasn't entirely sure where she was going either, but the more they talked about the dead, the closer she was to getting some answers. "I heard he and your father were close. He must miss him."

Robert took a sip of his drink. He smacked his lips together and shrugged.

Annabelle's eyes widened. "You don't think his ghost is still here, do you?"

Robert's eyes flickered from his wife to Abby and back to Annabelle. "What on earth are you talking about?"

"Abby has found a way to communicate with *ghosts,*" Annabelle whispered excitedly.

"Nonsense." Robert's brow furrowed. "Tell me you didn't waste money on this quack like you did those psychics in New York."

"I'm not a psychic," Abby said, attempting to defuse the situation. "And Annabelle hasn't paid me anything. I don't do this for a living. I'm a magician."

"Oh so much better." His tone oozed sarcasm.

"And occasional part-time barista," Abby added. "But anyway, the point is I don't charge money to see ghosts. I was attacked by a ghost here, in this house. I got some equipment that lets me communicate with them. If you're interested, I've been told your dad is still around—"

"I don't want to hear it. What's this?" Robert turned his back to Abby, reaching for a worn book on the coffee table. It wasn't until he was already flipping through it that Abby realized it was Lucas's sketchbook.

She reached forward, snatching the book from Robert's hands. "That's private."

Firelight danced off Robert's eyes as he gave Abby an appraising nod. "No need to be embarrassed. They're good."

Abby hugged the sketchbook protectively to her chest. "They aren't—"

A scream cut Abby short. It sounded close, from the kitchen.

Robert cursed as he spilled his drink, and attempted to dab the alcohol off his pale shirt.

Abby's stomach lurched. She shoved past Robert and ran down the hall, the memory of a scream throbbing in her ears.

Abby pushed open the kitchen door and found Sandra standing in the opposite doorway, her hand over her mouth. In the center of the kitchen, Mrs. Kensington hunched over the sink, washing a delicate tea-cup. Her dark shawl draped her shoulders, and oversized headphones rested on her ears. If she had heard Sandra's shout, she showed no indication. Her head bobbed right to left, nodding along to a song Abby couldn't hear. This oddly domestic moment for such a grouchy old woman would have been comforting, if it wasn't for the chef's knife suspended in midair, pointed directly at her back.

Abby lunged for the knife's handle. A cold wind knocked her back as the knife jerked out of reach.

Abby quickly surveyed the kitchen, looking for anything she could use against the ghost. The remaining knives rested in a wooden block, their handles gleaming under a cloth welcome sign. Fancy plates and stemmed glasses glimmered through glass cabinet doors. Jars of spices, coffee, and loose-leaf tea lined the counter—Abby considered searching for salt, but there was no time.

The knife surged forward.

Abby ran. Holding Lucas's sketchbook in front of her like a shield, she darted between the knife and Mrs. Kensington.

Crack.

The knife struck the sketchbook with such force, Abby nearly dropped it. Ignoring the tremble in her hands, she tightened her grip as the knife pulled back and repositioned.

This time, it aimed for Abby's face.

Sandra screamed.

"Salt!" Abby shouted, ducking behind the book. "We need salt."

The sketchbook reverberated as the knife struck.

Abby let out a dizzying breath. She winced as the knife screeched along the cover, hating that she was inadvertently damaging Lucas's prized possession.

She shoved the book toward her attacker, hoping it was possible to throw a ghost off balance.

The knife lurched as salt tore through the kitchen, raining over the tiles in a thick pale mist. The knife fell to the floor, crashing inches from Abby's feet.

Abby turned toward Sandra, who stood a few feet away, holding an empty box of salt in her trembling hands.

As the salt cloud dissipated, Sandra hastened past Abby and reached Mrs. Kensington. Tears streaming down her face, she embraced the old woman. Mrs. Kensington took on a shocked expression, sliding her headphones around her neck. The faint sound of New Age music drifted through them.

Before Abby could say a word, Sandra's lips were pressed against Mrs. Kensington's.

Robert ran in, throwing his hand to his heart. His eyes widened at the salt-strewn floor. "Jesus! What happened?"

The women broke apart. Shock flashed across Mrs. Kensington's face as her eyes darted from Sandra to her son. Abby wondered if Sandra's kiss wasn't a fit of passion brought on by a near-death experience—perhaps she and Mrs. Kensington had exchanged kisses before, but Mrs. Kensington wanted to keep them a secret.

Abby wasn't sure what Robert had caught—if anything— for Sandra was already stepping back, shouting in a trembling voice, "The knife! It flew off the counter."

"What do you mean, it flew?" Robert moved deeper into the kitchen, salt crunching under his shoes as he ran a hand through his hair. He stopped in front of the knife, staring between it and Sandra.

"Oh, leave the poor woman alone," Mrs. Kensington snapped, not meeting anyone's gaze. "I am perfectly fine."

In a sweeping gesture, she reached down and picked up the knife at her feet, and held it out for the others to examine, as if she were about to perform a magic trick and wanted to prove it was in fact a real knife. "An accident."

"An accident?" Robert's voice hitched. "That had you screaming like that?"

Annabelle hurriedly moved to his side, her face pale and stricken, attempting to soothe him. He shook his head, gently brushing her aside, his gaze fixated on his mother with growing concern.

With trembling hands, Abby peered through the binoculars and did a quick sweep of the room. Not a single ghost was in sight. Whoever had attacked Mrs. Kensington had vanished.

Mrs. Kensington slid the knife into the block and patted Sandra on the shoulder. "It's been a long day. Why don't you go lie down?"

"Of course, of course." As Sandra's fingers tugged at the sleeves of her beaded tunic, her gaze flickered to Abby's.

"Never in my life have I seen such a thing."

Abby refrained from making an 'I told you so' face as she turned to Robert, who was shaking his head in a state of disbelief. Abby couldn't blame him. It wasn't every day a ghost tried to stab your mother. Or you walked in on your mother kissing her 'roommate.'

Abby made a mental note to ask Robert what exactly he had seen when he was in a better state of mind—right now, he seemed only capable of repeating the word 'Jesus' to himself in various inflections, as if he were an actor practicing for a one-line role.

Abby inspected Lucas's sketchbook. Two large gashes marred the center, and there was a thick slash across the cover. She gulped. A few centimeters to the right and that gash would have done serious damage to her fingers. Hesitantly, she flipped open the book. Dozens of black and white sketches and several full colored drawings stared back at her, marred with a ghastly hole through the center. Abby's insides churned at the thought of how much work must have gone into each one, and how quickly she had ruined it.

With a shudder, she turned to Mina, who stood in the hall, arms folded across her chest. Despite her strong posture and stoic expression, Abby could sense her fear.

The danger hadn't ended with Dean Johnson.

Someone still wanted Mrs. Kensington dead. Tonight, they had nearly succeeded.

Chapter Fifteen

An overhead light flickered ominously as Abby stared at the kitchen sink, where Mrs. Kensington had nearly died moments before.

The stairs creaked, Mrs. Kensington and Sandra's voices fading as they retreated upstairs. Abby wanted to know more about their relationship. The thought that they were together—however informally—bumped Mrs. Kensington's late husband to the top of her list of suspects.

Abby's moment of contemplation was short-lived as yet another shout tore through the quiet. Her stomach lurched.

She ran into the main hall. Mrs. Kensington and Sandra were safely on the second-floor landing, looking as mystified as Abby. Across the living room, the back door hung open, letting in the cool evening breeze and the occasional flutter of snow. Michelle stood outside, her dark coat billowing around her waist, her gloved hands pressed to her lips as she stared at the yard in terror.

Abby hurried outside, ignoring the chill of snow against her bare feet. Shivering, she clutched the binoculars. She brought them to her eyes and swept the courtyard, fearing to see a ghost burying Lucas in snow.

But the only ghosts were the children, attempting to make snow angels on the patio.

Abby lowered the binoculars.

"What is it?" she asked. "What's wrong?"

"Look!" Michelle pointed to the middle of the backyard, where the snow had been cleared and replaced with a carpet of faux grass with a makeshift aisle that sprawled between rows of dark chairs to the base of a pale gazebo. There was no one in sight, neither living nor dead. Only the wind wandered the ground, howling like a lost puppy.

"At what?" Abby asked in confusion.

"The chairs," Michelle cried, clawing at her hair.

The others scrambled into the garden. David and Mina charged ahead while Annabelle and Robert hung back in the doorway.

Michelle let out a choked sob. "They're *black*!"

Abby frowned, taking in the others' reactions. Mina shook her head in a somber motion, while Robert sighed and turned away. Annabelle's hand flew to her mouth; she was clearly horrified.

Abby scratched her head. "And this is a problem because…?"

"They're supposed to be white." Michelle sobbed onto Mina's shoulder. "How am I supposed to have a wedding with chairs meant for a *funeral*?"

Mina tapped Michelle's shoulder as awkwardly as a cat-person trying to soothe a dog. "I'll call the company. See if we can get someone to replace them."

"Already on it." Taking out his phone, David retreated inside and began to pace.

Lucas rushed out of the doorway, breathing rapidly. "What is it? What happened? Who screamed?" His gaze swept over Mina and Michelle's solemn faces and he looked stricken. "Oh God, what now? Whatever Abby did, I can explain—"

"Hey!" Abby grabbed his arm from behind, receiving a startled yelp in response as she dragged him away. "I didn't do anything. The chairs were delivered in the wrong color."

"Oh." Lucas let out a sigh that created a fleeting, misty cloud in the cold air. "False alarm."

"*False alarm?*" Michelle repeated, furious. She stormed toward him waving her fist. "Oh, so *this* is no big deal to you? It's just a wedding, huh? Not something important, like your little comic con groups or video games."

"I didn't say that," Lucas said. "What I meant was—"

"What you meant was that you don't care about me or my life!" Michelle snapped. "Ever since you got here, you and Abby have been treating my wedding—*my life*—like it's some kind of game."

"What do you care?" Lucas countered. "You don't even want us here!"

Michelle's fists clenched at her side. She shook her head. For a moment, it looked like she was about to cry, but then she spoke coldly. "You're right! I *don't* want you here. You should go. Both of you."

Abby stepped between her friends. "Michelle—"

"Don't!" Michelle held up her hand, her diamond ring glistening in the evening light. "I'm going to dinner. I expect you to be gone by the time I wake up tomorrow. I don't want to see either of you again until I'm walking down that aisle!"

Michelle stormed inside, Annabelle at her heels.

Mina gave Abby an apologetic shrug and followed.

The door shut, locking Lucas and Abby out in the cold.

"Well," said Abby, painfully aware of Lucas's ruined sketch-book tucked into the folds of her borrowed jacket. "That didn't go so well."

"No." Lucas sighed with a note of dejection. "Guess we better pack."

Abby wanted to cheer him up. She tried to think of a relevant movie quote or a witty pun, but nothing came to mind. Her mind was too busy worrying about how they were going to protect Mrs. Kensington now that they'd been banished from the estate. She folded her arms across her chest and shivered.

Lucas sank into the nearest chair and hung his head. The way he stared out into the bleak horizon against dimly lit snow, it looked like he was attending a funeral for the sun.

Abby stepped beside him, wishing she had worn shoes. The faux grass kept the bite of snow away, but the breeze still stung. She gently nudged her friend's shoulder. "Let's see if there's any more of that fancy hot chocolate."

Lucas shook his head.

"The fancy candy, then?"

"No, Abby." Leaning back, he gazed at the smoky blue sky. "You know, I thought this was going to be different. I thought—now that we're both adults—Michelle and I could bond. But no, she's still just as cookie-cutter perfect as always and I'm just a rotten egg."

"I think you mean cracked."

"What?"

"The expression is 'cracked egg.'"

"No, it's rotten."

"Well, either way, you're not rotten or cracked," Abby said. "And Michelle is not perfect. And she's definitely not a cookie."

"She is! Look at this—" Lucas gestured down the aisle to the delicate arch and then around the garden. "She's marrying someone who's kind, handsome, and *loaded*. She's got a stable job, good career, and *all* my parents' adoration."

"Yeah, but she doesn't *appreciate* it the way you do. You know what I see when I look at all this." Abby flopped her arm in the direction of the estate. "People who have so much money, they worry about what to do with it. They spend it on what flowers they think other people will compliment, or how good the pictures they post online will be. Life's so easy for them they can't appreciate what they have. Like hot chocolate or snow or time with their super cool best friend." She pointed both index fingers at herself, receiving a small smile from Lucas. She grinned back in response. "And hey, one day, you're going to be some bigshot professor and meet an awesome girl—if you're lucky she'll be *almost* as cool as me—but for now, you've got a pretty sweet life going on, so don't knock it."

Lucas's smile faded. "I didn't get the job."

Abby blinked. With everything going on, Lucas's unemployment seemed like a low priority. But she knew it meant a lot to him, and she wanted to be supportive.

"That's okay," she said reassuringly. Taking a seat beside him, she crossed her legs, attempting to massage warmth back into her feet. "You'll get another one."

"Do you know how hard it is to get a job teaching English?"

Abby shrugged. "Shouldn't be too hard. Everyone speaks it."

"You'd think. But no, no, it's hard. You know what they want you to have in order to teach English? A degree in *education*.

You know what I have? A degree in *English literature*. Not a PhD, just a master's. You know what that qualifies me for? Nothing."

"You could write books."

"I know how to read, not write."

"What about your comics?"

"I haven't made one in years."

Abby frowned. "What are all those sketches in your sketch-book?"

"Just doodles," Lucas muttered.

Abby had a feeling they meant more to him than he was letting on. She chewed her lip. "Okay, well, don't be angry, but your sketchbook kind of, sort of, got stabbed…"

She slipped the sketchbook from her coat and held it out to him.

Lucas's eyes widened. His fingers trembled as he took the tattered book from Abby and ran his thumb over the damage.

"Your most recent drawings are still fine," Abby said. "Maybe a bit dented, but fine. It's only the first few that will need some major repair."

Lucas made a bitter sobbing sound so full of sorrow it was heart-wrenching to hear.

"The ones you did the other day are still as good as new."

Shadows danced across Lucas's face, magnifying his expression of horror. "You looked through it?"

"Only a bit, over Robert's shoulder—"

"Oh, so you're showing it around to everyone now?"

"No, I took it from him! He only saw a few pictures, but he said it was good."

"And now it's ruined." Lucas flipped forcefully to the most recent drawings and ran his fingers along the dented pages.

"Guess it doesn't matter anyway."

"They're gorgeous," Abby said gently.

Lucas shrugged. "They were supposed to be for Wanda."

"Your non-date to the wedding?"

"Yeah." Lucas sighed, his breath trailing white in the cold air. "I keep trying to draw our characters together, but I can never get it right. I don't know, I guess I was hoping to impress her or something. I thought maybe—but it doesn't matter."

"I bet with a little tape and—"

"Can you not?"

"Not what?"

"Not do *this*." He gestured between them. "This 'peppy coach-talk' thing you do."

"What am I supposed to do? Watch you sit here and be miserable?"

"Yes," said Lucas, removing the binoculars from around his neck and tossing them to a patch of slush at Abby's feet. "Because that's what adults do, Abby. We face reality—we accept our losses, give up on our dreams, sit in misery for a bit, and then we go back to whatever crumbs of warmth we have." He looked to the sky and groaned. "Which, for me, is nothing but my parents' guest room and half a dozen online friends. Thanks to Michelle."

Abby folded her hands in her lap, rubbing her thumbs together. "How is any of that Michelle's fault? Is this still because you blame her for not getting into that fancy high school?"

Lucas grumbled an affirmative response.

Abby's heartbeat quickened. Despite the cold, her palms grew warm and sweaty. She shoved them under her thighs, leaning toward Lucas. "That wasn't Michelle's fault."

"It was," Lucas insisted, slamming his book shut. "When I didn't get in, I went back and checked my application. My essay was gone. Instead, there was this BS essay about how my parents were making me apply against my will. And it was full of typos! No wonder they didn't let me in."

"Michelle didn't write it." Abby took a deep breath like she was about to dive headfirst into ice cold water. "I did."

Lucas stared at her. "What?"

"I thought I was helping you," Abby explained, thinking back. She never thought she would be apologizing for helping Lucas out over a decade ago. "You told me you didn't want to go, that you doubted you'd get in, but your parents were making you."

"I said that so I wouldn't hurt your feelings."

Abby blinked, heat rushing to her face. "Well I believed you."

Lucas groaned. He rubbed his eyes as if trying to convince himself he was awake.

"Are you upset?" Abby held her breath, hoping this wouldn't get in the way of their friendship.

Lucas made a fist and tapped the chair, as if he couldn't decide if he wanted to punch it or dig a hole to escape through. At last, he leaned back and sighed, shaking his head. "Go back inside. Pack your things. Get Mina's number, if you want it. We're leaving first thing in the morning."

Abby stared at him. "But we have to save Mrs. Kensington."

"You heard Michelle," Lucas said. "We're not welcome here. Someone else will have to deal with the ghosts. We have our own problems."

"But I've figured it out! In the kitchen——"

"I'm done, Abby." Lucas stood, tucked his damaged sketch-book under his arm, and turned his back to her. "Do what you want, just keep me out of it."

Abby wanted to argue, wanted to talk sense into her friend, wanted to find a way to restore his drawings. But he was already slamming the back door, leaving her alone in a sea of shadows and vacant chairs.

Chapter Sixteen

Abby tucked her bare feet under her jeans as the breeze enveloped her. She wished she could go back in time and stop herself from using Lucas's sketchbook—if only she had grabbed a cutting board, or a cookbook. Better yet, she wished she could have stopped herself from changing Lucas's high school application. This whole misunderstanding between Lucas and Michelle was blown out of proportion and Abby felt guilty for her part in driving a wedge between them.

It would take time for them to make up. And—Abby realized with a sickening feeling—it would take even more time for Lucas to trust Abby again. She had never considered that she and Lucas might one day grow apart. He was all that she had left of her childhood—of *herself*—that wasn't eroded by grief.

She shook her head, clearing her thoughts. This was *Lucas*—the same boy who had forgiven her for crashing his bike, and for using his library card without permission. He would come to his senses eventually, as always. The only difference was that this time, she didn't have the luxury to wait for him.

Abby reached for the fallen binoculars, wincing as the frosted metal stung her skin.

She wasn't ready to give up. Not when Mrs. Kensington's life was at stake, and when she felt so *close* to answers. Peering through the aged lenses, she glanced from window to window. The ghost kids were huddled around the TV, watching a football game over Robert's shoulder. Sarah was sitting in the living room, looking forlornly out the window. In one of the upstairs bedrooms, Archie was locked in an intimate embrace with someone—another ghost. It wasn't until they broke apart that Abby recognized his companion. It was none other than George Kensington.

Abby stepped back in surprise, watching as Archie caressed George's cheek. Talk about a night of surprise affairs. Did George's wife, Sarah, know about this? It was far more shocking than Mrs. Kensington and Sandra.

Archie turned from George and glanced out the window. Heart pounding, Abby swept her binoculars to a different section of the house, hoping Archie hadn't noticed. After a full minute of scanning the lower floors, Abby raised the binoculars back to the upstairs window where Archie and George had been.

The curtain was closed.

No light came from under the window, which made it unlikely someone living had gone into that room. Archie must have shut the curtains, which meant he was strong enough to move other objects—such as lace and a knife.

Abby recalled everything she knew about Archie and George. Sarah and George appeared to be happily married—she had seen them dancing together just the other day. But George and Archie also appeared very pleased with each other. Archie had designed the manor for George—had George hired him, or had he approached George?

Abby wished she had paid closer attention to Lucas's research. Now was not the time to ask.

After trudging back to the house, she savored the living room's warmth, heading straight toward the fireplace, where she rested her chilled feet near the dwindling fire.

When her feet regained their usual warmth, she paced. Remnants of sunset drifted through the darkening windows, lengthening her shadow. Her stomach growled. Abby doubted she would be invited to dinner.

She tried calling Glen once more.

No luck. That guy had bad service or bad hearing—possibly both. She left another quick message and turned on her phone's flashlight.

It was time to visit Mrs. Kensington's late husband in the basement.

IT TOOK ABBY a while to locate the basement. This was partially due to the fact Sandra distracted her with a plate of freshly baked cookies and partially due to the fact that the basement was not the dusty space full of storage and cobwebs that she had envisioned, but a well-furnished entertainment area.

The first time she set foot in the basement, she had promptly returned to the first floor, thinking she had taken a wrong turn somewhere. The second time, she spun around in awe, taking in the glorified bachelor pad.

It suddenly made sense why Michelle would use this as her backup wedding venue. It was nicer than many hotel ballrooms (though admittedly smaller). A full bar spanned one side of the room, while the other hosted a variety of comfortable seats, televisions, computer monitors, and arcade games. There was even a bowling lane, complete with electronic pins.

Abby checked behind the bar and found it fully stocked with dozens of beers, wines, and fancy liquors she had never heard of. At the end was an old-fashioned popcorn maker. She flipped a switch and it groaned to life.

As the kernels began to heat, she checked the doors on either side of the bar—the first led to a small closet filled with cleaning supplies, floor tiles, and large paint cans. Abby's flashlight flew across dozens of labels from midnight black to seafoam blue. Someone had clearly repainted in recent years. Would that count as a serious enough renovation to upset Archie? He was probably particular about his wall colors and floor tiles, but the question was if he cared enough to risk his life—well, spirit—to attack Mrs. Kensington in vengeance. Probably not. He seemed to value his relationship with George too much for that.

The second door led to a pantry brimming with packaged snacks, and extra baking supplies. Abby rummaged through them until she found several boxes of salt. She carried one to the counter, making a mental note to refill the salt gun when she returned upstairs.

The popcorn machine whirred as Abby took a seat on a barstool. Kernels popped, growing louder by the second, filling the room with the aroma of butter.

Lifting the binoculars, Abby searched for Mr. Turner's ghost. Tommy and Mary waved, running up and down the ramp of a Skee-Ball machine, while Elizabeth sat next to her, kicking her heels off the edge of the counter. They seemed to have picked up a habit of following her—Abby was both pleased and unnerved by this.

She continued scanning for someone who might look like an older version of David or Robert, but the only other ghost in sight was the nanny, who peered cautiously through the doorway. Her floral dress swayed gently around legs, the work of a nonexistent breeze. She frowned as she caught Abby watching her, then gave a timid wave before patting the top of her blonde hair.

There was something oddly familiar about her.

Abby's eyes widened in recognition. She turned on the walkie-talkie.

"You were at the florist!" She *knew* she had recognized that dress before, she just hadn't remembered where she had seen it. "You straightened my flowers."

Surprise—or embarrassment—caused a blush to creep across her face. "Your skills were atrocious."

"But how could you leave the house?"

The nanny rolled her shoulders back, lifting her chin with pride. "Not all ghosts are attached to the house. Some are attached to objects or even living beings."

"What are you attached to?"

"That's a very personal question." The nanny stiffened, her blush growing as red as her necklace. She lowered her gaze and added softly, "But, if you must know…the car."

"The car?" Abby tried to imagine this proper-looking nanny being so attached to the dark Ford sedan they had driven to the florist. Abby didn't know much about cars, but it hadn't seemed magnificent in any way, and it couldn't have been more than a few years old. The nanny may have died more recently than Abby had initially speculated.

"If you think that's bad, you should see what some of the others are attached to," the ghost continued quickly. "I hear George Kensington is attached to his golf clubs. Sarah said he disappeared for months at a time when Robert took them to college."

Abby nodded in acceptance. She hadn't considered that the ghosts could leave the house, and the thought disturbed her. How many others were attached to objects that moved often from location to location? Could that be why the attacks started recently? Perhaps something previously missing from the house had recently been returned—along with a murderous ghost.

Elizabeth's awed voice filled the static. "I always forget this exists. It wasn't here in my time."

"What do you forget?" Abby asked, turning toward her in curiosity. "Is there something new down here?"

"This whole place," Elizabeth said dreamily, waving her hand around the room. "It was just a cellar in my time. All dusty and gross."

"Have you seen a man down here?" Abby asked. "A ghost named Mr. Turner?"

Elizabeth shook her head. "Like I said, I forget this place exists. I'm never down here."

"I don't like it," the nanny said with a shiver. "I wish you children would come back upstairs."

Abby scanned the rest of the room. Seeing no other ghosts in sight, she scooped herself a bag of popcorn and played a few rounds of pinball, pausing to look through the binoculars between each game. At Tommy's request, she played two rounds of *Pac-Man*, ignoring the uncomfortable sensation of him floating over her shoulder.

When she finished, Elizabeth's voice crackled through the walkie-talkie. "There's a man in the dark room."

"What dark room?" Abby asked.

Mary pointed to a door at the far end of the room, opposite all the games, which Abby hadn't noticed because she had been too distracted by the popcorn and the games. The door was made of the same polished dark wood as many of the others in the house, complete with a gold knob that was all but hidden in shadow. Hesitantly, Abby turned the knob and pushed open the door.

Elizabeth's description of the room as 'dark' was accurate—the lights from the rest of the basement barely stained the carpet. The rest of the room was pitch black, without a single window or flicker of light. Squinting, Abby used the flashlight on her phone to examine the wall, looking for a light switch.

When she finally located one and flipped it on, she found herself standing between a large screen and a dozen plush seats complete with drink holders in what was clearly a miniature movie theater.

Abby's stomach knotted. She hadn't stepped foot in a movie theater since the day Chelsea died. This might have been a home theater, but it felt like the real deal. Even the aisle was lit with dim blue lights. Abby took a deep breath, trying to keep her thoughts from darting back to *that night*. She knew there was nothing dangerous about movie theaters but she felt like she was walking on the edge of a cliff, where the slightest wrong movement could cause her or someone she loved to end up dead.

She propped the door behind her open with a chair and steeled herself. Chelsea wasn't in this room, but another ghost was. A quick sweep of the binoculars revealed the ghost of a middle-aged man sitting in the second row, smiling at the blank screen.

"Mr. Turner?" Abby asked, placing the walkie-talkie on the edge of a front row seat. The man looked a bit like David, only older and with brown eyes instead of David's sea-green. This was definitely his father. And probably the one who had attacked her.

What was his name again? "Mark? Mason?"

"Shh." Mr. Turner pointed to the screen as if indicating she should be paying attention.

Abby frowned, stepping into his line of vision. "There's nothing playing."

"Of course there is." Mr. Turner blinked. "Or…there was. I must have fallen asleep."

He looked around as if just noticing his surroundings for the first time. "Who are you? Who let you in here?"

"I'm Abby. Abby Spector," Abby said, thinking a second too late that it might not be the best idea to give a murderous ghost her real name. "I'm here for the wedding."

"Ah, you're one of Annabelle's friends, are you?" Mr. Turner grunted. "Coming to size up the place? You tell that no good woman she may have won my son, but she's getting her hands on this house over my dead body!"

Chills ran down Abby's spine. He appeared to be thinking of Robert's wedding, not David's. Perhaps he was as out of it as Dean Johnson had been, forgetting his own death.

"Annabelle doesn't want your house," Abby said gently, cautiously nudging the conversation to the present time. "She and Robert have a nice house, or so I imagine. They're only here for the week, for David's wedding."

"David?" Mr. Turner blinked, then stroked his chin. "He's getting married?"

Abby placed her hand uncertainly on the back of a chair in the front row. Her pulse quickened. She felt the urge to run out of the room, to the safety of warmth and sunlight, where she could surround herself with the living and not the dead. But she thought of how much that entitled cat and sweet Sandra loved Mrs. Kensington, and steeled her nerves. "This weekend."

Mr. Turner nodded, slowly, recognition dawning on his features. "Of course, how could I forget? And Nancy has come to pout, has she?"

"Nancy?" Abby asked, frowning. The name seemed familiar, but she couldn't place it. "Are you referring to me? You think I'm like Nancy Drew?"

He shook his head. "Annabelle's horrid mother."

Oh right, Annabelle had mentioned that her mother and the late Mr. Kensington hadn't gotten along. "I'm afraid she's dead."

"Is she now?" Mr. Turner grunted. "I could have sworn I just saw her. Then again, my memory isn't what it used to be. Could have been her daughter. She's what, thirty now?"

Abby hesitated, wondering if he would provide more information if he knew his current state. If he didn't know he was dead, she didn't want to jar him into remembering and set off another death-loop.

"I actually wanted to talk to you about Mrs. Kensington," Abby said, sticking with neutral territory. "I think she may be in danger. Do you know of anyone who would want to hurt her?"

"Hurt her?" His eyebrow shot up. "Why do you ask? Is she in trouble?"

"Someone tried to stab her."

He stood so suddenly Abby jumped in alarm. His jaw tightened and his brow trembled, a fiercely protective gleam in his eyes. "Is she alright?"

Abby studied him. The concern he showed for his wife's well-being seemed *genuine*. If he was faking, he was an expert con artist. "She's fine. Not even a scratch."

Mr. Turner's fists clenched. "Who did it?"

Abby leaned back, lowering her binoculars to rub her eyes. "That's what I was hoping you could tell me."

The walkie-talkie creaked with static. When Abby returned the binoculars to her eyes, he was pacing the front of the movie theater, running his fingers through his short hair. "I wouldn't be surprised if we got an angry letter or someone cut up her roses, but stabbed? Good Lord! You're sure she's alright?"

The concern in his eyes made Abby's suspicions evaporate even more. Mr. Turner appeared to be a loving husband, even in death. "Yes. For the time being, at least."

"I should check on her." He stopped pacing. "But she doesn't know I'm here, does she? She doesn't know I'm——" He stuck his hand through a nearby chair and gestured to himself.

"She doesn't know you're a ghost," Abby validated for him softly.

He shut his eyes, a pained expression on his face. "Please tell her that I love her and not a day goes by when I don't think about her."

Abby was uncomfortable passing such a personal message from a ghost along to the living, especially when Mrs. Kensington had clearly moved on.

Sensing Abby's hesitation, Mr. Turner deflated. "Unless... she's with someone else now?"

Abby drew out her response, studying him. He seemed genuinely uncertain about how she would answer.

At last, Abby nodded. "I'm not sure how official it is."

Mr. Turner let out a relieved sigh. "Ah. Well, good for her."

"That's it? You're not jealous?"

"What's there to be jealous of? I can't be there for her anymore. I'm barely aware I exist half the time."

Abby shifted her weight. This was turning out to be more difficult than she had thought. "Do you know any of the other ghosts?"

Mr. Turner pinched the bridge of his nose and winced as if he was thinking so hard it pained him. "I don't leave the basement. When I first——" he cleared his throat, skipping over the word 'died' "——I checked on the others. A couple who claimed to be the original owners of the house welcomed me.

They were very kind. They suggested I spend some time down here, where I was less likely to be interrupted."

Interrupted by the living or by the other ghosts? Abby's brow furrowed. Had Sarah and George ushered Mr. Turner to the basement to give him time to process and grieve, or had their reasoning been more sinister in nature? It's possible they wanted him out of the way while they went after Mrs. Kensington.

Abby tried a different approach. "Is there anyone Mrs. Kensington hated?"

He rubbed the back of his neck. "No. Well, her grandfather, but he's not around. I'd have had some choice words for him if he were. That bastard—he was rude to Paige, furious she would inherit the house. He had some old-fashioned notion that it needed to go to a man. When her brother died, he wanted it to go to one of his cousins—can't remember who, Rudolph or something."

"I didn't know Mrs. Kensington had a brother," Abby said, wondering if she had overlooked a key suspect. "When did he die?"

"Years ago, when Paige and I were teenagers. He was only twelve, poor boy."

Abby thought of the ghost boy in the room next door. "Tommy?"

Mason Turner blinked in surprise. "Yes. How did you know?"

Abby felt a weight in her stomach. She had known Tommy had died young, but she had imagined it happening lifetimes ago; with such distance the tragedy was numbed by time. She hadn't considered his relatives could still be alive, could still mourn him. "He's still around."

"Really?" Mason frowned. "I shouldn't be surprised, but I am. I wonder if he remembers me."

"He's next door if you want to ask."

"Another time."

Abby lowered the binoculars, running the strap between her fingers. If Tommy knew Mrs. Kensington, that made him a suspect. She couldn't imagine the bright-eyed boy wishing anyone harm, but she had to admit this information troubled her. Were there any other connections to Mrs. Kensington that she had missed? She should have questioned the kids more closely.

"Did you know of any other children who died here?" she asked, returning the binoculars to her eyes. "Elizabeth or Mary?"

Mason shook his head. The children must have died before his time. Abby continued thoughtfully. "Did Tommy have a nanny?"

"Not that I know of."

Abby ran her fingers through her hair. The nanny's dress was too modern for her to have watched over Elizabeth or Mary during life. She made a mental note to ask David and Robert if they had a nanny growing up. That would explain her attachment to the car. Abby hoped she wouldn't have to break the news of her death to the Kensington boys. Lucas would surely call her out for being tactless.

She felt a pang of longing for Lucas to be here at her side. He would keep her on track, and know the right questions to ask. She tried to imagine what he would say—she could picture him saying '*I told you not to jump to conclusions*' now that halfway through the interview her confidence that Mason Turner was guilty had dropped to zero.

He would ask for something incriminating about someone else. Probably Archie.

"Have you met Archie?" Abby asked. It was as good of a place to start as any.

When she received a confused look from Mr. Turner, she continued, "The man who designed this house? He's tall, thin—complains a lot. He would have died before your time, but maybe you've seen him around since you've—" Abby cleared her throat, and finished her question more tactfully "—recently?"

Mr. Turner stroked his chin. "I may have. I forget his name, or exactly how long ago I saw him, but a man like that was sitting at my bar, complaining about the wallpaper."

"That sounds like Archie. Did he say anything about Mrs. Kensington?"

Mr. Turner's eyes sparkled eerily, reflecting light that didn't exist. "He did. He said, 'That woman will be the death of me.' I said, 'What woman?' He said, 'Mrs. Kensington,' and I told him, 'That's my wife you're talking about.' Then I got to drinking—or, remembering drinking, as ghosts do—and when I came to, he was gone."

"But he's already dead," Abby pointed out. "How can Mrs. Kensington be the death of him?"

Mr. Turner shrugged. "Figure of speech? He was upset about something she was doing with the veranda."

Abby frowned. Maybe his words were a figure of speech. Or maybe Mrs. Kensington's renovations included destroying an object that was keeping Archie's ghost around. If Archie wasn't ready to move on and Mrs. Kensington was about to force him to, that could give him motive.

"Was he upset? Do you think he'd want to hurt Mrs. Kensington?"

Mason's eyes glazed over as he turned back to the screen, where he was clearly locked in some memory.

"Mason?" Abby prompted.

"Huh?" He glanced at her as if being pulled from a daze. "Do I know you?"

Abby sighed. She was losing him, and she hadn't gotten much out of him besides a mess of information that may or may not be relevant and a reiteration of things she already knew. "Thank you, you've been very helpful."

"My pleasure," Mr. Turner said with a curt nod, lacking eye contact. "Tell the boys I'll be up after this movie."

Abby frowned, but she nodded as she moved out of his line of sight and turned off the lights. Her sneakers pattered across the carpet as she slipped out of the movie theater and turned off the walkie-talkie. Without it, the basement was silent as a tomb.

Abby flicked her bag of popcorn back and forth across the marble countertop. If Mr. Turner was innocent, that made Archie the most likely culprit. Which meant Lucas was turning out to be right.

Chapter Seventeen

Abby didn't like the idea of sneaking into Mrs. Kensington's room while the old woman slept, but she preferred it to finding Mrs. Kensington dead in the morning. Snores drowned out her footsteps as she crept around the four-poster bed. Marie Antoinette cracked one eye open, her tail switching against the duvet as Abby slowly poured a circle of salt across the plush carpet.

Abby put a finger to her lips, hoping the cat would sense that she was trying to help—not harm—Mrs. Kensington. Mrs. Kensington heavy breath filled the silence. As Abby circled the bed, she tried to picture the old woman as a young girl. Had she played with Tommy the way he now played with Mary? Had they been close, or did Tommy secretly resent her for inheriting all that was once promised to him? Abby shook the thought. Tommy seemed content with his ghost friends. Nothing in his behavior indicated he felt anything but respect toward Mrs. Kensington—certainly nothing indicated he would be desperate enough to strangle her in her sleep or stab her with a knife.

Maybe Lucas was right, and Archie was wrapped up in all this. He had clearly been keeping his relationship with George a secret. At first she had assumed that was out of respect for—or fear of—Sarah, but now she wondered if there wasn't something more to it. She needed to look into what was going on with the verandas.

With the circle completed and only a sprinkle of salt left in the box, Abby sealed it shut and slipped back into the hallway. Marie Antoinette sat up, watching her go, but made no move to wake Mrs. Kensington.

Abby was so focused on the cat, she nearly collided with someone.

"Abby?" Mina whispered, turning on a flashlight.

Abby shut Mrs. Kensington's door just in time to prevent the yellow glow from filling her bedroom.

Mina stood there in a pair of sneakers, yoga pants, and a baggy workout shirt, sweat beading at the base of her ponytail. "What are you doing?"

"Trying to fix things," Abby said, starting down the stairs.

Mina followed, her breath warm against Abby's neck. "How?"

Abby held up the box of salt. "Made a circle of salt around Mrs. Kensington's bed. If Glen was right, that should keep her safe until morning."

"You poured salt on her floor?" Mina snorted. "She is going to hate you tomorrow."

"But she'll be alive tomorrow." Abby pointed to Mina's reusable water bottle. "You went out for a midnight run?"

"Downstairs," Mina corrected. "They've practically got a gym here."

Abby merely shrugged. Nothing about this house surprised her anymore. "You should see the movie theater in the basement."

Mina shook her head, moonlight gleaming off her warm eyes. "This place is extra."

"Agreed." Abby frowned as she reached the living room. She had left the coat she was borrowing over the back of the couch, but someone had moved it. Quietly, she creaked open a closet door and peered inside.

"What are you looking for?" Mina whispered.

"My coat," Abby whispered back, selecting a coat on a hanger and holding it to her chest. It was way too big, the arms trailing down to her knees. "Or any coat I could borrow."

Mina stiffened. "Where are you going?"

"Outside."

"I got that." Mina's gaze flickered from Abby to the door and back, heavy with trepidation. "Where?"

"Backyard."

"You're looking for another ghost?"

"No— aha!" Abby made a triumphant sound and immediately covered her mouth with her hand. She waited a moment, preparing to dive into the closet at the slightest sound of angry footsteps. All she heard was the occasional drip of melting ice and the clock's steady tick. After several seconds, Abby removed the familiar peacoat. The wool hugged her shoulders like the embrace of an old friend. "I'm going to take care of the chairs first."

Mina's eyebrows twitched upward. "The chairs?"

Abby returned to the basement, her phone's flashlight casting a yellow glow over the ceramic tiles. She led Mina to the closet, where her flashlight darted from label to label until she found a can labeled 'snow.' "Michelle said she wanted white chairs, right?"

Mina's eyes widened. "You're going to paint them?"

Abby grinned. She picked up the paint can and carried it to the counter, massaging her shoulder. It was heavier than she'd thought.

Mina picked it up, in a gesture that was probably supposed to be kind but made it look *too* easy. Now she was just showing off.

"What are you doing?" Abby asked as Mina picked up a second can.

"Helping. The place is refusing to take them back, so it's actually not a bad idea. I'll carry the paint. You get the brushes."

Abby couldn't argue with that. Brushes in hand, Abby followed Mina back through the house, and into the backyard.

Golden lights peeked out of damp mulch beds, providing small patches of light. Abby rubbed her hands together for warmth. Though most of the snow was melting, it was still chilly. One day, she would get gloves. For now, she would focus on the task at hand.

Within minutes, they were leaving pale glossy strokes across the dark wood.

Within hours, the chairs glistened with a fresh coat of white paint.

This was turning out better than she had hoped. Maybe— just maybe—this would earn back Michelle's favor, and buy her a little more time to stop a murder.

ABBY WOKE TO the scent of coffee. A glance at her phone showed her it was almost 9 a.m. Though her body ached for more sleep, she forced herself out of bed and downstairs in a timely manner.

For a house filled with ghosts, there sure was a lot of life this early in the morning.

Annabelle replaced a vase of flowers with a fresh floral arrangement, while David stood on a ladder, straightening a heart-shaped wreath over the front door. Robert sat in the living room, sipping coffee while checking his phone.

Through the windows, Abby saw Sandra and Mrs. Kensington seated on a bench in the back garden—the very bench Abby had 'ruined' with the blowtorch. They didn't seem to mind. They were both grinning ear to ear, hands intertwined. Their feelings for each other were so obvious now; Abby kicked herself for not seeing it before.

Yawning, Abby entered the kitchen. Michelle practically tackled her into a hug.

"Mina told me what you did!" Michelle squealed. "Thank you, thank you, thank you!"

Abby struggled to breathe beneath Michelle's tight grip. She waited until she let her go to say, "I take it you've seen the chairs."

"They're *perfect!*" Michelle clapped her hands together. "Abby Spector, you are a lifesaver!"

After another quick hug, Michelle was running through the doorway and deeper into the house. Abby grinned. While Michelle hadn't *explicitly* said that she and Lucas were welcome to stay as long as they liked, she took Michelle's joy as an invitation. At the very least, claiming she was too tired to drive because she had stayed up most of the night painting chairs was a good excuse.

Lucas stepped into the room, rubbing his eyes. The faint redness at the edges stung Abby's heart as she recalled the damage she had caused to his precious sketchbook. "Am I dreaming or did I just hear my sister call you a lifesaver?"

"You heard right." Abby forced a cheery smile as she ushered him toward the window and pointed to the white chairs resting on frosted grass. "We fixed her chair problem."

Lucas's eyes widened. "You painted them?"

Abby wrung her hands. "I know, I know, you told me not to meddle in things, but——"

"That's ingenious!"

A tentative grin spread across Abby's face, faltering as she recalled their recent argument. She wasn't sure where that left them—Lucas wasn't acting like he was angry with her, but he wasn't exactly his usual cheerful self either. She felt like he was holding part of himself back.

A spark of static jolted Abby's right leg as she rubbed her toes across the rug, waiting for Lucas to ease the tension between them.

Lucas rubbed his chin. "I take it you're not planning on driving me home today?"

Abby shook her head. "No. But when I do, I promise I'll buy you a new sketch——"

"Which means you're planning on vanquishing another ghost?"

"Um, yeah." Abby shifted her weight, unable to get an emotional reading from him. He wasn't giving her much to go off—intentionally, no doubt. She tucked her hair behind her ear and asked hesitantly, "Want to hear what I found out?"

Lucas sighed. "Let me finish my tea first."

He didn't look at Abby, but his sentence came out fluid, with a casual tone. Abby's heart warmed. It was a genuine invitation to continue working together, a clear sign that she could count on him, and a sincere signal that they were still friends.

She waited until Lucas poured his second cup of tea and then led him to the basement, recounting her conversation with Mason Turner. When they reached the basement, Lucas's eyes widened. "Is that a Scooby-Doo pinball machine?"

"Yep." Abby stepped out of the way as he rushed forward to play.

"You are the best friend *ever!*"

Abby beamed at the compliment. While she couldn't take credit for the pinball machine's existence, she was enjoying this joyful carefree side of Lucas. It reminded her of the old Lucas, the way he had been when they'd hung out in high school, before he had started worrying about college and bills and prestige and such.

After two rounds, Lucas ran out of tea. Abby offered to get him another cup as she was craving a hot drink herself. She hurried out of the basement and down the hall, debating between hot chocolate and hot apple cider.

Abby stopped abruptly outside the living room and backtracked. Peering around the columned door-frame, Abby watched Sandra serve drinks to Michelle, Mina, Annabelle, and a woman in a sleek gray dress who looked suspiciously familiar.

She stepped forward, hesitantly. "*Mom?*"

The woman in the gray dress turned and Abby saw, without a doubt, that it was her mother, Rebecca Spector. As always, she looked like she was dressed for a business meeting, with her practical watch, excessively hair-sprayed curls, and fitted dress with a high neckline.

"Abby!" Her mother's hand flew to her heart as if Abby's presence had nearly given her a heart attack. "What a surprise!"

"Seriously." Abby's forced smile wilted into a grimace with the anticipation of an unpleasant exchange as she stepped forward. Her mom hadn't come to check up on her, had she? Talk about an invasion of privacy. She never should have called her on the drive up. "What are you doing here?"

"Why, I'm here for the wedding, of course." Her heels clacked against the polished floor as she stepped toward Abby, arms crossed. "What are *you* doing here? You're supposed to be looking after the house."

"I never agreed to that," Abby whined. "I said I'd think about it."

"Well, it's no big deal, I can find someone else." Rebecca waved a hand before placing it on Abby's shoulder and pulling her in for an awkward side hug. "It's good to see you. You could have told me you were coming, though. I've got a whole pile of clothes I'm about to donate—I'd have brought it for you."

Abby choked back an exasperated sigh, stepping out of her mother's embrace. "How many times do I have to tell you—we do *not* have the same style."

"I know, I know, you have flair. I respect that. But you could benefit from some more practical clothes."

"Mom—"

"I'm just saying, when you get tired of your magic gig or whatever it is you're doing now—"

"Mom!"

"It couldn't hurt to have a more professional wardrobe. Might open some new opportunities."

Sandra handed Abby a tall glass of a carbonated drink and Abby took a sip. It was so bitter, Abby winced and spat it out into the glass.

Rebecca Spector looked horrified. "What was *that*?"

Abby blinked. "What was what?"

"I did not teach you to spit out good champagne."

Abby shook her head at her mother in bewilderment as Sandra took the champagne glass.

"Perhaps I could bring you some sparkling fruit juice?" Sandra offered.

"Yes, please," Abby said, screwing up her face as she attempted to get the bitter taste off her tongue. "And Lucas wanted more tea."

Sandra retreated toward the kitchen. "I'll put on the kettle."

Abby's mother was still glaring at her in disapproval.

As Abby rolled her eyes, her gaze brushed Mina's and she saw a twinkle of amusement there, which fueled her rebellious spirit. She turned back to her mother with a shrug. "What was I supposed to do? Drink it even though it tasted like sandpaper?"

"Yes," her mother snapped.

Abby folded her arms across her sweater. "That's not what you said when we accidentally mixed up drinks at Amber's birthday party."

"Amber—" Rebecca's eyes narrowed. "Are you talking about the time when you were twelve? Where are your manners?" She reached toward Abby's wrist, as if she planned to drag her out of the room and chastise her for her behavior.

Abby stepped out of reach. "I don't know, maybe they got donated with the rest of my stuff."

Rebecca turned back to the coffee table, where she wrapped her fingers around the stem of a champagne glass and took a sip. She turned back to Abby, her harsh gaze scanning her up and down, as if she was searching for some hidden meaning in Abby's mannerisms the way she studied her former clients. "I told you we were selling the house."

"You didn't say you were going to give away all my belongings with it."

"Give away all your belongings? Don't be so dramatic. You hadn't lived there in years. What were you going to do with a bunch of stuffed animals and high school notebooks?"

"I had things—" Abby shook her head. She didn't want to have this conversation here, in front of Mina and Michelle and poor Annabelle, who was staring longingly at the kitchen as if she wanted to escape. She didn't want to talk about how some of those stuffed animals had belonged to Chelsea and how those high school notebooks had margins filled with her bubbly handwriting. She attempted to keep her voice as calm as possible, enunciating every word flatly to make it difficult for her mother to psychoanalyze her. "I don't expect you to understand."

Her mother opened her mouth to respond. "I—"

"Why are you here *now*?" Abby asked in a desperate plea to change the subject. "The wedding's not until Saturday."

Abby paused to take in her freshly ironed dress, her golden earrings that were only reserved for formal events, and the leather binder in front of the place she'd been sitting. "Wait, you're *in* the wedding?"

"Is that such a surprise?"

"Considering I didn't know about it, yes." Abby turned to Michelle. "Why is *my* mother in *your* wedding?"

Michelle tucked herself deeper into her cardigan. "She's been an invaluable part of my life."

Abby tried to recall any time she had seen her mother and Michelle together, outside of the occasional family cookout or graduation. She vaguely recalled Michelle coming over a few times to pick up Lucas, her final year of high school, and— Abby snapped her fingers. "She tutored you in psych."

"And so much more," Michelle said fondly. "Without her guidance, I'd never have gone to Boston and met David. I'd never have gotten such a prestigious career. Your mom believed in me during a time when no one else did."

Abby couldn't believe what she was hearing. They were talking about the same woman, right? The woman who had missed most of her school plays because she had classes to teach and donors to kiss up to.

"Oh, Michelle, your parents believed in you, they just didn't realize your full potential." Rebecca placed a hand on Michelle's shoulder. "I'm so proud of you, being the first of your family to go to college—finding your dream career and a wonderful partner to share it with. You should be proud of yourself."

"I'm so happy you could be here." Michelle's bracelets clattered as she threw her arms around Rebecca in a hug.

Abby felt like she'd stepped into a Hallmark movie in which her own mother was playing a role with someone else's kid. She raised an eyebrow. "See, now why don't I get speeches like that?"

"Because you never stick with anything long enough to see results," Rebecca said, breaking away from Michelle. "You don't think things through. When unexpected challenges come up, you quit."

Abby folded her arms across her chest. "Name one time that's true."

"Swimming, gymnastics, basketball—"

Abby rolled her eyes. "Okay, one time since I was eighteen."

"Every job you've ever had. Every relationship since—"

"Okay, okay, I get it." Abby collapsed into her mother's seat and propped her feet on the table. "Maybe I like trying new things."

"And you do that wonderfully, dear," Rebecca said in her overly polite 'I'm not having this conversation in front of the neighbors' voice. "But today is Michelle's big day, so let's focus on her, okay?"

"Technically Saturday is her big day," Abby muttered.

Rebecca's glass clanked as she returned it to the coffee table, empty. She cleared her throat and glanced at Michelle. "You didn't tell me Abby was going to be a bridesmaid."

"She's not," Michelle said, giving Abby an apologetic shrug. "She and Lucas are helping out."

"Oh?" Surprise flickered across Rebecca's face.

"She's been very helpful," Michelle assured her. "The chairs arrived in the wrong color and she stayed up all night painting them for me."

Rebecca arched an eyebrow, impressed. "All by herself?"

"Mina helped," Abby admitted.

"But it was all Abby's idea," Mina chimed in, encouragingly.

Rebecca patted the back of her hair, as if she didn't trust the excessive amount of hairspray holding it together. "What kind of paint did you use?"

Abby shook her head, refusing to play whatever game her mother was getting into. "Does anyone need anything from the kitchen? I'm going to—"

"What kind of paint, Abby?" Her mother repeated, more forcefully.

Abby clenched the back of the nearest armchair. She had half a mind to storm back to the basement that instant—tea be damned—but after their recent argument she didn't want to disappoint Lucas. She took a deep breath and answered, "White."

"Acrylic? Interior or exterior?"

Abby shifted her weight. "Whatever was in the basement. Does it matter?"

"It will when it rains. If you used the wrong kind, the paint's going to run and the chairs themselves are likely to be ruined."

Abby let out a heated sigh. "Good thing the forecast doesn't predict rain."

"There's a twenty percent chance of snow tonight. That'll do just as much damage."

Abby groaned. "Do you have to nitpick *everything* I do?"

"Why don't we take the chairs inside?" Mina stood quickly, nodding toward Abby. "That way, we don't have to worry about the weather."

"Good idea," Rebecca said, smoothing out her dress and returning to her 'polite neighbor' tone.

Abby wrinkled her face and followed Mina to the closet, where they slipped on their shoes. They headed out the back door. Abby took in a deep breath of refreshing air. It was still cool, but no longer frigid, the snow having melted in all but the deepest shadows. Sunlight fell across the yard, sparkling on the dewy evergreens and highlighting the imperfections in the painted chairs.

"So that's your mom, huh?" Mina's warm brown eyes bore into Abby's with compassion. Her usual curls were a bit more glossy and styled today, pulled back in a half braid. A thin layer of natural-looking makeup paired with a fitted sweater and dark skinny jeans made her look polished—almost formal. She must be trying to make a good impression on Mrs. Kensington.

Abby reached for the nearest chair. "I can't believe *she* is going to be in Michelle's wedding!"

"It sounds like they're close."

Abby snorted as she hauled the first chair under the stone overhang.

Mina followed her, a chair in each arm. "Closer than you two are, I take it?"

Abby huffed, returning for the next chair, the stone pathway crunching under her sneakers.

"Do you want to talk about it?"

"No." Abby stormed across the yard, hurling the next chair under the overhang a little harsher than intended. "It shouldn't surprise me, it really shouldn't. Mom's bragged about Michelle for years. I guess I just thought that was her way of trying to nudge me into what she envisioned as the perfect life: 'See, Michelle does all these grown-up things, how hard can it be?' I didn't realize Michelle was her adopted daughter."

"You're jealous?"

"Thankful," Abby grunted. "Finally someone can steal her attention away from nagging me."

"She's proud of you too, you know," Mina said softly. "At least, she should be. You're incredibly spirited and inspiring. She's an idiot if she doesn't see that."

"She's an idiot," Abby declared. Her sneaker skidded across a puddle and she tumbled forward, face-first toward the soggy grass. Mina's arms wrapped around Abby's waist, holding her steady.

Abby regained her balance, lingering in Mina's grip as the

nutty scent of lotion enveloped her. Mina's sweater brushed Abby's cheek, her hands warm against her back, brown eyes intense and concerned.

This was kind of romantic. *Too romantic.*

Abby pulled away, sinking deeper into her borrowed coat, and cleared her throat. "I should check on Lucas. See if he made any progress."

Mina's forehead crinkled. "With the ghost thing?"

Abby nodded.

"Okay." Mina turned her back to Abby and grabbed another chair. "I'll finish up here."

Abby left with a heavy feeling in her chest, as if her heart had been buried deep underground and was struggling to break through layers of caked mud and dirt. Mina was special. Mina sparked something in Abby that made her crave attention.

But Abby didn't do relationships. Her heart was buried too deep. Even if she somehow managed to uncover it, she was pretty sure it was too damaged to work properly.

Abby stomped up the steps to the back door.

It wouldn't budge.

She fidgeted with the knob. It was locked.

A breeze scattered pine needles at her feet as she pounded her fist against the door and waited for someone—anyone but her mother—to let her in.

Weak sunlight gleamed off the polished windows, reflecting a cloud-strewn sky. Wind whispered against Abby's ears.

The house was quiet.

Too quiet, considering how many people had been in that living room mere minutes ago.

Cupping her hands to the window, Abby peered inside. Her mother, Michelle, and Annabelle stood in the hall, expressions of horror on their faces. Abby followed their gaze to the shadowy outline of a figure hanging off the banister. At first, Abby thought it was a Halloween decoration—a scarecrow tied up by the neck—but she realized with horror that it was Mrs. Kensington.

Mrs. Kensington was suspended from the balcony, clawing at the garland wrapped around her neck, kicking furiously.

Abby pounded harder against the window, screaming for Lucas. If he was still in the basement, maybe he would hear her and bring up the salt gun. Abby clawed at her hair, searching her surroundings for a way inside.

"Stand back," Mina ordered, clenching her fists. Before Abby could ask why, Mina was hurling a kick at the glass door.

Glass shattered inward as the wooden frame slammed open.

Abby had barely a second to be impressed before Mina leaped over the shards, charging inside.

Abby followed her, hurrying past the terrified bridal party, a stunned Robert Kensington, and century-old portraits, until she was tearing up the stairs, two at a time.

Her mother shouted her name in warning.

Like that would stop her from saving someone's life.

Mrs. Kensington's gasps echoed through the main hall as her shadow swung across the polished floor. Her kicks grew weak as she attempted to free herself.

Abby reached the landing and knelt to the floor. Sticking her arms between the railings, she reached for Mrs. Kensington. Her hand brushed the old woman's collar as she wrapped her arms around her frail torso and pulled upward. With Abby's support, Mrs. Kensington managed to pry the greenery from her neck long enough to take a deep, raspy breath.

Pain seared down Abby's back, so sharp she lost her grip

and jammed her knee into the railing. Craning her neck, she saw a lamp hovering over her, preparing to strike. Abby rolled away just in time; the lamp shattered on the carpet, the metal pole denting the floor where she had been.

"Lucas!" Abby shouted. Their ghost-hunting equipment would really come in handy right now. Without knowing who or where her attacker was, Abby was low on options.

And Mrs. Kensington was low on oxygen.

Gritting her teeth, Abby reached for Mrs. Kensington again. She had barely brushed the woman's sweater when the garland snapped in half.

Mrs. Kensington screamed as she plummeted.

Chapter Eighteen

Mrs. Kensington's scream echoed through the halls, mingling with the gasps of the horrified onlookers. Her shadow washed over the stairs as sleek and steadfast as rain. Abby braced for the deadly impact, but it never came.

Mina had shoved a couch under her just in time. Mrs. Kensington landed safely—though rather ungracefully—on the cushions with an *oof*.

Robert ran to her side, running his hands through his hair in relief. "What the hell just happened?"

In response, Mrs. Kensington coughed.

"Michelle, call a doctor," Rebecca barked. "Annabelle, get her a glass of water."

Mrs. Kensington took several deep breaths and got shakily to her feet, stretching as if she'd spent a long day at the opera. "No need for a doctor. I'm perfectly fine."

Rebecca's manicured fingers tore at the roots of her high-lighted hair. "By sheer luck! You could have *died*."

"What were you doing hanging off the stairs?" Robert asked, kinder now, as if he thought Mrs. Kensington had decided to tie herself up for attention.

Mrs. Kensington studied her reflection in an antique mirror, running her fingers around the edge of a puffy pink line on her skin. "The greenery attacked me."

Abby's body gradually relaxed as she eased out of her crouched position, sinking back into a seated stance at the top of the stairs. Memories of the lace biting into her own neck resurfaced, bringing a sharp sting of recollection.

"What do you mean it *attacked* you?" Robert asked.

With pursed lips, Mrs. Kensington adjusted her collar and turned to him, with a shrug. "You know how it is."

"I don't." Robert's voice trembled. "I've never seen anything like that before."

"A hazard of living, I suppose," Mrs. Kensington said dismissively. Despite her tone, her hands trembled as she massaged the base of her neck. "Annabelle, please ask Sandra to bring a cup of tea to my room."

Annabelle nodded, rushing toward the kitchen.

Rebecca opened and closed her mouth, clearly at a loss for words. Her watch clattered against the brass buttons of her cardigan as she shoved her hands against her hips and began to pace. Her eyes met Abby's with a gaze so heated, Abby shied away as if it could physically burn her.

"What just happened?" Rebecca snapped.

Abby reached up the back of her shirt, assessing the damage. The spot between her shoulder blades stung, but she didn't feel any blood, and her bones were intact. Still, she winced as her sweater pulled against the bruise. "If I told you, you wouldn't believe it."

"Did *you* have anything to do with this?"

Abby slumped against the top stair. "Yeah, I thought it'd be funny to dangle Mrs. Kensington off the banister and see what happens."

Rebecca's eyes narrowed. "If I find out this is one of your pranks gone wrong—"

"It isn't." The soft tone in Michelle's usually confident voice deflated the tension faster than pricking a pin in a balloon.

Everyone turned to her.

"Michelle?" Concern burned through Rebecca's voice. "What is it?"

Michelle chewed her lower lip. "It's difficult to explain. It's— complicated."

Rebecca leaned forward, her composure cracking—likely under the weight of her curiosity, which was the one thing she could never resist. She grabbed Michelle by the shoulders and urged, "*What's complicated?*"

"The house is haunted," Annabelle declared ominously, returning from the kitchen as pale as a ghost. She slipped, trance-like, into an armchair and shivered. "It wants to kill Mrs. Kensington."

Rebecca's brow caved into a look of disapproval.

"One of the ghosts wants to kill her, not the house itself," Abby elaborated.

That made Rebecca frown deeper.

"Ask anyone," Abby said. "It's true."

"*Something's* up with this place, that's for sure." Robert shook his head, pouring himself a drink. "As soon as I inherit this shithole, it's going up for sale. I could buy something twice as nice in this market."

"The house is old," Michelle said, uncertainly. "She could

have slipped. And I wouldn't put it past Lucas to have hung the garland too low."

At the mention of Lucas, Abby stood, her gaze darting toward the basement. Surely, he would have heard the commotion. So why hadn't he come running? With a sinking sensation in the pit of her stomach, Abby hobbled toward the basement door.

"Where do you think you're going?" Her mother's words floated down the narrow hallway.

Abby ignored her, moving as fast as she dared with her bruising knee, until she reached the basement's entrance. The door was shut, the brass knob gleaming sinisterly in the sunlight. Abby attempted to open it, but the knob wouldn't budge. It was locked.

The door shook.

Someone pounded from inside.

Abby jumped back with a yelp.

"Help!" Lucas's muffled voice came through the iron door. "I'm locked in!"

Abby shut her eyes and took a deep breath. First she had been locked out of the house, and now Lucas was locked in the basement with their equipment. This had to be the work of the ghost. Whoever attacked Mrs. Kensington must have wanted her and Lucas out of the picture while they went after Mrs. Kensington alone. And they nearly succeeded.

A chill crept down Abby's spine. It seeped through her bones and settled in the hollow space between her ribs. She had been within inches of the culprit and still she had no idea who they were.

Chapter Nineteen

Abby had a tendency to take on too much. She knew this, but she also knew Lucas would always be there to help her out. When she tried to film a feature-length movie for their high school English class, he had loaned her his camera and stayed up editing footage with her all night. When she realized providing free ice cream to kids was not a successful business model, he'd helped her sell her ice-cream truck. When Chelsea died, he had been there to help Abby through the worst of it.

But now, instead of helping, he was packing his suitcases and shaking his head.

"I'm done, Abby." He slipped his ruined sketchbook carefully into a side compartment in his suitcase. "Being locked in the basement was the last straw. I'm out."

"Come on," Abby groaned. "So what, you got to play pinball for an extra half hour while David unscrewed the door. It's not like you're hurt or anything."

"Which is why I'm getting out now, when I'm unharmed."

Lucas slammed his suitcase closed and zipped up the sides. "I am staying at a ghost-free hotel tonight, where I don't have to worry about waking up dead tomorrow."

"If you were dead, you wouldn't wake up."

Lucas glared at Abby. He moved his suitcase to the floor, letting the wheels rumble against the creaky wood as he headed toward the door. He paused halfway across the room, glancing over his shoulder. "Are you coming with me or are you going to stay here in this mess?"

Abby considered his question. The idea of relocating to a place where they could talk and play games and watch movies all night, with no ghostly interruptions, sounded appealing. Hadn't that been why she had come here in the first place—to spend time with Lucas? Even though they had been sleeping under the same roof the past few days, it hadn't exactly been the joyful reunion she had anticipated. Maybe Lucas had the right idea.

She wanted to follow him, but hesitation kept her feet rooted to the carpet. "But we're so close. If we leave and Mrs. Kensington dies tonight, won't you feel horrible?"

"I'd feel worse if I ended up dead."

Abby frowned, unable to let go so easily. Even if she went with Lucas, she doubted she would be able to keep her mind from racing with theories and fears about the ghosts haunting the estate. "You're just going to sit there and let an innocent woman die because you're too scared to sleep in a haunted house?"

Lucas waved his arms at the ceiling. "This is *her* house. She's lived here for years without anything going wrong, until we showed up. I think she'll survive just fine."

Lucas reached toward the door.

Abby grabbed his arm, her palm closing around his scratchy sweater. "That's a good point."

"Thank you."

"Mrs. Kensington has lived here for years," Abby repeated, feeling close to a breakthrough—though what exactly that breakthrough entailed, she was still uncertain. "Why did the ghost attack *now* and not before? What's changed since we arrived?"

Lucas shrugged, but his expression was thoughtful. "The wedding decorations?"

Abby shook her head. While she doubted seashells and garlands were haunted, she wondered if something else about the wedding was the catalyst—something that was triggering an otherwise calm ghost into becoming murderous. "Mr. Turner wasn't a fan of Robert's marriage, was he?"

Abby couldn't picture the man she had spoken to going after Mrs. Kensington in his right state of mind, but the fact that he was missing periods of time seemed like a potential danger sign. She added, "Maybe he thinks this wedding is Robert's, and he's trying to stop it?"

Lucas shook his head. "It wasn't Mr. Turner. He was with me in the basement. When I realized I was locked in, I looked around. The kids were huddled in the corner and Mr. Turner was soothing them. They were all there when Mrs. Kensington screamed."

"All three kids?" Abby asked.

Lucas nodded. "Mary, Elizabeth, and Tommy."

Abby frowned. As relieved as she was to know they had just ruled out four suspects, it didn't seem to help. "You didn't happen to see Archie or George, did you?"

"You think it was one of them?"

Abby told Lucas how she had seen them together in one of the upstairs bedrooms, and how Mr. Turner had informed her that Archie had mentioned Mrs. Kensington would be the death of him.

"And you think they're trying to kill Mrs. Kensington because…?" Lucas's right hand still gripped his suitcase, but he was more relaxed, his mind churning behind his dark eyes.

Abby paced the length of the bed, moving in and out of a bright patch of sunlight. They didn't have a motive. They seemed happy together. Mrs. Kensington couldn't do anything to change that. Not unless— "What if she is making changes to the house that will separate them? Mason said something about a veranda. Are there any repairs planned for that?"

Lucas shrugged. "How should I know?"

Abby sighed. "Whoever it is that's after Mrs. Kensington, I suspect they're the one who locked you in the basement and locked me outside. That means they think we're a threat."

Lucas's eyes widened. "That means we're in danger."

"That means we're close."

Lucas tightened his grip on the handle of his suitcase. "I'm out. Sorry, Abby, I do *not* want to pick a fight with a dead guy."

The door creaked open and Annabelle poked her head in, her blonde hair pulled back into an elegant French knot, her cashmere sweater buttoned to the base of her ruby necklace. "Sorry to interrupt—Michelle is looking for you, Lucas."

Lucas groaned. "What does she want now?"

Annabelle said softly, "Your parents are here."

A look of pure horror flickered across Lucas's face.

Abby gently took his suitcase from him. "Go say hi. I'll see if I can figure anything out in the meantime."

"Go say hi?" Lucas's voice squeaked. "The last time I saw

them, I told them I could make my own decisions, stormed out of the house, and ordered a rideshare here. I expected to have a job by now. Or at least a place to stay—my God, am I *homeless?*"

He stepped backward, collapsed into a seated position on the edge of the bed, and cradled his head in his hands.

Abby stood beside him, her shoulder brushing the wooden bedpost as she gave Lucas's shoulder a reassuring squeeze and hoped he wasn't on the verge of a panic attack. "You're not homeless. Your parents would be happy to take you back in."

"That is *not* helping."

"And you can always crash on my couch, rent free."

"Only mildly helping."

"Lucas?" Mrs. Clark's voice called from the hallway. "Is that you?"

Lucas jumped to his feet, looking like he had been caught committing a crime. He combed his fingers over his hair and brushed the sleeves of his sweater before stepping into the hall to greet his parents.

Abby gave them a few minutes of privacy, trying her best not to eavesdrop but the walls were thin and Mr. Clark's voice was rather loud. The notion of avoiding the topic of Lucas's unemployment lasted all of about thirty seconds. His father was already reminding him he had a position waiting for him at the insurance agency he worked at.

Abby silently begged Lucas to respond, but he just made noncommittal sounds like he always did. Any second now, he would turn into an apologetic mess and give in to his dad's requests. He had given up his dog, ice-skating, and all hopes of going to Star Trek Las Vegas because they had insisted those things were not good for him. She hoped he wouldn't give up on his career so easily.

Thankfully, Michelle interrupted before he could sign his life away.

As the Clarks fawned over their little girl turned bride-to-be, Abby slipped into the hall and seized the opportunity to pull Lucas away. She led him downstairs, leaving his suitcase behind.

"The nerve!" Lucas grumbled when they were out of earshot. "They think they can walk all over me, make plans for my life without consulting me! And they think I'll just stand by and take it."

Abby bit her lip, holding back her opinion that he had reinforced that idea by giving in to almost every one of his parents' whims. Instead, she brought the conversation back to the ghost. "We need to know what else has changed in the past week. Something has upset a ghost—if we can't find out who, maybe we can find out what."

Lucas shook his head, his thoughts clearly not on the conversation.

"See if you can talk to David and Robert. Take notes on any recent or upcoming changes. See if there's anything we haven't thought about that might be a motive for Archie or George."

"What are you going to do?"

"I'm going to have a chat with our suspects."

ABBY WAS QUITE set on her plan. Briefcase in hand, she headed toward the living room, looking for Archie.

Instead, she found her mother.

"Abby, dear, come say hi to the Clarks!" Slipping a firm hand under Abby's armpit, Rebecca guided her into a reunion with the Clarks.

Unlike her mother, they knew how to dress for vacation *and* they greeted her with a warm embrace. They doted over her like she was still the eight-year-old girl she had been when they had first met—or perhaps they were thinking of the grief-stricken teenager that had showed up crying on their doorstep on more than one occasion. Either way, Abby would have appreciated the attention and the compliments, if it hadn't pulled her away from the very important task of preventing a murder.

Eventually, Mrs. Clark adjusted her thick silver glasses and leaned down to whisper to Abby. "Tell me, how's my boy doing, really?"

"Fine," Abby said, absently, glancing at the clock. She'd wasted over half an hour. Her only reassurance was hearing Mrs. Kensington's voice occasionally barking orders at David, and the calm manner in which Marie Antoinette slept curled by the fire.

"Is he even looking for a job?" Mrs. Clark whispered.

"Of course," Abby said, defensive of her friend. "He had an interview earlier this week."

"And did he get the offer?"

Abby chewed her lip. Answering that question was probably not helpful right now. She said instead, "He'll find one. It just takes time."

"Time he could spend earning money, working for me," Mr. Clark said, shaking his head. The way he settled into the couch with a beer in one hand and a bowl of nuts in the other looked like he was preparing to watch a sports game. "That boy is too prideful, sticking his nose up at a good career. I worked hard to be in a position to offer him one."

Abby opened her mouth to say that Lucas worked hard too,

but her own mother beat her to it.

"He's worked hard to get his master's degree," Rebecca offered. Sunlight sparkled off her wine glass, drawing attention to her manicure and solid gold wedding band. "Let him put it to use."

Mr. Clark cocked an eyebrow. "Where? In a bookstore?"

"Wherever he wants," Rebecca countered. "Anywhere he applies, he has an advantage now. I'm always telling Abby, education is an asset—"

"—no one can take away from you," Abby finished, rolling her eyes. "I know, Mom."

She flashed her mother a 'give it a rest' look. Couldn't she see that she wasn't helping? For an expert on psychology, her mom was terrible at interacting with other humans who weren't her students.

"Her father and I always thought she'd have her PhD by now," her mother continued.

Abby gritted her teeth, annoyed that her mom was speaking about her as if she weren't around. She flailed her arms in front of Rebecca's face. "Maybe if you didn't push me so hard, I'd have been more open to college."

"And what, have you attend that party school on the beach? Your SAT scores were too high for that."

Abby groaned.

Mrs. Clark reached out a hand and patted Abby's knee reassuringly. At least *someone* was on her side. Maybe she and Lucas should swap parents.

"Don't you think you're being a little hard on her? She's been through so much tragedy—"

Abby slid out of Mrs. Clark's grip and jumped to her feet. She wanted support, not pity. Why did everyone seem to think her whole life was dictated by the wake of Chelsea's death?

She was still herself. Still capable of making her own decisions.

"And it's time for her to snap out of it and get over it." Rebecca waved her hand dismissively. "If that girl was still alive, they'd have broken up by now and Abby would be moving on with her life."

The words hit Abby like a punch to the gut. She staggered back, staring at her mother. "*Mom!*"

"What? It's true. She was going to Harvard; you were looking at one of those party schools. Long distance is tough. Statistics predict—"

"I don't care about your statistics!" Abby snapped. "I don't care if we were on track to break up or get married—I care that she *died*. Chelsea *died*. And you want me to just 'get over it'?"

Rebecca straightened her shoulders and pursed her lips, preparing herself for a difficult conversation. Abby had watched her mother go through the same motions before every 'I'm not angry, just disappointed' diatribe and every 'death is a part of life' speech.

Abby raised her own emotional shield by folding her arms across her chest and glaring as menacingly as possible.

Rebecca sighed. "It's been nearly a decade, Abby."

Abby fixed her gaze on the twinkling Christmas tree, bracing for her mother to continue.

"It's time for you to get back on track."

Again, the words struck painfully. She couldn't just pick her life back up, as if Chelsea didn't matter—as if she could walk away unscathed from losing half her heart. She pictured moving into a dorm with a bunch of eighteen-year-olds, and sitting in a plastic chair while some professor droned on about a subject she didn't care about. There would be some cute girl beside her—in her imagination, this girl looked suspiciously like Mina—and Abby tried to imagine asking her out. At the thought, her stomach knotted with dread and betrayal.

She balled her fists. "I am *not* going to college."

Rebecca's gaze softened. "I've come to terms with that. But working part-time jobs, jumping from apartment to apartment, living alone—"

"I'm not alone!"

"You switch roommates so often, you might as well be. I'm not even sure you've been on a date in the past seven years."

Abby shot her a horrified look.

"What? I'm concerned about you, is all. Your father and I are getting old. You're so stuck in the past, you aren't taking any steps to secure your future."

"What am I, some damsel in distress in need of a husband?"

"You need some stability in your life—family, career, passion—I'm not sure you have any of it."

Abby's veins burned with anger and humiliation. How dare her mother criticize her life so harshly, as if it amounted to so little? She knew her mother could be pushy, but she had always thought it was because she was worried—not judgmental. "Well, I thought my family was pretty decent until now."

Rebecca frowned. "You know I love you, Abby."

"You could do a better job of showing it." Abby stormed out of the room.

Turning the hall corner, she let out a deep breath. How could her mother be so *irritating*? She suddenly had more empathy for Lucas's refusal to move back in with his parents. Spending a single day under the same roof as her mother was turning into a nightmare.

Running her fingers through her hair, Abby retreated upstairs to an empty room, where she let out a slow, shaky breath. How dare her mother speak ill of Chelsea? Chelsea *loved* Abby. Nothing could change that. Not even death.

A tear slipped down Abby's face. She twisted her bracelet, running her thumb along the faded braids. With all that had happened in recent days—with learning that ghosts were real—it felt like a cruel twist of fate that Chelsea wasn't among them. Some part of Abby had hoped that her love would have been strong enough to keep Chelsea tethered to the living. But it wasn't.

Chelsea was gone.

She had accepted it years ago, and she would have to accept it again. Sometimes it felt like that was all she ever did—accept that Chelsea was gone in a thousand little ways.

Wiping her eyes dry, Abby examined the contents on the nearest coffee table. Under various bridal and Christmas magazines, the stained edge of a leather-bound photo album poked out. It must be one of the albums Lucas scrounged up earlier.

Slipping into the nearest armchair, she began flipping through the album. The first picture was a sepia-toned photo of Kensington Manor. George and Sarah smiled fondly at the photographer, their hands intertwined. Abby was about to turn the page when she noticed a third person in the picture, leaning against the house's front porch. It was difficult to see him at first, but once Abby had located him, there was no mistaking his thin willowy outline.

Archie was standing behind George and Sarah, his expression lost to shadow.

Chapter Twenty

Abby yawned and attempted to massage the crick in her neck. She had fallen asleep in the armrest. She glanced at the clock. Her heart pounded furiously. It was nearly 8 a.m. She had slept through dinner and the entire night.

Abby jumped out of the chair and hurried to the stairs, her socks flapping against the hardwood. She peered over the banister, fearing to see Mrs. Kensington's body twisted on the floor or the glow of emergency lights through the glass windows. There was only faint sunlight brushing a white rug where the couch had saved Mrs. Kensington the previous afternoon and the heavy aroma of bacon and eggs.

Abby followed the smell to the dining room, where she found a large table fully set, and everyone digging into breakfast. Despite sunlight falling on their luxurious clothes and the numerous floral arrangements, they didn't look like they were preparing for a wedding—their silent faces and dismal expressions made it feel more like the eve of a funeral.

The Clarks avoided each other's gazes, carefully focused on their meals. Annabelle and Robert were seated next to each other, but had moved their chairs so far apart that they were nearly back to back. Mina's eyes were dark and vacant as she sipped her coffee, and Michelle picked at her food without eating a bite. She radiated such nervous energy, Abby was surprised she didn't combust.

David alone seemed to be enjoying himself, humming a Taylor Swift song while he sliced up his omelet.

Lucas was nowhere to be seen.

Abby's heart stung with his absence. He was truly gone.

Mrs. Kensington eyed her guests suspiciously, counting the silverware under her breath. David patted her arm and whispered, "Mom, relax. We're all family now."

Sandra shot Mrs. Kensington a flirtatious wink, and Mrs. Kensington muttered something to her son about still being careful, though her cheeks burned red from the attention.

Abby's mother was the first to notice her. She looked up from her coffee with pursed lips. "That flannel's too big for you. It's slipping off your shoulders."

"Good morning to you too," Abby muttered.

Mina held up her coffee cup in greeting.

Abby slipped into the empty seat beside the Clarks. "Who died?"

Annabelle gasped. Mina shot Abby a meaningful look, shaking her head.

"Not funny, Abby." Michelle tugged at her hair. "We've got less than forty-eight hours until we walk down the aisle. Annabelle, do you have the schedules printed up?"

Annabelle removed small slips of paper from her purse. She handed them to Michelle, who passed them out to everyone except Abby.

"Where's mine?" Abby asked.

"You have one task—stay out of the backyard."

"But—"

"No buts!" Michelle lowered her voice and stepped toward Abby, the pale rhinestones on her sweater sparkling in the morning light. "I know I can't stop you from…whatever it is you do. You have free range of the house. But the backyard is off limits. Don't make me regret this."

Abby reluctantly agreed, feeling she had little choice in the matter. She retreated into the kitchen, took one of the pristine glasses sparkling on the counter, and filled it with orange juice. Then she popped a bagel into a toaster. By the time the toaster dinged, she was feeling a bit more optimistic. At least Michelle hadn't assigned her any wedding tasks.

When she returned to the dining room—glass in one hand, napkin-wrapped bagel in the other—Michelle was addressing the rest of the room. "Now, if any of you need me, I'll be in the living room sorting through packages."

Annabelle promptly excused herself and hurried off after her.

Abby smeared cream cheese on her bagel while the others finished their meals in silence. By the time Abby had finished the first half of her bagel, only Mina remained.

"Some meal," Mina said, refilling her coffee. "I've had more lively conversations in nursing homes."

"That's because everyone's mad at each other."

Mina stared at her. "What do you mean?"

"Well it's obvious," Abby said with a shrug. "Lucas and his dad had a disagreement. His mom took Lucas's side, and consequently Mr. Clark is mad at her."

Mina's eyebrows drew together in contemplation. She nodded, encouraging Abby to continue.

"Annabelle and Robert are as distant as ever—" Abby recalled how far their chairs had been spread apart and how they both angled away from each other as they ate. "They've been having some disagreement since they arrived."

Mina's forehead creased. She whispered, "They're getting a divorce. Annabelle told me—they don't want the rest of the family to know until it's been finalized."

Ah, that would definitely explain it. Abby's heart went out to Annabelle for being in a wedding of a family she was about to break ties with. No wonder she was so stressed.

"My mouth is sealed." Abby mimed zipping her mouth shut. "And then there's Mrs. Kensington and Sandra."

"What about them?"

Abby lowered her voice, even though no one was around to hear them. "They're a couple."

Mina's jaw dropped. "No way."

"Yes way. But Mrs. Kensington hasn't told her family, and Sandra seems to be pushing the boundaries to see what she can get away with without anyone noticing."

"Well, damn," Mina said with a tone of approval. "Good for Mrs. K. And I'm impressed you've picked up on all this."

Abby beamed with pride, kicking her feet under the table. "Well, I saw them kissing, so that was kind of easy. Annabelle and Michelle—that one is a bit harder. I think Annabelle has been slacking on her wedding duties—or Michelle's simply overworked her—so there's tension there. And then there's you—you've got your usual thing."

Mina raised an eyebrow. "What's my usual thing?"

Abby opened her mouth, then shut it again. "Lucas doesn't like when I tell people things about themselves, even when they're obvious. He says it's an invasion of privacy and it upsets people."

Mina folded her arms across her chest. "I won't get upset."

Abby rolled her tongue across the roof of her mouth. She fiercely missed Lucas, who could tell her with a single look whether she should continue or not. Of course, she usually ignored his looks. But still, she missed them.

Sitting up taller, she risked speculating. "You're mad at life. At God or the Universe—whatever you believe in. You're mad that you're here right now, in this particular moment. You want to change the past, but you can't, so no matter what happens, you're unhappy."

Mina's face hardened into a scowl.

Abby winced. Maybe she had been too harsh. She hadn't meant to sound critical. She remembered what it was like to wake up every morning feeling like the world was *wrong*—full of shattered dreams and broken promises. She had hoped to convey to Mina that she understood—and even admired—her for persevering through such grief. Instead, she braced for Mina's denial.

"Okay."

Abby let out a tense breath, relieved and surprised that Mina wasn't about to close off or argue with her about her assessment. Most people did.

Mina moved toward the window, glancing at the thorny bare bushes as she twisted a strand of hair around her index finger. "That's pretty accurate, but not perfect. I'm not mad at God. I'm mad at myself."

She took a deep breath, staring into her reflection in the window. "When my mom was sick, I wasn't there for her the way I should have been."

She turned back to Abby, shaking her head, a pained expression flickering across her face. "I could have spent her last few days with her, but instead I was *too busy*."

"You had no way of knowing—"

Mina clenched her fists. "I *knew*. Maybe not the exact day, but I knew it was coming. I was a *nurse*. I knew the signs."

"You were a nurse?" Abby asked in surprise.

Mina nodded, her eyes downcast. "For almost two years. I knew what cancer could do to a person. And I just…I could have gotten on a plane and come home, but instead I stayed in Atlanta, pretending I cared about my damn job, when I was actually just too afraid to watch her die."

With a bitter laugh, she sank into a seat on the windowsill alcove, folding her arms across her dark sweater. "Joke's on me. I missed watching her live."

"That's understandable." Abby moved beside her, tentatively reaching out. Their fingers brushed, stirring dust along the windowsill. "Anger is often tangled in grief."

Mina let out a deep, shaky breath. "It wasn't just those final days. I should have moved back months before—I could have spent hundreds of dinners with her rather than watching stupid TV shows on my crappy laptop. God, I'm so selfish."

Abby let her fingers slip onto the back of Mina's hand. "You're not—"

"I am," Mina said sternly. She intertwined her fingers with Abby's and held on so tight, Abby nearly lost circulation. "My mother sacrificed so much for me, and you know how I repaid her? By abandoning her."

The radiator hummed to life, filling the silence as warm air churned around Abby's feet. She wanted to argue with Mina, to tell her that it's okay to be afraid of death, that it's not like she *caused* her mother to die. "You didn't—"

"I *did*," Mina insisted. "You know how often I spoke to her on the phone those last few months? Once a week. I knew she was dying and the only room I could make for her was thirty minutes *a week*."

Abby's heart hammered at Mina's nearness. She wanted to lean into her, to comfort her, but she knew this wasn't the time. "At least you talked to her."

Mina sucked in a breath. "Minimally. I used to think that by keeping my life in order—by sticking to a routine, following the rules, doing my job well—that things would work out for the best. I think part of me genuinely believed that if I was a good enough nurse, it would make Mom better."

Abby struggled to picture Mina in scrubs, tending fondly to sick or injured patients. "When did you quit nursing?"

"When I was fired." Mina sighed, her grip loosening to a pleasant sensation. "After Mom died, I just couldn't take it anymore. I couldn't stand to be anywhere near a hospital. I was stupid."

"That's not stupid," Abby reassured her. "It's a way of grieving. You must have loved her very much."

Mina nodded, faint tears glistening in her eyes.

Abby shifted her seat so she could meet Mina's gaze. "Then you didn't abandon her. Not in the way that counts most."

Mina leaned back, her jeans rustling like crisp autumn leaves. "I hope you're right."

Abby shut her eyes, needing to believe she was right more than Mina could possibly know. She untangled her fingers from Mina's to trace the bracelet on her left wrist. "My girlfriend—her name was Chelsea. Chelsea Summers. It's my fault she died."

Mina's eyebrows knitted together, clearly doubtful.

"The summer before college—" Abby paused to take a deep

breath as her heart pounded furiously against her rib cage. She kept her voice steady, afraid that if she let all her twisted emotions out, they would destroy what was left of her. "A new movie came out. Lucas and I had been dying to see it opening night. We got tickets to the midnight premiere. Chelsea wasn't into action films, but I begged her to come with us. She said she'd think about it. She never showed, so I figured she'd just stayed in. It wasn't until we saw her car flipped over at the intersection outside the parking lot that we realized what had happened. She'd tried to come, but she never made it."

Mina rested a hand on Abby's knee. The gesture gave Abby the strength to continue. "They said it was a drunk driver. Ran a red light."

Mina's hand moved to Abby's and she gave a reassuring squeeze. She started to pull her hand away, but Abby held it, savoring the soft warmth of her skin. They sat still in the window, surrounded by the steady ticking of a grandfather clock and the chill of deaths long past.

"It wasn't your fault," Mina whispered.

Abby shrugged. "Wasn't it? She wouldn't have been there if I hadn't insisted."

"You couldn't have known—"

"No, I couldn't have," Abby agreed, letting Mina's hand fall. "Sometimes, we blame ourselves for things that aren't our fault."

Mina shook her head. "And sometimes they are our fault. I made some bad decisions, there's no denying that."

Abby chewed her lip. Mina was being too hard on herself. "Everyone makes bad decisions sometimes. All we can do is make better ones from now on."

Mina frowned. "That's not going to do my mom any good."

"Maybe not, but it might do *you* some good," Abby insisted.

"And others—like Mrs. Kensington."

Mina's eyes narrowed. "What about Mrs. Kensington?"

"We can save her."

Mina leaned closer, the scent of coffee wafting off her lips. Sunlight gleamed off her dragon ring as she brushed a stray hair from Abby's cheek.

Abby's heart pounded frantically. She wanted to lean toward Mina—had the sudden urge to *kiss her*. But then she was thinking of Chelsea and how her warm eyes radiated in the sun and her lips felt so powerful and soft against her own, and she was pulling away from Mina as if she had seen Chelsea's ghost.

She cleared her throat. "What's on your schedule?"

Mina sighed, tucking her hair behind her ears as she slipped her folded schedule from her back pocket, and made a face. "Ugh, chairs? Again? Now she wants bows on them. You know what? I think I'm free."

Mina balled up the schedule and tossed it in the trash before flashing a smile at Abby that made Abby's heart flutter. "What should we do?"

Abby lifted the binoculars from around her neck and peered through them. They were alone. "Did you learn anything new from the Kensingtons?"

Mina shook her head. "Not much. I heard Lucas ask David about the veranda—he said he didn't know of any planned changes. But Mrs. Kensington got snappy when he asked her about it. She said it's her house, she doesn't need to be told how to run it."

The clouds parted and sunlight slipped through the window, washing the walls in a golden tint.

Abby jumped to her feet and paced, flinging shadows across the carpet. "Mr. Turner said he talked to Archie the other day, and Archie said Mrs. Kensington was going to be the death of him—maybe he meant it metaphorically, like the changes were going to ruin his masterpiece. Or maybe he meant literally—maybe the house is what's keeping him here and such substantial changes could sever his ties to the living."

"But if the house is what's keeping him here, how do we send him on?"

Her words sparked a thought in Abby that caused her to bounce with excitement. "That would be a problem, if what he loved most was the house."

Mina frowned. "Isn't that what he loved the most?"

"There's one thing he loved more."

"Than the house?" Mina raised an eyebrow. "What's that?"

The corner of Abby's lips lifted. "His *design* of the house."

Mina's eyes widened in understanding. "His blueprints."

"Exactly." Abby moved swiftly to the living room and began rifling through the drawers of a large desk. "It's got to be here somewhere. Are blueprints always blue?"

Mina leaned casually against the desk, trailing her fingers along the edge. "The house is a hundred years old. The designs are probably on display somewhere. Or in storage."

"Good thinking." Abby removed the flannel shirt that covered her tank top and tied it around her waist. "Let's start with the walls."

AFTER PAINSTAKINGLY INSPECTING all twelve rooms on the second floor, they moved on to the first floor, which proved rather difficult as they had to dodge frantic bridesmaids, a delivery man, and judgmental parents. By mid-afternoon, they had searched all the main rooms, except the kitchen.

Mina tapped the screen of her phone. "Two hours until rehearsal. I should go help Michelle."

"I'll find it," Abby assured her, stealing a mini quiche off a plate that was being delivered outside, to where Michelle and Annabelle were putting finishing touches on the decorations. Sandra's lips turned downward but her eyes twinkled. Abby took two more. "If it's not on display, you said it'd be in storage, right?"

Mina nodded. "Probably."

"So I should check the attic?" Abby asked, between mini quiches.

Again, Mina nodded. "Good luck. And…"

"And what?"

"Be careful," Mina whispered, concern clear in her voice.

Abby grinned, touched by the thought that she cared. "Always am."

As Mina retreated into the backyard, Abby lifted the binoculars to her eyes. To her alarm, Archie was seated at the desk in a study across the hall, going through the movements of drawing even though there was nothing in front of him. George sat across from him, reading a very real book, the pages fluttering as he turned them.

So *George* could interact with the real world. Perhaps he was protecting Archie. Or perhaps Archie and George were protecting each other.

Archie met her gaze with a look of disapproval.

She turned away abruptly. Hoping to avoid Archie's suspicions, she tiptoed past the empty living room and turned her attention to the frost-speckled windows that gave way to the garden, where her friends and family hung lanterns off leafless branches and poured sand over damp mulch beds. Abby's gaze lingered on Mina as she sprinkled paper rose petals down the aisle. Watching her do something so delicate and graceful felt like watching a tiger play with a ball of yarn. It filled Abby with a sense of wonder and pride, like she was special enough to witness something few ever had.

After nearly a minute, Abby realized she'd stopped to stare at Mina. Holding the binoculars to her eyes, she watched the ghost nanny straighten the flower petals. As Annabelle approached, the nanny moved a rock out of the way to keep Annabelle from tripping.

"The guardian angel," Abby whispered with a smile, recalling how Annabelle had mentioned a ghost—or what she had thought was her guardian angel—had saved her from a fallen tent. Could that have been the nanny? Abby found it likely.

The nanny glanced at Abby, a frown flickering across her face before she grinned and waved sheepishly. The thin straps of her floral dress looked even more out of place with her standing outdoors, her heeled sandals on top of a patch of slush.

Sweeping the halls with the binoculars, she saw no signs of Archie or another ghost. It was time to head to the attic.

To her surprise, the attic stairs were already down.

Abby hesitated. It was possible someone had opened it to bring down wedding decorations—or to bring up decor to make room for more wedding decorations. It was also possible that Archie *wanted* her to go there, and this was some sort of trap.

"Hello?" Abby called, hoping to hear a familiar voice reply.

There was no answer.

Cautiously, Abby started up the creaky stairs. They trembled under her steps, making her move faster despite her rising fear. Sunlight pierced a window with a cracked seal, seeping golden light across the finished though dusty floorboards.

As far as she could tell, the attic was vacant. At least of the living.

Sidestepping a box of candles, Abby moved deeper inside. She was able to stand at full height in all but the outermost edges of the room. Large boxes loomed in the corners, sagging and tearing with age. Someone had taken great care of this space before, but whoever had cared for the attic had long since perished or left it to wither away from neglect.

In the far corner, a floorboard creaked.

Abby stiffened. A faint sound reached her ears. Behind her, someone was breathing.

Ghosts didn't breathe.

"Who's there?" she demanded, her hands trembling around the binoculars. If she had to use them as a weapon, maybe she could knock someone out with them.

Someone popped up from behind a box.

Abby screamed.

The person hiding in the attic screamed.

Abby brought a hand to her heart. "Lucas?"

"Abby!" Lucas cried, removing his glasses to wipe the sweat from them. "You nearly gave me a heart attack!"

"You nearly gave *me* a heart attack!" Abby replied, sagging with relief and joy at seeing her friend. "What are you doing up here? I thought you left yesterday?"

Lucas shook his head. "I decided you were right. I couldn't live with myself if I gave up now and abandoned Michelle and my own parents, leaving them defenseless in a haunted house. I still can't believe you used my sketchbook as a shield! But then I thought about what would have happened if you *hadn't* used it and…well, I can replace a book. I can't replace you."

Abby rushed forward, flinging her arms around him in a hug. Lucas hugged her back before squeaking, "You're crushing my windpipe."

"Sorry." Abby stepped back. "When I saw your parents at breakfast and you weren't there, I thought you'd left."

"I was planning on it," Lucas admitted, tugging on his rolled-up sleeve. "But I thought better of it. I've been up here for hours, looking for something that could be keeping Archie here. Maybe his designs of the house."

Abby beamed. "Great minds think alike. I'm glad you stayed."

"Me too." Lucas adjusted his glasses. "I just hope some good came out of it."

"Have you found anything?"

"Not much. But there's a bunch of photo albums. Start on that side, I've done this one. I found an obituary for Archie—he was unmarried, but buried with George and Sarah—how about that?"

Abby started toward the far wall on the side Lucas had indicated. A kid's bike, sticky with cobwebs and dust, blocked her way. Abby flicked the tassels before moving it aside. It crashed to the floor, tossing the seat to her feet.

"Careful," Lucas warned, reaching for his water bottle. "A bunch of stuff up here is valuable. I've found like six laptops. They know they can trade those in, right?"

Abby moved, more carefully, toward the closest box. Toy cars, army figurines, and comic books peeked out through the plastic. The lid was labeled *David, 2004*.

She grinned. "Aww, it's David's kids' stuff. I wonder if he still plays with toy cars."

"He's thirty-two."

"So? We're twenty-six and we still play Nintendo."

"That's different."

"How?"

"It just is." Lucas clicked his tongue and pulled down another box, as if this conversation was beneath him.

Abby moved to an old wooden crate. Inside were papers, which looked promising. She flipped through them quickly. They were mostly financial documents and health records of those long dead.

"No way!" Lucas exclaimed.

Abby rushed to his side, excited and fearful of what damaging evidence he had discovered. "What?"

Lucas held up a comic book. "This is a *collector's edition!*"

Abby shook her head in amusement. "You could probably ask David if you could have it. I bet he's forgotten about it. You thinking of selling it?"

"No way! This is one of my favorites!" Flipping through the first few pages, Lucas made a dreamy sigh.

"Look now, read later," Abby called as she moved aside a stack of old golf clubs to get to the next box. A small tag dangled from the side of the suede bag. It read 'GK.' Abby sucked in a breath. She recalled the nanny saying George Kensington's tether was a set of golf clubs—probably the very ones she held in her hands.

This might be easier than she thought.

She could bring the golf clubs with her to confront Archie and George, and see who attacks first. They would definitely bring salt.

"I just don't get it," Lucas said, glancing out the window to where the rehearsal was beginning in the backyard. "He thinks he knows everything, like his plans are perfect and anyone who does something the slightest bit different is screwing up all his hard work. Like it was even *his* hard work in the first place."

"Who, George?"

"No." Lucas pried a lid off a box and threw it to the floor. "Dad. He thinks I have to be *exactly* like him or I'm a failure."

"You're not a failure."

"I know!" Lucas thrust his hand into the box, rummaging around without looking. "He acts like I'm a criminal because I got a *master's* degree. Most parents would celebrate that about their kids, but no. He made up his mind a long time ago about what he wanted for us."

Lucas yelped as he pulled out a skeleton hand. He jumped in alarm before realizing it was plastic. Glowering, he tossed it back in and stomped toward the window. "They wanted Michelle to marry a good Black man and be a teacher, but I guess marrying a rich white man and having a marketing career was a reasonable alternative. Meanwhile, following my calling and finding out what I really want in the world isn't good enough for them. I can't apply for a job without hearing Dad's voice in my ears, haunting me, telling me I need to go work in insurance, just like him."

Abby's mind raced. "What did you just say?"

"I can't apply for a job without hearing Dad's voice telling me I need to work in insurance."

"You said *haunting*."

Lucas shrugged. "Metaphorically."

Abby joined him at the window, bringing the binoculars to her eyes. The backyard was full of wedding guests and empty of ghosts. "Yeah, but you might be onto something."

"Onto what?"

Abby didn't respond, her attention focused on a rather unpleasant smell. "Do you smell something?"

Lucas sniffed. A look of confusion crossed his face. "Smoke?"

They turned to one another as a loud *crack* resounded through the attic.

Lucas grabbed Abby's arm, a look of panic in his dark eyes. The floor trembled. Abby turned toward the ladder, and found it folded up, the hatch shut.

"Oh no you didn't," Lucas muttered as he flung himself across the room and started trying to shove the hatch open.

It didn't budge.

"Don't tell me I got locked in *again!*" he cried, pulling and shoving against the hatch door.

Abby's eyes darted to a box behind him. Flames sprouted from an overturned lantern, blackening papers as they inched toward the cardboard edges. The scent of wax filled the air as the flames rose higher, showering the wooden beams with sparks.

Lucas let out a cry of alarm as the flames caught his attention. He ran forward and snatched away his precious comic book. Tucking the comic under his sweater, he pounded against the attic door so forcefully, Abby feared his knuckles would break.

But she didn't have time to worry about Lucas. She ran toward the flames, thinking quickly. If the exposed beams caught fire, the whole attic would be in flames within minutes, and they would be trapped inside. That fire needed to go out *now*.

She reached for Lucas's water bottle, but he was already unscrewing the lid. He ran forward, emptying the bottle onto the fire.

A few sprinkles trickled out, hissing against the flames.

"That's it?" Abby asked. "That thing is huge!"

"I was thirsty!" Lucas cried, shaking a few more drops onto the flaming box. At best, it slowed the spread by a few seconds.

Abby scanned the attic, looking for anything that could douse the flames for good. Beside George's golf clubs, an old mop rested against the wall. She grabbed the metal handle—it was dented and covered in cobwebs, but it would do. Clenching the handle in her fist, she shoved the opposite end into the fire, knocking the flaming lantern out of the box. Sparks shot out as it bounced against the floor, splattering wax in every direction. Abby covered her eyes, momentarily fearing that by moving it out of the box and onto the floor she had miscalculated and was only serving to speed up the inevitable process of setting the whole place on fire. But then the lantern hissed against their damp footprints, suffocating into smolders.

Abby let out a breath of relief.

"The box!" Lucas shouted.

Abby turned her attention back to the box as the flames fanned across the contents, blackening papers and melting plastic.

It's probably best if David *doesn't* still play with toy cars.

Lucas trembled, staring at the flames as if expecting them to rise up to the ceiling, consuming everything in sight. He pounded harder against the hatch door, screaming for help.

Abby dashed to the window. She pulled it open and reached out, sliding her hand across the cold windowsill. Though most of the ice had melted, several piles of slush lay at the corners. Cupping her hands, Abby grabbed as much of the frigid slush as she could and turned, dumping it on the fire.

After three trips, the fire died to a single burning paper, which Abby stomped on until there were only smoldering fragments.

Lucas peered out from behind his fingers. "Is it gone?"

Abby inched forward, hesitantly tapping the box with the end of the mop. After several seconds passed under diminishing smoke, she nodded.

Lucas's breath sounded loud in the now quiet attic. He slipped the comic from under his sweater and held it up, inspecting the cover. Finding it undamaged, he kissed the spine and placed it tenderly on the attic floor. "Thank you, Lord!"

"Seriously? You risk your life for a book?"

"I already lost my sketchbook; I'm not going to lose this baby in the same day."

"You *just* discovered it."

"And I'll never part with it." Lucas sank against an exposed beam, unbuttoning his collar. "I don't get it. If Archie is the bad guy, why would he risk burning the house? And if he isn't the bad guy, why would the real culprit want us dead if we aren't even onto them?"

Abby scrambled to the fallen pack of golf clubs and ran her hands along the bag. It was hot, coated in the scent of smoke, but undamaged. If this was what was keeping George here, George wasn't their culprit. And if Archie loved George, surely he wouldn't risk losing George's ghost.

Abby turned back to the lantern, frowning. Gingerly, she picked up the handle. It was still warm. "Did you bring this up here?"

Lucas shook his head. "Isn't that from Michelle's wedding?"

Abby nodded, musing aloud, "If the ghost brought this, then they must have carried it up three flights of stairs and into the attic. At that rate, why didn't they just stab us with that old hunting knife or shove us down the attic stairs?"

"Don't give them ideas!"

"My point is, I don't think they wanted to kill us."

"Then why did they lock us in an attic with an overturned candle?" Lucas snapped.

Abby frowned. Indeed. If the ghost didn't want to kill them, maybe they wanted to scare them or—*distract* them.

An image of Mrs. Kensington popped into Abby's mind as she rushed to the window and pried open the glass. Refreshing air cleared the smoke from her lungs. Despite the bitter chill, she breathed in deep, savoring each sweet breath.

Music drifted from the garden, soothing and melodic.

It grew louder as she leaned out the window and assessed the scene below. Michelle and David stood under the arch, her mother between them. Robert stood on one side, while Mina and Annabelle stood on the other. She was relieved to see Mrs. Kensington seated in the front row, beside Lucas's parents.

"I can't believe it!" Lucas cried, leaning over Abby's shoulder. "They started rehearsal without me!"

Abby kept her gaze on Mrs. Kensington. If the lantern had been a distraction, that meant the old woman was in danger— or would be, as soon as the ghost's strength returned. She reached for the binoculars—to her horror, they were nowhere to be found.

Neither was the salt gun.

After rummaging through several boxes and retracing her steps, she came to the conclusion that they were gone.

She turned back to the window in frustration.

"Did you get Mina's number?" Lucas asked.

Abby stiffened at the abrupt change of subject, surprised by a fluttering sensation in her chest at the thought of getting Mina's number. "Wouldn't you like to know."

"If we have to call someone to get us out of here, I'd rather not call my sister in the middle of her wedding rehearsal.'"

Abby sighed, the fluttery sensation sinking to one of regret. She hadn't asked for Mina's number. She had started to, but the moment she had opened her mouth, her lungs ached with a foreboding sense that this was too forward, too much of a commitment. She wasn't *ready* for a relationship. She wasn't sure she was even ready for a date.

Abby delayed her response by scanning the scene below, looking for subtle signs of interference. The ribbon on Mrs. Kensington's chair fluttered while she exchanged a smug gaze with Sandra across the aisle. Abby's mom directed Annabelle and Mina to move closer to the altar, while David whispered something in Michelle's ear that made her giggle.

Seconds passed. Just when she was hoping she could be wrong, she saw it.

A decorative torch jerked out of place. It hovered over the grass, drifting toward the aisle, smoke slithering from the flame like a deadly snake.

"Look out!" Abby cried.

Her voice was lost in the wind.

Slipping out her phone, she texted her mom 'TORCH!' and turned back to the window, where her mother continued to direct the bridesmaids, showing no indication of checking her phone. Abby groaned. Of course she would choose *now* to silence it. It was usually glued to her palm.

The torch drifted closer to the aisle, and the unsuspecting Mrs. Kensington.

"What's going on?" Lucas asked. "What's wrong?"

Abby shook her head, stumbling back as she scanned the attic for something—anything—that could stop a ghost. Or fire. Preferably both.

Finding nothing, she searched for a ladder. If she could get down there, she could put the fire out while it was still small.

There wasn't one, but as her gaze brushed the rusty spokes of the bike, an idea occurred to her. It was either ingenious or terrible.

She didn't have time to ponder which.

Abby picked up a helmet, flicked a dead spider out of it, and shoved it onto her head.

"What are you doing?" Lucas asked, clearly concerned.

Abby snapped the helmet in place and reached for the bike, guiding it toward the open window.

Lucas's eyes bulged. "Tell me you're not planning to ride that on the roof. You can't. The tire's flat. And it's a roof!"

"I don't need the bike," Abby said, wriggling the handle until it came apart. She held it up, grinning. "Just this."

With that, she jumped out the window.

Chapter
Twenty-One

A bby landed on the roof, heart pounding. She moved to the edge—it was a steep drop, three stories down to the stone patio. Abby tugged hard on the nearest row of string lights. They groaned, but held, thanks to whoever had nailed them to the roof. Abby hoped they could hold her entire body weight. If not, she would be in for a lot of broken bones.

Before she could take another step, the aisle went up in flames.

It happened in mere seconds. The torch devoured paper rose petals, turning them to ash. Flames spread down the aisle, licking the chairs with an orange glow. Shouts broke out as the wedding party scrambled out of the path of destruction.

Abby's heart burned with fear as the flames reached Mina's boots. She shouted her name in warning. Mina was already running. She grabbed Michelle, who stood petrified, mouth agape as her precious work went up in flames. Mina got her moving, pulling her deeper into the backyard.

Annabelle stumbled onto the bench, her face drained of color as she stared at the flames.

Abby's hands trembled around the cold metal of the bike's handlebar. She inched toward the edge of the roof, wishing she had her binoculars—or better yet, a hose. Peering over the edge, she made the mistake of looking straight down into the tangle of bushes below. Her stomach lurched. The sharp scent of burning foliage and billowing smoke were the only things between her and a thirty-foot drop.

As the crackling of flames grew louder, heat radiated toward her. She raised her gaze to the far side of the garden, where David joined Mina and Michelle on the garden wall. Sandra joined them a second later, shouting for Mrs. Kensington. Rebecca dashed deeper into the backyard, pulling her phone from her pocket.

Better late than never, Abby supposed.

Mrs. Kensington alone remained rooted to her chair in the front, struggling against her knotted shawl.

David called out to her.

When it became apparent she was stuck, Robert hurried toward her. He was halfway toward the flames when he toppled over as if tripped, falling face-first to the earth inches from the burning aisle. He rolled away, coughing in a cloud of smoke.

Sandra raced forward next, but Mina held her back. She zipped up her leather jacket, a determined look on her face, as if she was preparing to run into the flames.

Abby could get there faster.

At least, she hoped she could.

Abby placed the handlebar over the string lights and took a deep breath. It was just like the zip line she used to use behind her grandparents' house. Or that's what she told herself. As the thin wire trembled beneath her hand, she knew that wasn't exactly true. This wasn't some reinforced cable designed to carry her safely to the ground. There was a decent chance she'd fall.

But there was also a chance she could save Mrs. Kensington and vanquish this ghost, once and for all.

She jumped.

Keeping both hands on the broken handlebar, she glided down the makeshift zip line toward the blazing backyard. Wind whipped past her, stirring a rush of adrenaline through her veins. The wire sagged and swayed, yanking her arms. Her muscles ached as she tightened her grip, her palms stinging. Miraculously, the wire held.

Mrs. Kensington was not so lucky. Flames pooled around her chair, forming a thick blaze. Abby suspected the ghost had coated it in oil or kerosene. A bone-chilling cry broke through the fire's roar.

Abby's stomach lurched, both from the shaky lights holding her and pure dread. She was too close to fail now. She let go of the zip line, falling the remaining few yards to the grass.

She landed on her hands and knees, less than a yard from Mrs. Kensington. Smoke filled her vision as sweat broke across her skin. Across the yard, she recognized the dark coils of a hose, but there wasn't any time. Mrs. Kensington was already burning.

Abby lunged toward the old woman and pulled her—chair and all—out of the flames.

Sandra hurried to Abby's side, a pocket knife in hand. She sliced through Mrs. Kensington's shawl as Mina grabbed the old woman and held her close, rolling her over the damp grass until the flames on her clothes went out.

Abby's vision grew faint. Her lungs ached, the scent of smoke so thick she could taste it.

Taking deep breaths, she moved away from the others and surveyed the backyard. The place was a mess. Abby's freshly painted chairs were cracked and charred. Decorations hung askew. Ash clung to Mina's skin, her makeup distorted by sweat.

A hissing filled the clearing. Abby turned around to see the flames doused in a thick white substance. Rebecca stood behind them, a fire extinguisher in her hands.

Abby collapsed on brittle grass, her back pressed against the rock wall. Of course her mother had gone for the fire extinguisher. Why hadn't she thought of that?

For once, Mrs. Kensington didn't protest as the paramedics arrived and helped her into the back of the ambulance. Robert and Sandra escorted her, while David comforted a weeping Michelle.

Amidst the chaos that followed, both Mina and her mother found the time to tell Abby her rescue attempt was stupid.

"Breaking your bones is the worst thing you could do at a time like this," Rebecca insisted, her thick heels clanking against the stone porch. If it weren't for the way her hand trembled as she patted the back of her hair and the slight widening of her eyes, Abby would have thought her mother was angry. But she had seen Rebecca angry enough to know that this was something else—this was fear.

"I'm fine, Mom. I didn't—" Abby's protest was cut short as Mina reached toward the lights she had used as her zip line. They sagged lower than the others. Mina yanked on the wire. It snapped, falling free from the roof.

Abby winced as the lights hit the ground with a sickening crunch. That could have been her, moments ago.

"You're lucky you aren't dead," Rebecca snapped, before storming off toward the ambulance. "Let's hope Mrs. Kensington is forgiving enough she doesn't hold us accountable for the damages."

"She's right." Mina stepped forward to squeeze Abby's shoulder. "I'm glad you're lucky. Don't do that again."

With a sad smile, she turned and hurried back to Michelle's side, leaving Abby alone with the smoky breeze.

IT WAS NEARLY half an hour before Abby remembered Lucas was still trapped in the attic and she was able to rope Mina into helping free the jammed attic door. The ghost had used her binoculars to jam it. Abby took personal offense to that, although she was relieved to be reunited with them again.

The salt gun lay on the floor, as if it had been tossed aside. A small crack ran down the outside. She picked it up and pulled the trigger, relieved to see salt sprinkle the floor.

Michelle's sobs permeated the walls, sinking their spirits like a mermaid drowning sailors at sea. Once Lucas stopped shaking, Abby helped him toward a roaring fire, and Annabelle brought them large mugs of hot chocolate.

As Abby leaned against the couch, dry air scraped her nose and an unsettling chill froze her stomach. This second chill had nothing to do with the air and everything to do with the knowledge that Mrs. Kensington had come closer than ever to death.

Mina poured herself an amber ale from the bar. She sipped it slowly, lips pressing together between each gulp. Dirt clung to her jeans, and her sweater now bore a dark smudge of mascara on the shoulder where Michelle had been crying.

"How's she doing?" Lucas asked.

Mina winced as Michelle let out a rather shrill sob. She took another sip of her drink. "She's coping."

With Mrs. Kensington in the hospital, the wedding would likely be postponed. Abby wondered if it would happen at all.

Mina's footsteps echoed through the quiet house as she paced, her shadow raging across the hardwood. Annabelle moved closer to the radiator, shivering in her pale blue cardigan. Lucas cupped his mug between his hands, as if it were a shield, his gaze darting from corner to corner.

Abby hated seeing her friends look so frightened and unnerved. She turned the binoculars over in her hands. Mrs. Kensington may be safe at the hospital for the time being, but there was still a murderous spirit among them and it wasn't above hurting them all to get to Mrs. Kensington.

Abby chewed her nails. She doubted George would have risked his golf clubs burning, and Archie wouldn't either.

The only ghost Abby had seen interact with anything—besides George, Archie, and Mr. Turner—was the nanny. But what motive could she have?

Rebecca stormed in through the front door, an accusatory glare in Abby's direction. "Abigail Rachel Spector, if I find out you were behind any of this, you will never hear the end of it."

Abby leaned back against the couch with a groan. She didn't have time to worry about her mother when there was a killer at large. But she couldn't resist replying, "How could you possibly think this is *my* fault?"

"Mrs. Kensington goes up in flames and you come swooping down like a hero? What am I supposed to think?"

"Gee, I don't know. Is it really that hard for you to believe that I helped someone in danger?"

"When you're usually the one putting people in danger, yes, it is."

"When have I ever put anyone in danger?"

"Last time Lucas came to visit, you got him bike-riding down that mountain."

"He was fine!"

"He pulled a muscle," Rebecca said. Her heels clicked against the polished floor as she continued, "And you're lucky it wasn't worse. When you made that so-called 'treehouse,' Chelsea twisted her—"

"Don't you *dare* talk about Chelsea!" Abby replied. She wished she could rewind time and leave the room before her mother ever stepped foot in it. But she was too deep into arguing to give up now, so she continued, "Stop criticizing my life! If you care about me, then why don't you *trust* me?"

Rebecca blinked. She pursed her lips before parting her mouth to speak.

Annabelle burst into tears.

"I'm sorry." Annabelle sobbed. "This is all my fault."

Abby and Mina exchanged glances of confusion.

"How is this your fault?" Mina asked.

Annabelle wiped at her eyes. "The curse."

"Honey, there's no such thing as—" Rebecca began.

"What curse?" Abby said, shooting an angry glance at her mother.

"Robert and I are getting a divorce," Annabelle whispered, as if she was confessing some great evil.

Abby wasn't surprised. Mina had mentioned it before, and Annabelle and Robert seemed distant. It was understandable they would want to go their separate ways.

"I'm so sorry," Lucas said gently. "But that doesn't make any of this your fault."

"It does." Annabelle's shoulders heaved with her sobs. "Every member of the Kensington family has gotten married here since it was built. Now that we're about to break that, what if the house is taking vengeance on us?"

Abby scratched her head. The thought of a curse on top of ghosts was too ridiculous to consider, but Annabelle might be onto something. Someone didn't want the wedding to happen, or they didn't want Mrs. Kensington to attend.

Abby thought back to her conversation with Mr. Turner. He had said Annabelle's mother was the most likely culprit, but in all their searching, they had never once come across the ghost of Annabelle's mother.

"Do you have a picture of your mother?" Abby asked as her muddled suspicions started to come together.

Lucas shot her a puzzled glance.

Annabelle's eyes widened in surprise, but she gracefully slipped her phone from her purse. She scrolled for a minute, before turning the screen so Abby could see. On the screen, a thin blonde woman in a bright red dress and with ruby earrings grinned mischievously. Chills spread down Abby's neck. She recognized that face.

"Your mother didn't happen to have a twin, did she?"

Annabelle shook her head. "No."

"What about a near-identical sister?"

Lucas elbowed Abby, reaching for the phone.

"She was an only child," Annabelle confirmed.

Lucas gasped. "She's the nanny!"

Abby picked up the binoculars and scanned the room. Thankfully, the nanny was not in sight. Only Mary, the youngest ghost, was with them. She was warming her hands by the fire. Abby turned on the walkie-talkie.

"Mary," she said slowly. "Do you know this woman?"

"Who on earth are you talking to?" Rebecca asked.

Abby shushed her as she held up Annabelle's phone.

Mary took one look at the picture and nodded, grinning.

"Who is she?" Abby asked.

"Nan'y," the girl replied.

Rebecca jumped, startled by the response.

Lucas frowned. "I don't get it. Why is she mistaking Annabelle's mother for their nanny?"

"She's not saying nanny," Annabelle said softly. "My mother's name is 'Nancy.'"

Mary nodded. "Nancy," she said again, slower so everyone caught the 'c.'

The chills spread deeper down Abby's spine. Annabelle's mother had been haunting them from the beginning, but they hadn't thought to question her because they hadn't realized who she was. Abby tried to recall everything she had heard about Nancy. She hadn't gotten along with the Kensingtons. Mrs. Kensington accused her of stealing. Mr. Turner had said she was after the house. She had always wanted to marry into the Kensington family. Now that her daughter was on the verge of divorce, she would do anything to keep the house in her family—even kill.

Chapter
Twenty-Two

Abby loved acting, but she was used to acting for entertainment, not to prevent a murder. Her stomach churned as she stepped into the living room. She and Lucas nodded at one another, moving to opposite sides of the room.

"The blueprints must be here somewhere," Abby said, trying to keep her voice calm. In the light of the roaring fire, she ruffled through some bridal magazines, pretending to continue their search for the house's blueprints. If Nancy was indeed the murderer, it was best to let her think they were still after Archie.

The front door opened.

Robert hurried inside.

Abby's stomach knotted. This wasn't part of the plan. Annabelle greeted him tentatively, like a cat checking out a new plant. She touched his arm and immediately took her hand back as he removed his jacket, revealing a row of pale bandages along his right arm.

"I swear, this place hates me." He tossed his coat to Annabelle and headed toward the bar. "The next time we're back here, I expect a for-sale sign out front."

The hair on the back of Abby's neck prickled at his words. She tensed, preparing for the ghost of Annabelle's mother to attack, but no attack came.

Had they gotten it wrong? They would know soon enough.

"Why is it so dark?" Robert asked, reaching for the light switch.

Annabelle grabbed his arm. "Michelle has a migraine," she whispered. It was good thinking.

For a moment, Abby thought Robert was going to go through with turning the lights on anyway, but he sighed and removed his shoes in the dark.

As Annabelle hung Robert's coat on the brass coat rack, the front door opened again.

A cold gust of wind shook the candles, sending shadows scuttering across the floor like spiders.

David stood on the front porch, a grim expression on his features. Beside him, Mrs. Kensington stood in her dark fur-lined coat, complete with a black hat that spilled lace over her face. Her gloved hands gripped a wooden cane.

"Let me help you to the couch," David offered, extending his arm.

Mrs. Kensington shook her head, grunting as she started forward, her cane clacking against the wood as she moved.

The binoculars felt warm against Abby's chest. She reached for them, preparing to scan the room, but thought better of it. The less attention she drew from the ghosts at this point, the better. It was all about surprise.

Mrs. Kensington's breath became more and more labored as

she inched across the entry hall.

Abby moved away from the coffee table, giving David space as he helped Mrs. Kensington into a seated position on the couch.

Marie Antoinette started toward them, then stopped, hesitantly, making a pained meow.

"She'll be okay," Abby whispered, thinking quickly. They'd come too far for the cat to give them away. She knelt down beside Marie Antoinette and added, "She won't smell like the hospital forever."

Marie Antoinette gave her a confused look as Michelle rushed in from the kitchen. She looked like she would collapse at any moment. She ran toward David and stopped cold as she saw Mrs. Kensington's limp figure, on the couch.

Through the lace, Abby noticed an oxygen mask pressed over Mrs. Kensington's lips.

"What's this?" Robert asked, frozen by the bar, blinking at his brother and mother as if they were strangers.

David helped Mrs. Kensington lay down, and covered all but her face with a blanket. Her frail raspy breaths were so loud and pained, Abby could hear them from yards away.

Robert drained his glass and ran his hand through his hair. "I don't get it. She was fine when we left. What the hell happened?"

"She collapsed in the parking lot." David said the lines Abby had fed him. She had to give him credit—he was a decent actor. "The doctors said it's just the shock of everything she's been through at her age. As long as she keeps the mask on overnight, she should be fine in the morning."

"Jesus." Robert poured himself another drink.

"How awful—" Michelle half-collapsed against Lucas. He made a muffled squeaking sound in response. Abby flashed him a look of sympathy. She had wanted to fill Michelle in on their plan, but there hadn't been enough time.

The stairs creaked as David retreated to the second floor.

Abby moved to the corner of the room where her supplies gleamed on the bookshelf. Lucas was supposed to be at Annabelle's side, but he was still caught up with Michelle, and Robert wasn't supposed to be here at all.

"There's leftover dinner in the kitchen," Abby said, looking directly at Robert.

He rubbed his hand over his eyes, his face softened by the gentle glow of the Christmas tree lights. "I'm too tired to eat."

"Then why don't you go to bed?" Abby asked, moving toward him.

Abby stopped mid-step as the woman on the couch began removing her oxygen mask.

That wasn't part of the plan.

Abby looked closer, squinting against the dim firelight. What was she doing? Abby studied the figure, who lay still against the couch, gloved hands folded across her chest. *She* wasn't removing her mask—the mask was removing itself.

Or rather, a ghost was removing it.

Abby reached for the binoculars, but before she had lifted them to her face, a cry of alarm rang through the room.

Michelle ran forward, screaming as she attempted to return the oxygen mask to Mrs. Kensington's mouth. She was met with strong resistance, shoved back as if someone had kicked her in the shin.

"What the—?" Michelle cried as the oxygen mask fell to

the floor and skidded under the table, kicked by an invisible shoe. Understanding flashed across her face. "Holy frick, it's a ghost!"

Michelle lunged for the mask. This time, she stumbled and fell as the ghost shoved her sideways.

She lunged for the mask once more as Mrs. Kensington bolted upright.

Abby saw the shock play across Michelle's face.

The woman sitting on the couch in Mrs. Kensington's clothes was *definitely not* Mrs. Kensington. Firelight flickered over her youthful dark features, her black hair peeking out from the edges of a gray wig.

Michelle's mouth fell open. "*Mina?*"

Abby sucked in a breath as Mina ripped off her wig. She had expected the charade to last longer, to catch the ghost in the act of attempted murder—she hadn't expected Michelle to intervene. Of course, she had to choose *now*—the most inconvenient time of all—to believe.

"What the hell is going on?" Robert asked, glancing around the room in confusion. "Where's Mom?"

There was no time to answer. Abby peered through the binoculars. Sure enough, the nanny—Nancy—stood over Mina, her face twisted with confusion and horror.

Abby wasted no time in handing the binoculars to Annabelle, whose fingers shook as she raised them to her eyes.

Annabelle took a few wobbly steps forward, stopping behind the couch, her usually soft features hardened into a pained expression. "Mother?"

Static crackled from the base of the stairs. Abby ran forward and picked up the walkie-talkie. She turned the volume up as a scratchy voice said wearily, "Annabelle."

"So it's true?" Annabelle's fists shook. "All this time, *you've* been trying to kill Mrs. Kensington?"

Abby held her breath. This was the moment of truth.

"Oh, honey, I was just helping her," the voice crackled. "Fixing her mask."

"I always knew you loved this house." Annabelle's voice trembled, growing in volume. She stepped deeper into the living room until she was practically at Michelle's feet. "I just didn't realize you loved it more than me."

"That's not true." Nancy's voice cracked through the walkie-talkie, echoing off the staircase. "I'm doing this for you, for your future."

"Stop lying to yourself," Annabelle shouted. For someone so small and quiet, she had a lot of fight in her. Abby made a mental note never to get on her bad side. "All this time I thought you were gone, you've been here with me. And instead of trying to speak with me and make amends, you tried to kill someone—for what? For some stupid dream you had for me when you were alive."

She lowered the binoculars long enough to wipe tears from her eyes.

"Annabelle, honey—"

"Goodbye, Mom." Annabelle clenched her necklace and pulled down, stressing the clasp.

Her necklace was the one thing Abby could think of that could be keeping Nancy here, considering Annabelle claimed it was the only thing she had with her that had belonged to her mother, and she had been wearing it when she was at the florist. It couldn't have been the car, as Nancy had wanted them to believe, for Michelle had driven it miles away while Nancy had remained at the florist.

Before the clasp could break, a terrible scream hurled through the walkie-talkie. Abby trembled as it rose to the rafters.

With a cry, Annabelle lurched backward, tumbling against the wall. The binoculars slipped through her fingers and clattered to the floor, skidding down the hall.

Robert ducked under the stairs, shouting 'Jesus!' as he covered his head with his hands.

Beside him, Lucas fumbled with the salt gun. If she'd known it would take him this long to position it, she'd have done it herself.

Adrenaline pounding through her veins, Abby ran forward, and snatched the fallen binoculars before someone stepped on them—or worse.

The room took on the monochrome look as she raised them to her eyes, the golden trim fading to a washed gray. Across the couch, Nancy hovered over Annabelle, her floral dress fanning out around her, fury reddening her face.

"You have no idea what you're throwing away!" Nancy's words crackled through the walkie-talkie.

Abby watched in horror as the ghost clasped her hands around Annabelle's neck. Annabelle made an awful choking sound as she clawed furiously at the air.

Abby winced, remembering what it felt like to be strangled. How could someone do that to their own daughter? She ripped open a packet of salt and hurled it at the ghost. It pelted Nancy like acid rain, sizzling through her.

Screaming in agony, Nancy dropped Annabelle and threw herself at Abby.

"You stupid girl!" Nancy's voice crackled over Annabelle's raspy gasps. "Stay out of this!"

Abby ignored her, running away from Annabelle, hoping

to distract Nancy long enough for Annabelle to unclasp her necklace.

Staying away from the salt that glistened off the polished floorboards, Nancy retreated to the corner of the room, glaring. The misty holes in her appearance began to mend themselves, making her more solid. She reached for a cord, but her hands passed through it. Scowling, she swooped back and tried again. Abby's gaze followed the cord to a lamp that rested on an end table inches from Annabelle.

"The lamp!" she shouted, pointing as it teetered.

Nancy finally grew solid enough to pull the cord and the lamp toppled over.

Robert shoved Annabelle out of the way as it crashed toward her. Mina dashed forward, catching the lamp before it shattered.

Lucas *finally* fired the salt gun. It spewed salt, thrashing through Nancy until she dispersed into a patchy mess like butter on a skillet. Her tattered remains retreated to a far corner of the ceiling, over the stairs. Abby winced just looking at her.

But when the ghost's voice came through the walkie-talkie, it was as clear and strong as ever. "You should have stayed out of this! This place would be yours!"

Annabelle pried the necklace from around her neck. The ruby glistened in her trembling fingers before she tossed it into the fire.

Howling, Nancy's remains swooped across the room. She charged through the couch and coffee table as if they were shadows. Hovering over the fire, she reached for the necklace, but it slipped through her hands. She tried again, her movements frantic and desperate. When her second attempt failed, she reached for the fire poker, but her hands wouldn't close around the metal—they slipped right through, like fingers through smoke.

The salt had made her weak. How long would that last? Long enough, she hoped.

"No matter." Nancy composed herself into a patchy form that resembled her former ghostly state, reminding Abby of mist seeping through a burned photograph. "It'll take more than this pathetic fire to destroy a ruby. You don't have the heat to even damage it."

Abby glanced at the fire, waiting for the ruby to burn.

Lucas stared at Abby. "Seriously? *This* was your plan?"

Abby bit her lip. She had worked it out. The ruby *had* to be what Nancy's spirit was tied to, and that fire would destroy it. Right? She could swear she saw a fire destroy a gem before, in a movie once. "It worked in *The Lord of the Rings*."

Lucas grasped his head, hands digging into his hair. "That wasn't a fire, that was a volcano!"

Abby gestured to the fire. "Well this is the closest thing we had."

Lucas's voice hitched. "You threw a *ruby* into a fireplace and expected it to burn?"

Abby glanced back at the fire, hoping to see at least a subtle change in the stone. There wasn't one. "Do you have a better idea?"

"Throw it in the ocean! Drop it off in a desert! Take it to a jeweler far away from—"

His words were cut short with a cry as Nancy grabbed the fire poker and knocked the salt gun from Lucas's hand. Lucas dropped to the floor, covering his head as the gun flew across the room and slammed against the window. Shattered glass cascaded over the Christmas tree.

Everyone screamed. Everyone except Mina. She was too busy wrapping her hands around the fire poker and prying it from the ghost.

"What now?" Annabelle whispered, ducking behind the couch between Abby and Lucas.

Abby pressed her back to the couch, thinking furiously. Lucas's plans were sounding better by the second. Someone could make a run for the salt gun, while someone else snatched the ruby, and they could all run out as quickly as possible. But Nancy would follow whoever had the ruby. She could slam on the brakes, or move the wheel, or crash the car if she wanted. There had to be another way to stop her.

"What's wrong with you?" Mina shouted as the sound of clanking metal filled the living room.

Abby glanced up to see Mina locked in something like a sword fight with the ghost. Mina used the fire poker to fend off an attack from Nancy, who was attempting to slam metal tongs against Mina's head.

"I would give anything to see my mother again," Mina continued, parrying the attack. "Here, you have a chance to reunite with your daughter, and you're using it to *fight* her?"

"I know what's best," Nancy countered in a cold harsh tone.

Lucas reached into his pockets and cried triumphantly, "I have a saltwater taffy!"

Abby shut her eyes. If there was enough salt in that to slow the ghost down, it could buy them enough time to get the gun.

Mina gave a shout of pain as the tongs slammed into her arm. She jumped back, dangerously close to the fire.

"How is this happening?" Annabelle sobbed, tears streaming down her face. "She's not like this. She *wasn't* like this."

Mina's words echoed in Abby's mind. She glanced at Annabelle and felt a burst of hope. "Do you think you could talk to her?"

Annabelle took a deep shuddering breath, massaging her elbow. "And say what?"

Abby remembered what Glen had said. "Sometimes a ghost's unfinished business isn't an object, but a person. Maybe she wasn't following the necklace around—maybe she was following *you*."

Mina cried out again. Lucas muttered a prayer, kissed the saltwater taffy, and chucked it at the ghost. The clanking stopped.

Abby knew they didn't have much time. She clenched the binoculars at her side and turned to Annabelle. "She cares about you. In some twisted way, she thinks she's doing all this for you."

Firelight glistened off Annabelle's tear-filled eyes. "Why?"

"I don't know," Abby admitted. But one thing she did know about families was that a lot of the drama could be solved if people would just sit down and listen to each other. Abby handed her the binoculars. "Why don't you ask her?"

Annabelle took a deep breath and stood on trembling legs.

"Mother," Annabelle said in a manner that sounded like a warning.

"Annabelle," her mother replied with a tone of disapproval.

"*Mother*," Annabelle said again, harsher this time. "Why are you doing this?"

"For you, of course." Nancy's voice echoed around the dim living room. "For your future."

Abby stood beside Annabelle, surveying the room. While she couldn't see Nancy, she assumed the ghost was starting to recover from being hit by a piece of salt candy.

Annabelle's hands shook, but her voice was steady as she scolded, "No. You've spent your whole life claiming to look out for me, but you've been looking out for *yourself*."

"Don't be ridiculous. I gave you the perfect life."

"There's no such thing! This so-called 'perfect' life—" Annabelle gestured to the trashed living room. "This is what *you* wanted, not what *I* wanted. I'm miserable. I'm leaving it, Mom. I'm done trying to be the perfect daughter. It would never have made either of us happy anyway."

Nancy's voice broke. "All I wanted was for you to be happy."

Annabelle took a deep shaky breath. "And I am. Or at least, I will be. It's time you move on and trust that I'll be okay, house or no house."

Annabelle's hair fluttered back from her face. For an instant, Abby could see the faintest outline of Nancy embracing Annabelle. Gray light surrounded them, faint and dull like moonlight pulsing against a sea.

Just as quickly, it was gone.

Static filled the walkie-talkie.

Annabelle lowered the binoculars, her eyes brimming with tears.

"Is she gone?" Abby asked.

Annabelle sobbed in response, sinking to her knees. Robert tentatively moved to her side, placing a comforting hand on her shoulder.

Michelle clutched the roots of her hair, her manicured nails trembling against her scalp. "What the hell just happened?"

"Annabelle put her mother's spirit to rest," Abby explained. "Mrs. Kensington is safe to return home."

Mina groaned, examining an abrasion on her arm.

Abby hurried to her side. "Are you alright?"

Mina leaned against the couch. "I've been through worse. That ghost was better than a lot of actors. You won't believe how many black eyes I've gotten from some pretty boys trying to stage fight."

"But—but—" Michelle's eyes darted around the disheveled room. "All this time, this place was really *haunted?*"

"Technically, it still is," Lucas said, stepping carefully around the broken glass. He rested the salt gun on the table and leaned against the couch, rolling up his sleeves.

Michelle ran forward, pulling Lucas into a tight hug that caused him to let out an *oof* of surprise.

When she stepped back, relief poured through her expression. "You mean, all this time, when I thought you were just playing stupid games, you were risking your life for me?"

Lucas shook his head. Abby imagined he had seen it more as protecting his own life. He was too humble.

"Exactly!" Abby came to Lucas's rescue, clapping him on the shoulder. "He did all this for you. That's a pretty good brother, don't you think?"

Lucas scuffed his socked foot against the floor before shrugging sheepishly. "I did want you to be happy."

Michelle made a sound that Abby thought was better suited toward adorable kittens than Lucas, before she hugged him again. She stepped away, beaming, then saw the salt gun. Her eyes narrowed. "What's this you said about the house *still* being haunted?"

Lucas tugged on the end of his sleeves. "Don't worry about it."

"The rest are friendly ghosts," Abby added.

Michelle opened her mouth, her brow furrowed. Before she could say anything else, David descended the stairs. In his dark button-down shirt and slimming dress pants, he looked ever the role of a charming groom.

Michelle dabbed at her smeared makeup and gave him a hesitant look, as if uncertain what to do now that their wedding had been derailed by a hostile ghost. Abby didn't blame her. She doubted this scenario was listed in any etiquette book.

David hurried forward and took Michelle in his arms. She buried her face against his chest, her shoulders sagging in relief.

When they broke apart, David cleared his throat and said, "We should get some sleep. I believe we have a wedding to attend tomorrow."

Michelle beamed like she had never been happier.

Chapter
Twenty-Three

Michelle and David's wedding was beautiful, despite the faint scent of smoke, and blackened chair legs. A sandy aisle led them to the gazebo, where they exchanged vows under the glow of early sunset. The sand was a nice touch, enhancing the beach theme while hiding the ashes of charred petals.

Burrowing deeper in her borrowed peacoat, Abby could almost imagine they were at the beach—one of those rocky northeastern shorelines where wind bellowed off the sea. She had a harder time imagining the sun-kissed shorelines that Michelle had been going for, but the ceremony was lovely nonetheless.

Mrs. Kensington sat near the dance floor, Marie Antoinette purring in her arms, while she toasted the happy couple. The back of her hand was bandaged, but—according to Michelle—the burns were mild and should heal in a few weeks. Sandra strolled to her side, planting a kiss on her cheek as she handed her a glass of champagne.

Even though the ghost of Annabelle's mother had been put to rest, Abby peeked through the binoculars now and again, just to make sure everything was in order. When David walked down the aisle, Mr. Turner had appeared by the gazebo, smiling apprasingly. The Gardners had also attended the ceremony, holding each other as the couple exchanged vows.

Archie and George now stood on the back porch, side by side. They had watched the ceremony with Sarah, who was now across the yard, exchanging whispers with Mrs. Gardner while pointing from guest to guest. Even without the walkie-talkie, Abby could tell she was criticizing fashion choices. Archie met Abby's eyes and raised a ghostly drink as if toasting, then turned to head inside with George. The curtains closed behind them.

"I gotta hand it to Michelle—" Lucas said between bites of bruschetta "—she knows how to plan a party."

Abby nodded in agreement, watching the ghost kids play limbo with the cake, which hung like a chandelier from a suspended stand. The ghost dog circled them, tail wagging. She slipped the binoculars into her coat and let her eyes adjust to the world of dangling seashells and dancing couples.

Lucas bobbed his head in time to the jazz music that floated through the clearing. In his white button-down shirt and purple vest, he looked every bit the man of honor—a title Michelle had thrown upon him last minute. The purple was a slightly different shade than the bridesmaid dresses, but it looked good on him and—with everything that had happened the previous day—matching garments were the least of Michelle's concerns.

"I can't believe a ghost almost ruined it. And the ghost of *Annabelle's* mother at that—I don't know how we missed her."

"We didn't pay enough attention," Abby said, annoyed with herself. Nancy had been one of the first suspects they had interviewed, only she hadn't thought to even take down her name.

"That was a good catch, asking Annabelle for a picture. But how did you know she was the one after Mrs. Kensington? She had no motive."

"She did," Abby countered, slipping off her peacoat. The outdoor heaters were warm enough; she didn't need it over the black dress she had borrowed from her mother. "Once we realized who she was, that is. If Mrs. Kensington died, Annabelle was first in line to inherit the house. But that would change when she and Robert went through with their divorce. Nancy had a short window to kill Mrs. Kensington before the divorce would be finalized and Annabelle wouldn't see a penny of Mrs. Kensington's inheritance."

Lucas leaned forward with his shoulders hunched. "It seems obvious, now. But I could have sworn it was Archie. Didn't he say she was going to kill him?"

"He said Mrs. Kensington was going to be the death of him," Abby corrected.

"But he isn't fighting her? He just accepted her renovations?"

"I don't think there are any planned."

"But the veranda—"

Abby shook her head. "I don't think Archie was worried about Mrs. Kensington's plans for the veranda. Or Mrs. Kensington at all, for that matter. We assumed that. I think he was upset about Sarah Kensington. When I first saw her, she was dancing on the veranda with George. I think the poor ghosts are locked in some kind of century-long love triangle, and he's worried he'll lose George to Sarah."

Lucas's eyes widened in understanding. "Ooh."

Abby took a sip of lemonade. She nearly spat it out as Lucas's parents came into view. "Your parents are headed toward us."

Lucas raised his hand and waved at his father. Mr. Clark smiled and waved back, before moving on to greet another of David's relatives.

Abby raised an eyebrow. Last time she had seen Mr. Clark and Lucas in the same room, there was practically smoke billowing from their glares. "He's in a good mood."

"He is." Lucas sat up taller, fiddling with his cufflinks. "I had a talk with him last night. I told him my plans, talked to him about finance, showed him my emergency savings. He seemed a lot calmer after that. I think he was just worried I didn't know how to take care of myself."

"Tell me about it," said Abby, thinking of her own mother.

Lucas loosened his tie. "In a weird way, I think seeing what lengths Nancy went through to so-called 'help' Annabelle made me appreciate what my parents did for me more. It also made me realize I needed to make it very clear what I want and don't want from life. I do *not* want my father's ghost sabotaging my career down the road so I'll take over his old job or something."

Abby rolled her eyes. "He's not that bad."

"You can never be too careful." Lucas shrugged, sipping his beer. "I also think it helped that Michelle backed me up. Explained that it's perfectly acceptable to work odd-jobs these days. Most people don't find one company—or even one career—and stick to it for life. I'm not sure if that helped him be more flexible in supporting my career choices or in making him think there's a chance I'll switch to insurance one day, but at least he's off my back for now."

"That's good. Maybe they'll be more supportive of your new career."

"What new career?"

Abby beamed. "Paranormal investigator."

Lucas made a face like Abby had smacked him.

Abby winked. "Think about it."

Lucas cleared his throat. "I should get back to my date."

"How is she? Do you like her in person as much as you do online?"

Lucas shrugged, swirling his drink. "She's alright."

The grin spreading across his face gave away that he thought she was a lot more than 'alright.'

Abby nudged him. "Well, go dance with her."

He frowned. "But then you'll be here all alone."

Abby felt a pang in her heart. Lucas didn't need to worry about her. She wasn't the same grief-stricken girl she'd been eight years ago. She could handle a wedding without falling apart. "Don't worry about me."

Lucas met her gaze and nodded. He finished his drink, squeezed her hand, and rushed off to dance with what's-her-face under a sky of twinkling string lights.

Michelle's laughter carried across the field as the band began to play an upbeat song and David took center stage performing a breakdance. Annabelle clapped as Robert and Mina hollered. Mrs. Kensington carried Marie Antoinette to a quieter, more secluded spot.

As the crowd formed a circle around David, Abby watched Mina's eyes shine with joy. Her dark hair was pinned at the back of her neck, revealing studded earrings. She wore her lavender bridesmaid dress with confidence and danced with remarkable rhythm. Abby considered joining her, but the music was too fast—she would probably trip trying to keep up with the steps.

"Some wedding, huh?" Abby's mom unbuttoned her white leather gloves and dropped them on the table beside Abby.

Abby's groan was lost in the loud music. The last person she wanted to spend time with right now was her mother.

"I have to tell you," Rebecca said, cutting straight to business as always, "I have no idea what happened with Mrs. Kensington and this so-called 'ghost' nonsense, but the others are all proud of you, so—I figure you must have done something."

Abby did a double take. "Is that a compliment?"

"Don't act so surprised, I compliment you all the time."

Yeah, between orders and complaints. In the interest of keeping civility at Michelle's wedding, Abby choked back her retort and said instead, "There *was* a ghost. Want to see?"

Her mother pursed her lips together in an expression of disbelief. "Sure."

Abby handed her the binoculars. "Scan away."

Rebecca marveled as she scanned the wedding. She lowered the binoculars and examined them. "What is this? Did you make it? How do you get the pictures to show up over the live feed?"

Abby rolled her eyes as she pulled the binoculars back. "It's real, Mom. From a paranormal investigator."

Abby's phone vibrated in her back pocket. She pulled it out to see the caller ID showed Glen Ashford. So the man did know how to use a phone. He just had terrible timing.

Stepping away from the table, she shrugged her mom off with a wave and moved as far from the music as possible before answering.

"You missed all the excitement," she said into the phone.

Glen cleared his throat. "Is this Abby?" The voice came out lighter and softer than the man she had met with.

"Yeah," Abby said, double-checking her caller ID. "This is Glen, right?"

The un-Glen voice cleared his throat again. "This is his brother. I'm afraid Glen is no longer with us."

Abby blinked. "I don't understand."

"My brother, Glen, died a few weeks ago."

"What?" Abby shook her head in disbelief. The man must be mistaken. There must be another Glen Ashford. Maybe Glen Ashford Senior had died and she had met Glen Ashford Junior—

"It was a tragic accident. A tree fell on top of him, poor guy. They say he didn't suffer. The service was a few weeks ago. I can send you the recording."

A chill crept up Abby's spine. She recalled the overturned tree in his driveway and the damp scent of decay in his house. If Glen was dead, then who met her in the cabin? Who gave her his things?

When Abby next spoke, it was a struggle to keep her voice calm. "That won't be necessary. But do you think you could text me a picture of him? So I can remember him by," Abby added, not wanting to reveal the true reason behind her request.

"Of course. It's good to know Glen had friends."

The silence that followed was becoming uncomfortable. Not having anything else to say, Abby thanked him for calling and hung up. Seconds later, a text from an unknown number came through.

It contained a single picture of a gruff old man with a scruffy beard and familiar deep-set eyes.

It was the very same man who had given her the equipment.

Abby gulped. Thinking back on their meeting, she felt dizzy. Glen's cabin had been so cold, Lucas had called it 'unlivable.' She recalled striking a match, lighting the logs in the fireplace, watching dust rise with the flames. Her hands reached for the binoculars as she remembered sliding the briefcase from the shelf. She tried to recall if Glen had touched anything the entire time they were there. His words echoed in her mind. Some ghosts are so powerful they can be seen by the naked eye.

Goosebumps trailed up Abby's arms. She returned to her table and reached for her lemonade, wishing she had selected a hot drink.

Her mother studied her, eyebrows pinched together. "What happened to you?"

Abby blanched. Her mother wouldn't understand.

Rebecca looked at her critically now, as if trying to squint past her exterior and read her innermost thoughts. After several excruciating seconds in which Abby felt like she was under interrogation for treason, Rebecca said, "Besides this 'ghost' haunting Mrs. Kensington, did you see any others?"

Abby studied her mother, trying to tell if she believed her or thought she was losing her mind. Cautiously, Abby proceeded, "A few."

Rebecca held Abby's gaze. "Chelsea?"

Abby's heart twisted. Ever since she'd found out about the existence of ghosts, Abby had longed to talk to Chelsea as much as she feared it. But Chelsea's ghost simply wasn't around.

Abby glanced away from her mom and twisted the bracelet at her wrist. "No. She isn't here."

"Are you going to go look for her?"

The question was like a knife to her ribs. Maybe, one day, she would return to 103 Blackthorn Lane to see if Chelsea's ghost haunted those halls, but not yet. And she sure wasn't going to tell her mom that.

"No," Abby said, focusing on a nearby candle.

"That's probably for the best." Her mother patted her shoulder. "You've come so far, you know. I'd hate to see you slip."

Slip where? Into grief? People slip back into bad habits, addiction—not grief. Grief was something stitched into Abby's veins—sometimes it stung and sometimes she barely felt it, but it was always there.

"You'll find someone," Rebecca said in a chipper tone. "You know, one of my colleagues—Professor Mathison—has a granddaughter about your age. She's pretty. Blonde."

Abby stared at her. "Are you...trying to set me up on a date?"

"I'm just saying, if you're interested, I can give her your phone number—"

"Mom, no!"

Rebecca waved Abby off. "Alright, alright. I'm just saying, you don't have to spend the rest of your life alone."

"I'm not alone," Abby said, thinking of her friends.

Rebecca looked as if she wanted to say more, then decided to sip on her pineapple martini instead. "I'm glad I got to see you here," she said at last. "Enjoying yourself."

"You know, you might not believe it, but I'm actually pretty happy with my life right now."

Her mom arched an eyebrow.

"Really," Abby said, sincerely. "I like my job. I like my apartment. I have friends."

Rebecca opened her mouth, then turned back to her drink. Abby sighed. "Just say it."

"Say what?"

"Whatever it is you want to say."

Rebecca plucked the cherry out of her drink, ate it, and twirled the toothpick between her fingers. Nearly half a song passed before she finally said, "I know what happened with Chelsea was…difficult."

"You mean her death?"

Rebecca nodded. "Yes, that. She was a lovely girl. Who am I to say she wouldn't have been your one true love and you wouldn't have lived happily ever after were she still alive."

Abby nearly choked on her drink. Was this an attempt at an apology?

"However," her mother added. Of course there was a 'however.' "I hope that's not the case. It was tragic enough losing Chelsea that night. I hope we didn't lose you too."

A lull in the music caused a crowd to retreat from the dance floor. Abby moved aside to make way for Robert and some of his friends as they joined the growing line for drinks. "What does that mean?"

Rebecca set her glass down and met Abby's gaze. "Exactly what it sounds like. Now, I promised to bring a drink to your father. Make sure you say hi before you head out."

As Abby watched her mother retreat into the crowd, her fingers tugged at the bracelet on her wrist. For years she'd worn it, cherished it. At first, she'd thought that it might house Chelsea's ghost, but if Chelsea had any unfinished business, Abby was not involved. Maybe the only unfinished business around Chelsea was Abby's.

It was time to let Chelsea go. Shutting her eyes, Abby unclasped the bracelet.

She let it fall, watching as the wind swooped it up and carried it away.

A sense of calmness washed over her, like catching her breath after stepping off a merry-go-round. She rubbed the pale patch of skin that the bracelet had left behind.

Mina caught the bracelet, frowning. Her eyes met Abby's and she moved toward her, holding out the bracelet.

"You might want to keep this."

Tucking her hair behind her ears, Abby shook her head. "I'm done holding on to the past."

Mina nodded, her eyes filled with understanding. "Maybe. But one day, you might want to look back. And that's not a bad thing."

Her fingers brushed Abby's waist as she tucked the bracelet into the pocket of Abby's dress. She waited there a moment, the scent of champagne on her breath, her lips hovering inches from Abby's.

"Are you ever jealous?"

"Jealous?" Abby blinked. "Of what?"

Mina sighed, her fingers lingering against Abby's waist. "That Annabelle got to reunite with her mother, while our loved ones are—" she waved her hand "—not around."

"A little," Abby admitted. "But as much as I'd love to talk to Chelsea again, I'm glad she's not stuck reliving her death. Or worse." An image of Chelsea as a ghost flashed through her mind; only, instead of Chelsea's joyful inquisitive eyes, she wore an expression of anger not unlike Nancy's. Abby shook the thought with a shudder.

"I suppose you're right." The corners of Mina's lips twitched as if she wanted to say more, but she stepped back in silence and started to turn away.

Abby caught her hand. "Wait."

Mina turned back to her, her eyes suspiciously bright.

Abby shifted her weight, Mina's palm warm against her own. "Do you...want to dance?"

A smile radiated across Mina's face, crinkling her eyes. "I thought you'd never ask."

She pulled Abby toward her, pressing her firm hands against Abby's hips as Abby entwined her arms around Mina's shoulders. Music pulsed around them. Some part of Abby was aware that the dead and living alike surrounded them—that the glow of string lights fell on more than just bare branches and their own warm skin. But the way Mina looked at her, the way she held her close with her hand steady against Abby's back and her breath tickling Abby's nose—Abby felt like they were the only ones dancing, the only ones who mattered in this moment.

"Kiss her," Lucas's urgent whisper behind Abby's shoulder brought her back to reality. She attempted to elbow him, but by the time her elbow shot out, he was already moving to a different part of the dance floor.

Mina laughed, a sweet melodic sound.

Abby blushed. "I take it you heard that?"

Mina's eyes twinkled. "I did. I don't think it's a bad idea."

Abby inched closer, letting her hand slip up to caress Mina's cheek. "I don't think so either."

Mina's hands tightened around Abby's waist. "Then what are we waiting for?"

Abby didn't answer the question. Instead, she stepped forward, trailing her lips softly, hesitantly toward Mina's. Her heart pounded. This was the closest she had come to kissing anyone in years. The first kiss she would have since Chelsea.

Mina leaned closer, brushing Abby's lips with her own.

Their mouths parted, sinking into each other in a warm, passionate kiss that made every inch of Abby's skin feel alive and eager for more.

For the first time in a long time, Abby longed not for the past, but the future.

Author's note

This book is filled with ghosts.

Obviously, it's a ghost story.

But beyond the fictional characters that roam the halls of haunted mansions, there are *real* ghosts. Smaller, personal ghosts—the kind that drift inside our memories and linger bittersweetly in our dreams. Sometimes they are echoes of departed loved ones, while other times they are remnants of former homes or shattered relationships. To me, they are a longing—a longing to reunite with what has been lost. A longing to return to a comforting time, place, or person. A longing to experience joy.

Several years ago, my best friend tragically passed away. I struggled to write, churning out pages too dark or too forcefully light—until Abby. Abby's optimism and love of life in the wake of such a tragedy created room for the perfect tale of a joyous adventure set against the harsher realities of life. I hoped that it would reflect our own while offering space and comfort to heal through a bit of whimsical wish fulfillment.

In the weeks leading up to this book's publication, I faced another profound loss when my dad was killed. He was my greatest supporter, and I am devastated that he won't have the chance to hold this book in his hands. But the ghost of his love is strong and lives between the pages of this and all the future stories I will write. He inspired my sense of imagination, passion for storytelling, and enthusiasm for adventure. I can honestly say I would not be the person I am today if it weren't for him. His ghost will live on in me, always.

I hope you enjoyed your time with this book and its ghosts. They can't wait to bring another reader to life.

Acknowledgements

I want to express my heartfelt gratitude to everyone who has supported me along my writing journey. From classmates in my creative writing programs who praised and encouraged my words, to my coworkers who make my day job enjoyable—I wouldn't be where I am today without you. Thank you!

An extra huge thank you goes out to my family. You have always loved me and supported my dreams. Mom, thank you for helping me strike the perfect balance between humor and darkness. Dad, your scientific insights and suggestions made the ghostly physics feel more believable. April, thank you for being the best sister and beta reader throughout the years. To my wife, Kiran, thank you for being my rock and listening to me ramble about my stories for hours on end. Your support and encouragement have been invaluable. To my cats, Inigo and Sazed, for your cuddles and purrs on hard days (and for teaching me that sometimes a good keyboard smash is necessary).

I am immensely grateful to Anna for providing in-depth feedback on my messy first draft and helping me find the right direction. And to my line editor, Hannah McCall at Black Cat Editorial Services, thank you for your keen eye and insightful feedback. Your expertise has truly elevated this book.

A special shoutout to my beta readers and critique partners. Your honest feedback and constructive criticism have been instrumental in shaping this story and its characters into the version we see today.

Of course, what's a book without its cover? Holly Dunn beautifully captured the tone and essence of the book with her delightful artwork. Thank you, Holly!

A big thank you to my dear friend, Kristi Langli, for not only listening to my writing ramblings but also assisting me with the publishing process, including the meticulous task of formatting.

To the artistic and writing communities that have inspired and supported me, thank you. Your camaraderie and shared experiences have enriched my writing journey and kept me going when times were tough. And a special thank you to those of you who created character art—you have no idea how much it warms my heart to see Abby and her friends come to life!

Lastly—but certainly not least—I'm extremely grateful for my readers. This book seriously would not be here without you. Your belief in my work has given me the confidence to share my stories with the world, and I can't thank you enough for being a part of this incredible journey.

Abby and her friends will return in Book 2...

coming 2024!

Visit MorganSpellman.com to learn more.

About the Author

Morgan Spellman (she/they) writes whimsical stories sprinkled with magic and wonder. She holds an MA in Creative Writing from Oxford Brookes University and works in Marketing at a technology company. She lives in North Carolina with her wife, two attention-seeking cats, and an entire cabinet devoted to tea. When not crafting stories, Morgan can be found hiking through scenic trails, indulging in freshly baked cookies, or embarking on epic tabletop role-play game quests with friends.

She can be found online at **morganspellman.com**

Printed in Great Britain
by Amazon

27737266R00189